Jenni Fletcher was born ⸻
and now lives in Yorksh⸻
and two children. She w⸻
child, but got distracted by reading instead, finally
getting past her first paragraph thirty years later.
She's had more jobs than she can remember,
but has finally found one she loves. She can
be contacted on X, @JenniAuthor, or via her
Facebook author page.

A MARQUESS
TO REMEMBER

Jenni Fletcher

MILLS & BOON

First published in Great Britain 2025
by Mills & Boon, an imprint of HarperCollins*Publishers* Ltd,
1 London Bridge Street, London, SE1 9GF

www.harpercollins.co.uk

HarperCollins*Publishers*, Macken House, 39/40 Mayor Street Upper, Dublin 1, D01 C9W8, Ireland

A Marquess to Remember © 2025 Jenni Fletcher

ISBN: 978-0-263-34546-9

12/25

This book contains FSC™ certified paper
and other controlled sources to ensure responsible forest management.

For more information visit www.harpercollins.co.uk/green.

Printed and Bound in the UK using 100% Renewable Electricity
at CPI Group (UK) Ltd, Croydon, CR0 4YY

For the 3Ms

As Marquess, your first and most urgent task is to secure the future of Rainton through marriage and the siring of an heir. Therefore, act swiftly and with discretion. Select a bride whose fortune will enhance the estate, whose temper will benefit your domestic harmony, and whose bloodline is worthy of our illustrious family. Above all, choose with your head, not your heart. Any mistake in this matter could lead to the ruination and collapse of everything I have spent so many years striving to achieve...

Extract of a letter from Augustus Claridge to Leopold Claridge upon the latter's elevation to the marquessate,
January 1814

Chapter One

Dorset, six months later...

A persistent buzzing sound filled the air.

From her recumbent position, Florence lifted a hand to swat the side of her head, where some kind of winged insect was making a nuisance of itself, hovering right beside her ear. Although…on second thoughts, the buzzing was actually louder than that, as if the noise was coming from *inside* her head. She had a sudden, horrifying mental image of a large, fluffy bee crawling inside her ear and flying about inside her skull, but that was impossible, surely? Bees didn't just go crawling up ear canals. There was no pollen there. Ergo no point. And even if there were, theoretically yet horrifyingly, a bee inside her head, she would be able to feel it crawling around, wouldn't she? Whereas all she felt right now was tired.

So very tired…

She gave a wide yawn, about to bury her face in

her pillow and let herself drift back to sleep when she remembered the date. The twelfth of June! She didn't have the luxury of lying in bed, not today of all days. The Wadlows' ball was tonight and there was no time to waste, certainly none to spend thinking about bees and ears. Amabel, her dearest friend, neighbour and confidante since childhood, needed her!

It was thanks to Amabel that she was in London at all, since her parents, though eminently respectable, were a long way from being members of the *ton*. Left to themselves, they would never have dreamt of sending her any further afield than the assembly rooms in Carlisle. Amabel, however, had somehow convinced her own parents, Lord and Lady Wadlow, that, as such a 'dreadfully ancient' debutante—her entrance into Society having been delayed, first by an outbreak of scarlet fever, then by the demise of, and subsequent mourning period for, her paternal grandfather—it was imperative that she bring a companion for the Season. And who better than Florence, who was so capable and good-natured, not to mention perfectly content to wear the same gown on half a dozen occasions? If anyone was loyal and level-headed enough to help Amabel negotiate the back-stabbing world of the *ton*, not to mention identify eligible suitors, it was her!

And so Florence had travelled with the Wadlow family all the way from Cumberland to Mayfair, a fellow 'dreadfully ancient' twenty-one-year-old, to enjoy all of the balls and picnics and soirees the great Marriage Mart had to offer, albeit largely from the sidelines since her own lack of dowry rendered her effectively invisible. All things considered, it had been an eye-opening and entertaining experience, yet somewhat fraught over the past fortnight, ever since the tall, dark and glowering Marquess of Rainton had arrived on the scene and begun paying special attention to Amabel.

Naturally, the Wadlows had been over the moon at this development, scrambling to organise a ball that would provide the perfect opportunity for a proposal. And today was the day! It was going to be a most splendid occasion, one of the finest and most lavish events of the Season, and Florence's role, as outlined in somewhat exhaustive detail by Lady Wadlow the previous evening, was to keep Amabel calm, composed and in the correct frame of mind to say yes.

A betrothal announcement was expected before midnight.

As requested, Florence had their activities for the day all planned out. First, they would enjoy a leisurely breakfast of tea and buttered muffins, then they would visit the modiste to select some fabric for a new day gown for Amabel, followed by Hatchard's bookshop for a copy of Fanny Burney's new novel, *The Wanderer*, for Florence. Then, after attending to any correspondence (her mother, in particular, would be thrilled to learn about Amabel and the marquess), they would have luncheon, do some reading and piano practice, take a walk in Hyde Park, and then finally return to Grosvenor Square to eat a small dinner prior to the ball. At some point, they would also need to bathe, have their hair styled and dress in their ballgowns, but she would leave that part for Lady Wadlow to worry about.

In order to do any of that, however, she needed to rouse herself sufficiently to get out of bed. Which she wanted to. Very much. Only actually doing so appeared to be more of a challenge than usual. How late had she gone to sleep? She honestly couldn't recall. Instead, she was struck with the strangest sensation of having lain in one position for a long time.

Prising her eyelids open only made matters worse, since the world appeared to be a great deal brighter than usual—dazzling, in fact. Meanwhile, her vision was so blurry, it was like looking at the world through opaque glass. She had to blink a few times just to focus. Now she could see more clearly and yet everything around her was wrong...and right. Which was to say, the bedchamber in which she found herself was more luxurious than any she'd ever slept in before—elegantly decorated in shades of pale blue and yellow, with a selection of curved walnut furniture, all embellished with carvings of feathers, and the most exquisite goldfinch-and-cornflower-patterned wallpaper she'd ever seen—but unless the Wadlows had decided to redecorate during the night and not told her, which seemed distinctly unlikely, she'd never seen it before in her life.

Where was she?

Her heart thumped with alarm as a woman's face poked its way into the edge of her vision. Thankfully, it didn't look particularly threatening. On the contrary, its hazel eyes were somewhat anxious-looking, but she didn't recognise it either. She didn't recognise anything! A flurry of questions burst into her mind. Who was it? What were they doing there? *What was going on?*

Fortunately, it didn't take her long to guess the truth. It was a dream! Thank goodness. Of course she was dreaming. It was an odd dream and frankly, she didn't have time for it, but she supposed it could be worse. There were no snakes or lizards to frighten her. And now that she understood the problem, the solution was obvious. She needed to wake up, that was all, simply wake up.

Wake up, she ordered herself. *Wake up. Wake—*

'Can you hear me?'

Her heart thumped again, even harder this time, like a hammer blow against the side of her ribcage. The voice sounded real. Much more real than she would have expected for a figment of her imagination, speaking in an unfamiliar accent too. It seemed curious that a person could talk with such clarity, not to mention in an entirely new accent, in a dream, but perhaps her imagination was more vivid than she'd previously given herself credit for?

Wake up! she told herself more sternly, wishing that something outlandish might happen, like a unicorn falling down the chimney or an elephant bursting through the ceiling, anything to reassure herself that this really was a dream, because what if…?

'My lady?' The voice was also persistent. 'Shall I fetch the doctor?'

My lady?

The words took a couple of seconds to penetrate her consciousness and when they did she almost laughed aloud with relief. Well, she'd wished for something outlandish and there it was. The idea of anyone calling her, plain Miss Florence Lowrie, 'my lady' was laughable! Ha!

Only, for a dream, everything still looked alarmingly real… Ha?

'I'll fetch the doctor.' The woman edged towards the door. 'Hopefully he hasn't left yet. Don't move, my lady. I won't be long!'

Please, please, please wake up, Florence pleaded with herself, squeezing her eyes shut and counting to ten before opening them again to find the room… exactly as it had been before. As if it was, in fact… actually…real.

A cold sweat broke out on the back of her neck, sending a shiver straight down her spine. How was this happening? If it was real then she was lying in a strange bed in a strange room being watched over by a strange woman who was now on her way to fetch a strange doctor. Was she sick? Injured? She didn't remember any kind of illness or injury, although, now that she thought about it, her nose was blocked, her throat was scratchy, and her head was filled with a strange kind of grey fog, in which blurry images and silhouettes seemed to float like phantoms, fading away whenever she tried to focus, as if they were deliberately taunting her. Her body felt unusually sluggish too, but she couldn't let that hold her back. She had to get up, had to find out what was going on…

Summoning all her energy, she flung the counterpane aside and heaved her stiff legs over the edge of the bed, intending to stride to the door. No sooner had her feet touched the floor, however, than she gave a powerful sneeze, followed by a short, sharp yelp of alarm as her ankles crumpled and she plummeted downwards.

'Ow!' She glared resentfully at the carpet, as if it were somehow responsible for her position, then braced her hands and knees against it, crawling the short distance to a nearby dressing-table to heave her protesting body, with yet another gargantuan effort, up onto a stool.

The face she saw reflected in the gilded mirror before her gave a violent jolt and then opened its mouth wide with an expression of shock and horror. In most respects, she looked just as she always had. Her shoulder-length, light brown hair was twisted into its usual night-time braid and her eyes were still a summer-sky shade of blue, but her cheeks had a feverish glow and her nose was a positively startling shade of red. More shockingly, there was a jagged gash, surrounded by a purple and yellow patch on her forehead, half hidden in her hairline.

Body shaking, she leaned forward to trace a finger around it. How—when—had *that* happened?

'My lady?' The door opened abruptly and another stranger, an elderly man this time, strode into the room, dressed sombrely in black like an undertaker, accompanied by the woman who'd just left.

'Who are you?' Florence spun around on the stool, then clutched a hand to her head as the buzzing sound returned with a vengeance. Worse, her mouth was so dry, it actually hurt to speak, as though the words themselves were scraping the inside of her throat.

'Dr Pritchard, my lady.' The man made a bow. 'I've had the honour of attending you. I was just getting into my carriage when Nurse McKay here stopped me.' He pulled his shoulders back and tugged at the hem of his waistcoat. 'Permit me to say how heartened I am to see you awake. Might I ask how you're feeling?'

'I don't know you.' She threw a glance at the door, wondering if her legs were strong enough for her to make a run for it. Somehow she doubted it. 'My doctor is called Ogden. He's a friend of my father's.'

'I see.' The man rubbed a hand across his chin, a strange, evaluating glint in his eye. 'Would Your Ladyship care for a tonic? It might help to steady your nerves.'

'No.' She inhaled deeply, trying to get her frantic breathing under control. As much as she wanted something to ease her sore throat, she needed to know what was going on first. 'And stop calling me that.'

'Stop calling you what, my lady?'

'*That!* My lady!' She winced as the buzzing sound grew stronger again, accompanied by a sensation like hundreds of needles trying to push their way into her skull. If she wasn't careful, the panic was going to engulf her completely. None of this felt like a dream any longer. It was much, *much* more like a nightmare!

'Where's Amabel?' she asked, raising her voice in the hope that her friend was near by. 'I need to see her.'

'Amabel?' Dr Pritchard sounded confused.

'Yes. Miss Wadlow.'

'I'm afraid I haven't been introduced to anybody of that name.'

'But she must still be in London?'

'Ah…' A shutter seemed to descend over the doctor's face. '*She* may be. *We*, however…'

Florence felt the colour drain from her face as he let the sentence trail pointedly away. Now that she thought of it, the streets outside did seem unusually quiet. She couldn't hear voices or hooves or the usual rumble of carriage wheels across cobbles. Slowly, she craned her neck towards the window. The view outside was of rolling parkland. She could see a small hill in the distance, with some kind of folly on top, but other than that, there wasn't a single other building in sight. Definitely *not* London, not unless the house the Wadlows had rented for the Season had somehow been lifted up by its foundations and transplanted in the centre of Hyde Park. Again, distinctly unlikely.

'Where are we?' Her voice was reduced to a rasp. 'What date is it?'

'Rainton Court in Dorset, my lady, on the twelfth of July.'

'July?' Her stomach dropped. 'But that's a month from now!'

'I'm afraid not, my lady.' The doctor cleared his throat. 'Would you care for something to eat? Or some tea perhaps? You need to regain your strength. It's been three days since the…ah…accident.'

A cold draught seemed to blow through the room, chilling her through her white silk and lace nightdress, something else she'd never set eyes on before. '*What* accident?'

He didn't answer, turning to address the nurse instead. 'Please go and inform His Lordship of the situation. Tell him that I need to speak with him as speedily as possible.'

'What accident?' Florence repeated, louder this time.

'Perhaps you might wish to return to bed, my lady?'

'No, I do not wish it.' She pushed herself back to her feet, keeping one hand on the dressing-table in case her ankles buckled again. Her whole body felt ice cold suddenly, as if her blood were freezing in her veins. 'I *wish* to know what's going on. Why am I in Dorset? What accident? And who is this lordship you're talking about?'

'I think it would be best if he explains that himself, my lady.' The doctor gestured towards the bed. 'Now I really must insist…'

'I am *not* going back to bed!' She took an unsteady step forward, beginning to feel desperate. Her ribs felt too tight and there was a lump rising in her throat, but she wasn't going to cry. She needed answers a lot more than tears. And if she didn't find out what was going on soon, she was going to start shouting. At the top of her lungs and at length until somebody gave in and explained everything.

'There's no call for hysterics, my lady.'

'Who is he?' She grabbed a hairbrush from her dressing table and flung it across the room. She had no intention of striking the man, but if he was going to accuse her of hysterics, she'd show him just how hysterical she could be.

'My lady, I must protest!'

'*Who?*' She reached for an empty vase. It was actually quite pretty, cream-coloured with a pattern of trailing violets and strawberries. It would be a shame to smash it, but what else could she do? 'Tell me!'

'The Marquess of Rainton!' the doctor exclaimed, backing up against the door. 'Your husband!'

Chapter Two

Leopold Augustus Oliver Ralph Maximilian Claridge, fifth Marquess of Rainton, stared across the imposing width of his mahogany pedestal desk at his steward, Sewell, and wondered if the man was capable of answering a question with any word other than no. Every single suggestion that Leo had made for the improvement of his estate that morning had been met with the same stark response. At least on the question of crops, the man's clenched brows suggested he was at least thinking about it. That was some progress, although he suspected he already knew what the answer would be.

'No.' *And there it was...* 'I'm afraid that's impossible, my lord.'

'Of course it is.' Leo pinched the bridge of his nose between his thumb and forefinger. 'Why exactly?'

'The estate's main income has always come from sheep farming.'

'I'm aware.' He lowered his hand, fighting the urge

to pound his fist against the desk. 'And as I've said before, I've no intention of giving up sheep farming completely. However, the price of wool continues to fall, while the price of grain only goes up. All I'm suggesting is that we set aside a few fields for wheat and corn.' He paused before delivering the final blow. 'And cattle.'

'Cattle?' Sewell reeled backwards as if he'd just proposed a herd of elephants.

'Yes. Red Devons. That's not so outlandish, surely? Since we are, in fact, only thirty miles from Devon.'

'That may be, my lord, but the estate has never—'

'Sewell,' Leo interrupted him. 'Just because the estate has never done something in the past doesn't necessarily preclude us from doing it now, does it?'

'No-o, but—'

'Some might, in fact, call that progress.'

'Some might.' Sewell lifted his chin. 'But it strikes me as reckless.'

Reckless? Leo lifted his eyes skyward. Admittedly, he'd been feeling increasingly that way since his premature return from London, but good grief, it wasn't as if he was wagering the estate in a game of cards. All they were talking about was a few cows, thirty at most!

'One herd isn't likely to bankrupt us.'

'Perhaps not, but your father's instructions on the

maintenance of the estate were most explicit. If he were here now, he would advise—'

'That's enough.' Leo's patience snapped. He was well aware what his father would have said on the subject. On every subject, for that matter. The letter lying on his desk was never going to let him forget. The absolute last thing he wanted or needed was another reminder.

'Forgive me, my lord.' Sewell bowed his head. 'I only want to guide you.'

As your father wished me to do... The words seemed to hover unspoken between them, irritating Leo even more. Spending time with his father's old steward always made him feel this way, like a ten-year-old boy instead of a man of twenty-four. The man's lecturing, intractable attitude was infuriating, especially since he showed no inclination for retirement, but it was also well intended. Sewell had served his father loyally for almost fifty years. In half a century together, they'd produced a thriving and prosperous estate. No doubt he regarded himself as the defender of a great legacy. And the most annoying part was that he was probably right and Leo ought to heed his advice. After all, it had only been six months since he'd been summoned home from Cornwall to his father's deathbed, just in time to see him before the crushing weight of his inheritance had descended onto his shoulders. It might be prudent not to make too many changes just yet, especially considering how much of a mess he'd made with the very first instruction his father had given him: *Select a bride whose fortune will enhance the estate, whose temper will benefit your domestic harmony, and whose bloodline is worthy of our illustrious family...* The new Marchioness of Rainton was definitely *not* the kind of woman his father had had in mind.

'Very well.' Leo heaved a sigh. 'We'll leave it for now. However, I want work to begin on the new estate cottages as soon as possible.' He held a hand up as Sewell opened his mouth, presumably to object. '*That* is non-negotiable.'

'I still think repairs would be a much cheaper alternative.'

'Non-negotiable,' Leo repeated, turning gratefully towards his study door at the sound of a knock. 'Yes?'

'Pardon the interruption, my lord.' Rimmer, his butler, looked almost flustered. 'But Dr Pritchard wishes to speak with you as a matter of urgency. Apparently Her Ladyship is awake.'

'Ah.' Leo leaned back in his chair, taking a moment to let the news sink in. He was relieved, of course— as relieved as he'd be for anyone who'd sustained a serious head injury and then lain unconscious for the past three days—only he was also acutely aware of his bad mood plummeting even further. Because if his wife was awake, he supposed that now he'd have to go and talk to her, to make sure she was all right and then find out why the bloody hell she'd been riding in a storm by herself in the first place.

And he'd rather keep banging his head against a brick wall with Sewell than do that.

'Thank you, Rimmer. Tell him I'll be there shortly.' He nodded to the butler before turning back to his steward. 'Make the cottages your priority. I don't care how much it costs.'

'Very well, my lord.' Sewell's expression was pained. 'If you really think it's for the best?'

'I do.'

He waited, drumming his fingers on the green leather top of his desk until Sewell finally dragged his feet through the door, before flexing his neck from side to side, straightening his cravat, and reluctantly pushing himself to his feet.

Mounting the great oak staircase, he couldn't help but wonder what his father would have done in his situation, stuck with the wrong—not to mention, entirely unsuitable—woman for a wife, but it was impossible to imagine his father ever getting himself into such a mess in the first place. He would have known better than to fall into the marriage trap Leo had so blindly and foolishly walked into. None the less, it was a trap he now had to live with, which meant that he also had no choice but to keep on walking. As if this house didn't feel like enough of a prison already…

'My lord.' Dr Pritchard met him in the corridor outside his wife's bedchamber. 'Thank you for coming so swiftly.'

'Doctor.' Leo inclined his head. 'How is Her Ladyship?'

'She has a bad cold, as expected, given the circumstances, but in general she appears to be making an excellent physical recovery.'

'I'm glad to hear it.' He took hold of the door handle and frowned. 'Why is this locked?'

'That's what I wished to speak to you about, my lord. It was for her own safety. I'm afraid that Her Ladyship's behaviour was becoming somewhat hysterical. I thought it best to give her some time alone.' He glanced nervously at the door, as if he were afraid she might walk straight through it like some kind of phantom. 'Unfortunately, her accident appears to have had some unusual consequences.'

'What kind of consequences?' He held out a hand. 'The key?'

'Of course.' The doctor placed the item in his palm. 'Amnesia, my lord. It's not uncommon in the case of head injuries, although in Her Ladyship's case, the timing is unusually specific.'

'How so?'

'She appears to have forgotten the entire past month.'

'The past…' Leo paused as he slid the key into the

lock. 'But we were married on the seventeenth of June. That would mean—'

'I'm afraid so.' The doctor coughed. 'She seems to have no recollection of being married, or even engaged. She recognises your name, only she appears to find the idea of marriage somewhat…ah…distressing.'

'Indeed?' He arched an eyebrow. *She wasn't the only one.*

'Not the idea of being married to you, I'm certain.' The doctor backtracked hastily. 'Presumably just her current predicament. Memory loss can be most disorienting.'

'I'm sure. Is it likely to be permanent?'

'Not usually, although each case is different. Her memory may return gradually, or…in some cases… not. It's impossible to be certain.'

'I see.' Leo turned the key finally. 'Well, I appreciate the warning. Has she had anything to eat or drink since she woke?'

'Not yet, my lord. As I said, she was becoming hysterical, but it would be a good idea for her to have some nourishment after such a long period of unconsciousness. I've already sent the nurse to fetch some soup, after which Her Ladyship really ought to rest. A good night's sleep can often work wonders. However, if you could set her mind at ease in the meantime, it would be most beneficial.'

'Quite.' Leo kept his expression blank with an effort. Given the circumstances, he was quite possibly the last person in the world qualified to set his wife's mind at ease, but he supposed he ought to try.

Cautiously, he opened the door and stepped into the room, just in time to catch the former Miss Florence Lowrie, now Lady Florence Claridge, preparing to hurl what appeared to be a collection of tied-together sheets out of the window. As escape attempts went, it struck him as disappointingly unoriginal.

'Florence?' Her name felt strange in his mouth, but then he hadn't had a great many occasions to use it. They'd barely spoken since the wedding. Or at least *he'd* barely spoken to *her*. She'd spoken to him, or tried to, but he hadn't been in the mood for listening.

'You!' She spun around instantly, her whole body bristling like that of a cornered animal, albeit one with a bright red nose and dressed in a white silk nightgown. He wouldn't have been surprised if she'd bared her teeth, shaped her hands into claws and started growling at him. 'You can't come in here. It's my bedchamber!'

'So it is.' He felt a pang in his chest as he looked around at the marchioness's suite. It adjoined his own new set of rooms and yet, aside from three days previously, when he'd come to speak with the doctor, he hadn't set foot inside it since his mother's death eighteen years ago. 'Although it's *my* house.'

'It can't be.' She shook her head and then flinched

as if the movement hurt. 'I mean, you're not…we're not…what he said. It's impossible.'

Leo picked his way carefully across to the fireplace, stepping over a variety of items on the way: the shattered remnants of a vase, a brush, a jewelled trinket box, a scattering of hairpins… 'By *it*, I presume that you're referring to our marriage?'

'Yes!' She thrust her chin out, one end of her makeshift rope still clutched tightly in her hands. 'It's absurd. We've barely said more than two words to each other.'

He tipped his head in acknowledgement. If she had no memory of the past month then that was true. He'd been so busy courting Miss Wadlow, he hadn't spared a great deal of attention for her companion. He certainly hadn't made any attempts to engage her in conversation; deliberately so, since he'd found himself far too distracted by her on their first meeting. It had been at a musical soiree, a week after he'd first met Miss Wadlow at a picnic, and the captivating brightness of those large blue eyes, combined with a lively wit and down-to-earth manner, so at odds with that of most of the *ton*, had meant he'd listened to the performance without taking in a single note. Instead, he'd sat just two seats away, heart pounding, feeling as if something inside him had shifted.

It had been an altogether discomforting experience, almost enough to put an end to his burgeoning courtship of Miss Wadlow. Since he'd always known what kind of wife he was expected to marry, he'd never permitted himself to consider what kind he might personally prefer, but in the two women, he'd suspected he'd found prime examples of each. Once the music had finished, he'd made an excuse to leave the soiree early, then gone home, plunged into an ice bath, and consigned the image of his intended's companion firmly to a box at the back of his mind.

It hadn't been easy. He'd been particularly concerned that Miss Wadlow might want her friend to visit them once they were married, but he'd reassured himself with the knowledge that Cumberland was a substantial distance from Dorset and that he could always absent himself should the occasion arise. And so that had been that. The next time he'd allowed himself to look at Miss Lowrie properly had been on the night of the Wadlows' ball, otherwise known as the most humiliating night of his life, when he'd become a laughing stock to the whole of the *ton*. Now any attraction he'd once felt was more than outweighed by resentment.

'I agree that it's absurd.' His tone was harsher than he'd intended, but just the memory of that night caused his anger to spike all over again. 'However, it's also the truth.' He rested one arm on the mantel and jerked his head towards the window. 'Incidentally, you're not a prisoner, so there's no need to scale the walls. Dr

Pritchard overreacted. You're perfectly welcome to use the staircase.'

She swallowed visibly, looking from him to the now unlocked door, before dropping her sheet-rope to the carpet. 'It wasn't long enough anyway, but I had to do something.'

'I understand.'

'Do you?' Her eyes flashed. 'Because I don't. I don't understand any of this.'

Leo studied her face, his own a mask of impassivity. When Dr Pritchard had first mentioned amnesia, he'd wondered if it was simply a ploy on her part, another cunning trick to compel him to talk to her, only, looking at her now, he didn't think so. The bruise on her head was certainly genuine. And behind her defiant expression there was a definite look of panic; fear too, though he batted away any feeling of sympathy. No matter how vulnerable she might seem, she was still the woman who'd deceived and trapped him into marriage and he still resented her. Frankly, if anyone deserved to feel panicked, it was her.

But she was also his wife and if he didn't explain, who would?

'Shall we sit?' He gestured towards two wicker chairs set on either side of the fireplace, telling himself it was for his own comfort, not hers.

She hesitated, swaying backwards as if she didn't want to come any closer, before visibly steeling herself, clenching her fists and eyeing him warily as she edged forward and slid into one of the chairs.

He took the one opposite, determinedly averting his gaze from the way her nightdress clung to her legs as she moved. 'I'll get straight to the point. There was a bad storm a few days ago. It arrived suddenly and was stronger than usual for this time of year. My steward believes you took a severe blow to the head from a falling branch while you were out riding, though, since you were alone, there's no way for us to know for certain. It appears to have affected your memory.'

She blinked slowly, her expression shifting from surprise to confusion. 'I was out riding in a storm?'

'Yes.'

'Alone?'

'Yes.'

'Why?'

'I have no idea. To be honest, I'd hoped you might be able to explain that to me.'

'It sounds like madness.'

'I agree. Moreover, since you failed to tell anyone your plans, and managed to take a horse from the stables without alerting the grooms, it was some time before anyone noticed your absence. The alarm was only raised when the animal returned to the house with a saddle and no rider. Then your maid remembered something about you mentioning a trip to the village.'

'How…odd. Did *you* find me?'

'No. I was away on business. I came back when I received word, but by then you were under Dr Pritchard's care.' He felt a twist of guilt at the admission. It sounded distinctly ungallant. As her husband, he should at least have been part of the search, but instead he'd been forty miles away, talking to a man about cows. 'I'm afraid it's possible that you were lying injured in the rain for several hours, hence your cold. To be frank, you're lucky to be alive.'

'I see...' She gave a heavy sniff and pressed a hand to her forehead, as if she was struggling to take the words in.

'Here.' He reached into his pocket for a clean handkerchief and then leaned forward, dropping it into her lap. 'I know it sounds alarming, but at least you're safe and awake now. If you stay warm and get plenty of rest, hopefully you'll feel better soon.'

'*Better?*' Her eyes flew back to his, widening incredulously. 'How can I feel better? None of that explains how we're married! How can such a thing have possibly happened?'

'I've asked myself the same question several times.' He sat back again, clenching his jaw. 'What exactly is the last thing you remember?'

'Going to bed the night before the Wadlows' ball.' She answered without hesitation. 'I remember brushing my hair at my bedroom window, looking out over

Mayfair.' She turned her head accusingly towards the window. 'This isn't Mayfair.'

'True. We left London immediately after the wedding.'

'The wedding…' She pulled her hand away from her face, as if noticing the gold band around her ring finger for the first time. 'Oh!' She gave a sudden start. 'Are we in love?'

Love? The idea was so ridiculous, he let out a guffaw of laughter before he could stop himself.

'It's not so unreasonable.' She flinched, sounding embarrassed and defensive at the same time. 'I've no dowry or connections. Why else would you have married me?'

'Why indeed?' He cleared his throat, folding one long leg over the other. His laughter had been ungentlemanly, but there was no way he was going to apologise for it. 'In short, because I had to. I was obliged to obtain a special licence the morning after the Wadlows' ball.'

She gave a sharp intake of breath, all the colour seeming to drain from her face in a matter of seconds, leaving her lips and cheeks entirely bloodless. Only her crimson nose stood out sharply in contrast. 'You mean, we were compromised?'

'Yes. A wedding was unavoidable, though it wasn't much of a celebration, I'm afraid. More of a formality.'

'Did I give my consent?'

'*Consent?*' He felt another flash of anger, grinding his teeth at the hypocrisy of it. 'I didn't drag you down the aisle by your hair, if that's what you're suggesting.'

'No, of course not.' She shook her head. 'I didn't mean to accuse you. It's just so much to take in. Were my parents there?'

'No.' He took a deep breath to regain his composure. 'Since you'd already reached the age of majority there was no need to obtain permission from your father and it would have taken too long to send a message and wait for them to arrive.'

'But do they know about…us?'

'They do.' He dropped his gaze to her hands. At some point she'd picked up his handkerchief and was twisting it almost frantically between her fingers. 'I wrote them a brief letter after our wedding, and from what I understand, you've written to them since.'

'Have they replied?'

'No, not yet anyway. However, I presume that you fully apprised them of the circumstances.'

'*What* circumstances?' Her voice cracked on a note of frustration. '*How* were we compromised?'

He hesitated, a raft of accusations on the tip of his tongue, but now wasn't the time. Dr Pritchard had asked him to set her mind at ease and, so far, he only seemed to be making things worse. In any case, what difference would more accusations make? They wouldn't turn back the clock and *un*marry them.

'Now isn't the time to discuss it.' He pushed himself to his feet. 'We'll talk again in a few days when you've recovered your strength.'

'I can't wait that long!' She thrust a hand out, grasping his forearm as he started to walk away, her voice fierce now. 'You were going to propose to Amabel. Everyone was expecting the announcement at the ball.'

'Everyone was right.' He looked down at her fingers. Considering her recent ordeal, her grip was surprisingly strong. 'That was my intention.'

'Then what went wrong? How did *we* end up married instead?'

It was quite remarkable, Leo thought, looking down at the anguished expression on her face. If he didn't know what she'd done, hadn't witnessed it for himself, he might actually have believed that she was an innocent party in this whole mess, not the instigator of an elaborate marriage trap. She appeared to have no recollection of any of it. Somehow she made *him* feel like the villain.

Which was palpably absurd.

'Later.' He drew his brows together. 'You need to rest.'

'How can I rest knowing that I somehow ruined the prospects of my oldest and dearest friend?' Her eyes glittered. 'None of this makes any sense. I would never have allowed myself to be compromised!'

'*Allowed* yourself?' He wrenched his arm away in disgust.

'Yes.' Her head jerked backwards. 'Why do you say it like that?'

'We'll discuss it later.' He resumed his progress towards the door, his jaw already aching from the effort of clenching it so hard. If he didn't get out of there soon he'd say something he might really regret.

'No!' She pushed herself to her feet so fast, her body obviously wasn't ready. Her arms flailed in the air for a few seconds, as she tried to maintain her balance, before her knees buckled and she tumbled headlong towards the floor.

'Look out!' Leo reacted instinctively, leaping back to catch her.

'Oof!' She gave a muffled cry as her cheek landed heavily against his chest. 'I'm sorry. I did that when I stood up before, but… I forgot.'

He didn't answer, forgetting to breathe for a moment. In this position, with only his shirt and waistcoat and her silk nightdress between them, it was impossible not to notice how snug her body felt against his, her soft curves aligning perfectly to his hard lines. It was the first time he'd touched more than her hands and, despite everything, an unexpected bolt of heat shot through him.

'You should be more careful.' Quickly, he lowered her back down into her chair, ruthlessly suppressing the feeling. His imagination was already running riot at the thought of how her body might feel with *no* clothes between them… 'A bump on the head and a bad cold are enough to contend with.'

'Just tell me one thing.' Her eyes were wider and brighter than ever, peering up at him from beneath thick, dark lashes. 'Does Amabel forgive me?'

He hesitated, briefly considering the potentially devastating effect of an honest answer, before turning on his heel and stalking away. 'I've no idea, but I suspect that your food is ready by now. I'll send Dr Pritchard back in.'

Chapter Three

Florence lay on her back, staring up at the periwinkle-blue silk canopy above her head. After watching over her like a pair of hawks while she ate a bowl of chicken broth, Dr Pritchard and the nurse had finally tucked her into bed and departed with firm instructions to sleep.

Sleep?

It was the most ridiculous idea she'd ever heard, and not just because of her blocked nose. How could she possibly sleep when she had so much to think about? She was married! To a marquess! And not just any marquess, but the Marquess of Rainton, the sternest, stiffest, most humourless man she'd ever had the misfortune to come across. She remembered their first meeting quite clearly. Lady Wadlow had talked so much about the 'delightful' gentleman they'd met at a *ton* picnic, an event she'd missed due to some task she'd been performing for Amabel, that she'd expected some paragon of male virtue. Instead, he'd stared at

her as though she'd had food on her face and then pro-
ceeded to ignore her for the rest of the evening, not to
mention every evening afterwards. And now he was
her husband! Which made her a marchioness! *Her!* It
was utterly preposterous, as though she'd woken up
to find the world had tipped upside down, sending her
plummeting downwards onto his broad and—given
his cold demeanour—surprisingly warm chest. So
how on earth had it happened?

She scrunched her face up in frustration. Try as
she might, she couldn't remember anything about a
compromising situation, let alone a wedding. All she
knew was that there must have been some kind of terrible—no, catastrophic—misunderstanding! And if
his clipped tone and stony expression were anything
to go by, her so-called 'husband' wasn't particularly
happy about the situation, but surely there was no need
for him to glower at her quite so severely? It wasn't
as if she was dancing for joy either.

From what she remembered, however, he glowered
most of the time, his dark eyes filled with permanent
thunderclouds. Most ladies of the *ton* thought him
handsome despite it—there had been a rumour about
one debutante actually swooning after he'd danced
with her at Almack's—and she couldn't deny that his
classically sculpted features and perfect bone structure
were *somewhat* attractive, but personally she preferred
a man who didn't look quite so furious with the world.

In fact, now that she thought of it, Amabel had actually commented about his frowns once over breakfast, but her parents had laughed the comment away…

Amabel. The thought of her friend made her heart ache. Amabel should be the one lying here, preferably not with a head injury of course, but as the marchioness. She was perfectly suited to the role: beautiful, elegant and refined, with gleaming sable hair, doe-like brown eyes, a minuscule waist, and an ability to keep her thoughts to herself that Florence sadly lacked. *Of course* the marquess had wanted to marry her. And Amabel had wanted to marry him too, presumably, although she'd been uncharacteristically quiet on the subject, no doubt due to nerves. They would have made a perfect couple, exactly what you'd expect in two peers of the realm, and yet somehow *she*, a gentleman farmer's daughter, a companion and complete outsider to the world of the *ton*, had taken her place!

And what of the Wadlows? They'd never exactly been welcoming to her. In truth, they'd always treated her as a kind of unpaid servant, tolerating her without displaying the slightest interest in her life, but they'd still been generous enough to bring her to London. They'd even had some of Amabel's old gowns altered so she could accompany them to events without looking entirely out of place. What must they think of her now?

She blew her nose for what felt like the hundredth

time and then closed her eyes at the sound of her bedchamber door opening, in case it was the nurse back to check on her. As much as she appreciated the care, another lecture on the restorative benefits of slumber was definitely not what she needed right now...

'Are you awake?'

She opened her eyes again. That wasn't the nurse's voice.

'Yes.' She twisted her head sideways to find yet another new face peering at her. This one, however, was eager and friendly-looking, with huge green eyes and wisps of chestnut hair poking out from beneath a maid's cap.

'You're really awake!' The face broke into a wide smile. 'Mr Rimmer said so, but you know what he's like, always has to be the first to know and tell everyone everything. But then your nurse came and confirmed it, so I thought I'd sneak up and see for myself if it was true and it is! I'm *so* relieved! I've been worried out of my mind. And don't worry, your secret's safe.' The woman, whoever she was, held up a brown leather saddlebag. 'I've got your things right here. As soon as I heard that your horse had come back on its own, I raised the alarm, then went straight to the stables, distracted the grooms and whipped it away before anyone could notice. I've been hiding it in my room because I knew you wouldn't want it falling into the wrong hands, no matter what had happened, but now you're awake I'll just pop it in here.' She went over to the wardrobe, slipped the bag inside and then rubbed her hands together briskly. 'Now then, how are you feeling?'

'Um…' Florence hauled herself up against her pillows, struggling to take in such a large volume of words. Even without a bump on the head, she thought she might have had trouble. Some of them made no sense either. Why would she give two figs about a saddlebag?

Fortunately, her companion didn't seem to require an answer, coming to perch on the edge of the bed. She looked, Florence thought, about the same age as her, while her informal manner suggested they were on friendly terms.

'You're bound to feel delicate for a little while, so I brought you these to cheer you up. I know ginger's your favourite.' The woman drew a napkin out of her apron, opening it up to reveal a couple of biscuits. 'That nurse will have you on broth for the next week, so you'd better hide them if you're not going to eat them straight away. And make sure not to leave any crumbs or she'll be on to us.'

'Thank you.' Florence took the napkin and slid it under her pillow. 'That's very kind, only… I'm sorry to ask, but…' She cleared her throat awkwardly. 'Who are you?'

'Who am…? Oh!' The woman's friendly expres-

sion turned to one of utter horror as she sprang off
the bed and dropped into a curtsey so deep, it looked
as if she were sitting cross-legged on the floor. 'I beg
your pardon, my lady. They said something about you
being forgetful downstairs, but I assumed it was just
pretend or I would never have spoken so freely.' She
peeked upwards, her face crimson. 'Please don't tell
Mrs Fitch.'

'I won't say anything to anyone, I promise.' Florence shook her head quickly. 'And there's no need to
curtsey. The problem is, I seem to have no memory.
I remember nothing about the past month, so if you
could just remind me who you are…?'

'Jane, my lady. Your lady's maid.'

'Jane.' Florence repeated, in what she hoped was
a reassuring manner. 'It's nice to meet you. *Again*, I
suppose.'

'You too, my lady.' Jane straightened up slowly.

'And perhaps you could tell me…are we friends?'

'Oh, no!' Jane shook her head so violently, it looked
in danger of spinning straight off her shoulders. 'I
would never presume.'

'But it seemed like we were a few moments ago,'
Florence protested. 'And I think, if we were—*are*…
I would like that.'

'You would, my lady?' Jane's expression wavered.

'Yes. And please, call me Florence.' She smiled en-
couragingly. She supposed it *was* somewhat uncon-

ventional for a marchioness to be friends with her lady's maid—Lady Wadlow would never have permitted a servant to even sit in her presence, let alone on her bed—but then, she didn't feel much like a marchioness and she definitely wasn't Lady Wadlow. Besides, at this moment, she had a feeling she needed as many friends as she could get.

Jane scrunched her mouth up for a few seconds before breaking into another smile. 'All right, then, but I'll tell you now what I told you before. It's only for when there's nobody else about. Mrs Fitch would have a fit if she heard.'

'Who?'

'Gracious, you really have lost your memory.' Jane sounded impressed. 'She's the housekeeper here and she'd say that I was being disrespectful.'

'Understood. In that case, it'll be our secret.'

'You said that the last time too.' She chuckled. 'So it's really true? You've forgotten everything about your marriage to the marquess?'

'I'm afraid so.' Florence tilted her head to one side. 'But why did you think I might be pretending?'

'Because of, you know… Actually, I suppose you *don't*…' The maid's face took on a look of consternation. 'Oh, dear. The thing is, it's not my place to say, my lady.'

'I don't care about that.' Florence held her hands out imploringly. 'Nothing I've learnt since I woke up makes any sense. The last thing I knew, the marquess was about to propose to my best friend and now here I am instead. He said something about us being compromised, but he wouldn't tell me how.'

'Well, I only know what you told me, and I have to say, it all sounded very peculiar…' Jane started, then froze at the sound of footsteps in the corridor outside. 'That'll be your nurse coming back. I have to go.' She clasped hold of her hands and squeezed them. 'Take a look in the bag! That should explain some of it.'

'The saddlebag?' Florence looked across to the wardrobe.

'Yes.' Jane let go and took a step backwards, bowing her head as the door opened. 'Will that be all, my lady?'

'What's this?' The nurse stopped on the threshold, her gaze accusing. 'Her Ladyship is supposed to be sleeping.'

'I called for a maid.' Florence spoke up quickly. 'I had a question about the…um…chamber pot.' She cleared her throat as Jane snickered. 'But that will be all, thank you. You may go.'

'Very good, my lady.' The maid bobbed a quick curtsey, winking at her as she slid out past the nurse.

'Lady Rainton…' The nurse gave Florence a reproving look.

'I know, I know.' She slid back down under her coverlet. 'Sleep is the best medicine…'

* * *

One of the most docile breeds of cattle, the Red Devon also has one of the thickest hides, making it more resistant to external parasites, such as flies, gnats and lice. Consequently... Consequently...

Leo sighed, slamming the large agricultural tome shut with a thud. It was no use trying to read and make notes. He was too preoccupied, running over his earlier conversation with his wife and giving himself a throbbing headache in consequence.

He'd been distracted ever since he'd walked out of her bedchamber. Not guilty—because why should *he* feel that?—but uneasy, and not just because of how lost and confused she'd looked. In retrospect, his own behaviour bothered him too. He shouldn't have laughed when she'd asked if they'd been a love match. The hurt expression on her face had given him a brief, savage moment of pleasure, but the laugh itself had been callous and ungentlemanly. He shouldn't have been so cold towards her overall, but damn it, he wasn't accustomed to offering comfort, least of all to a person he resented. And this was the exact reason he'd avoided talking to her since they'd been compromised together at the Wadlows' ball. He'd been too angry to be anything *but* cold and ungentlemanly!

It wasn't as if he'd intended to remain silent forever. As her husband, he'd known that he'd have to converse with her eventually, but he'd planned to give it a few more weeks until his temper had cooled. Right now, less than a month after he'd reluctantly said 'I do', he still wasn't ready, and the inevitable result was that he'd vented his anger and resentment on a person— worse, a patient!—who had no idea why he was behaving that way. It was like punishing a person for a crime they didn't know they'd committed. Which left him with a quite singular dilemma.

What the hell was he supposed to do with her now?

And why was he *still* thinking about the way her body had felt pressed against his chest?

'My lord?'

He started, almost jumping out of his chair at the sound of his housekeeper's voice. *Hell's teeth.* He was beginning to think the woman crept up on him on purpose. She seemed to float over the ground like some kind of spectre, never making a whisper of sound. He narrowed his gaze, searching for a glint of anything like amusement in hers, but no, those stony eyes, the same pale grey shade as her hair, were a complete blank. She even looked like a spectre. He could almost swear the temperature dropped whenever she was close by.

'Mrs Fitch.' He sat back in his chair. 'What can I do for you?'

'I've come to enquire about the summer fair, my lord.' Her voice was its usual expressionless monotone.

'The fair?' He snapped his brows together. Was it really that time of year again already?

'It's only three weeks away.' Mrs Fitch bowed her head, as if her supernatural abilities extended to reading his thoughts. 'I refrained from enquiring whilst Her Ladyship was unwell, but now that she's awake...'

'Awake, but not recovered,' he clarified. 'Given that, I don't think it's entirely appropriate to hold the fair this year.'

'Naturally, I understand your reluctance, my lord.' The grey head dipped lower. 'But the fair is a Rainton tradition. It has always gone ahead, no matter how... unfortunate the circumstances.'

Leo twisted his face towards the window, looking out at the row of sycamore and horse-chestnut trees that lined the main drive. Between his housekeeper and steward, he could barely get through an hour without some reminder of the way things had always been and, by implication, *should* always be done. The fair had been held on the first Saturday in August ever since the days of the first marquess, his great-great-grandfather and, in all that time, it had never been cancelled, not even when his mother had passed away two weeks beforehand—that, presumably, being the 'unfortunate circumstance' Mrs Fitch was referring to. Despite being in mourning, his father had still made his usual appearance, acting as though nothing had happened and insisting that everyone else do the same. Only Leo, as a foolish and sentimental six-year-old boy, had had the temerity to cry, earning himself a thrashing as punishment.

'My lord?' Mrs Fitch gave a none-too-discreet cough.

He turned back with a sigh, wishing that he could simply give the woman her marching orders. Only he couldn't, and for the same reason he couldn't sack Sewell. Because irritation at their hectoring—occasionally borderline despotic—ways didn't seem like a good enough reason to deprive two people of their livelihoods, especially when they were, in all other respects, excellent employees. Besides, keeping them both in their current roles had been another of his father's instructions.

As if on cue, Mrs Fitch's eyes moved to the letter on his desk. 'Forgive my presumption in saying so, but I believe that your father would have wished for the fair to go ahead.'

'I'm sure he would,' Leo agreed, fighting the urge to say something truly ungentlemanly. 'However, Her Ladyship is obviously in no state to make any arrangements.'

'That won't be an issue, my lord. I shall arrange and oversee everything myself, both for the fair *and* in the household…' She paused, as if she was waiting for him to say something, before lifting her chin in the air. 'As I have done for the past eighteen years.'

'Good.' Leo reached for his book again. 'Then I'll leave it in your capable hands.'

'As you wish.' For a moment, a look of something like victory flitted across the housekeeper's features. 'I'll start making the arrangements today.'

Chapter Four

Finally!

Florence wriggled her way out from under the bed-clothes, placed her feet on the floor, took a few moments to steady herself—having finally learned from her two previous tumbles—and then crept quietly across her candlelit bedchamber towards the door.

It had taken *hours* for the nurse to fall asleep. Literal hours. So many that she'd begun to wish the doctor had provided somebody a little less diligent in their role. Through half-closed eyelids, she'd observed at least half a dozen false starts, when the nurse's chin had dipped forward onto her chest, only for her to give a startled jerk and then yank it back up again. The sky outside, narrowly visible through a gap in the curtains, had long ago faded to darkness before the nurse's head had finally tipped sideways and her breathing had turned to gentle snores.

Although frankly, it was no wonder it had taken so long, Florence thought as she wrapped a woollen shawl around her shoulders and slid her feet into a pair of silk slippers. The nurse's straight-backed wooden chair looked almost painfully uncomfortable, especially compared to the *much* softer armchair by the window, whilst her position on the far side of the bed was about as far away from the fire as she could possibly get, as if she was reluctant to steal any warmth from her patient. As if she genuinely had Florence's best interests at heart.

Drat!

The realisation made her stop with one hand on the doorknob and sneak silently back to the bed to remove a blanket and lay it gently across the nurse's lap. *There.* That was better. Now all she had to do was tiptoe back across the room, pick up a candle, slip outside, and then close the door behind her as quickly and quietly as possible.

One step, two steps, three, four, five, six, seven… Freedom!

She released a long breath, savouring a rush of triumph at her long-anticipated escape. Of course she wasn't technically a prisoner, or so the marquess had told her, but she had a strong suspicion the nurse would feel duty-bound to accompany her wherever she went, and right now she wanted to be alone. Admittedly, she had no idea where she was going, but she refused to lie in bed any longer, going slowly mad thinking about what might or might not have happened in London. The least she could do was get her bearings and look around.

The wood-panelled corridor in which she found herself contained five other doors, all closed. She hadn't heard any footsteps or voices during her time spent waiting for the nurse to doze off, which suggested the rooms weren't currently occupied, but she wasn't about to take any chances by peeking inside them either. If she was going to explore, she was at least going to make it to the ground floor...

Turning a corner, she found herself on a gallery overlooking a cantilever staircase that led down to a grand entrance hall. The walls on each side were painted with pastoral scenes, although it was hard to distinguish details in the candlelight, while the floor below was made up of hundreds of squares of white, black and orange decorative marble, all arranged to form the image of a majestic-looking swan.

She leaned over the gallery railing, her eye caught by a dark shape suspended in the air in front of her, hanging from the centre of a ceiling rose, not a chandelier, but what appeared to be a large, gilt birdcage. From what she could tell, it was empty, but immediately below it, curled up over the eye of the swan like some kind of gatekeeper, was a large grey wolfhound.

A *very* large grey wolfhound, practically the size of a pony. Oh, dear...

As if it sensed her alarm, the dog lifted its head,

fixing her with a baleful yet expectant stare. Florence gulped, contemplating retreat, before stiffening her spine. She hadn't waited so long for the nurse to fall asleep just to be thwarted at the first hurdle, even if that hurdle had paws the same size as her hands. Besides, it wasn't barking or showing its teeth. Surely that meant it recognised her smell and was friendly? She hoped so, because she really didn't want to consider the alternative...

Warily, she placed a foot on the top step of the staircase, wincing as it creaked beneath her weight, then made her way slowly downstairs, keeping her eyes fixed on the dog the whole time. The dog, in turn, watched her, its head tilted to one side, as if it was wondering what she was doing, creeping about the house in the middle of the night.

'I'm exploring,' she whispered, because he or she looked as if they required an answer. 'Not running away,' she clarified, although now that she thought about it, she could see the huge front door up ahead.

Maybe she *ought* to try running away?

The moment the thought hit her, she had the strangest sensation of having thought it before. A plan was already unspooling in her mind. She could go to the stables, 'borrow' a horse and ride off into the night. Obviously she'd need to put on a greatcoat, or at least something less conspicuous than a nightdress, and she'd have to raid the kitchens for supplies, but she *could* do it. Then she could ride north, forget all this nonsense about being married to a marquess and go home, back to Cumberland and her family.

Except… Her plan hit a wall. If she really *was* married to a marquess then this house was her home now. And she had no idea how to get from Dorset to Cumberland. Also, no money. Never mind the prospect of highwaymen and…

'Sleepwalking?' A deep voice made her heart jump so high, she thought it might be trying to escape through her throat.

She whirled around, almost extinguishing her candle in the process, to find the marquess standing in an open doorway, arms folded and legs planted wide apart, watching her without the faintest hint of emotion on those chiselled features. Despite the lateness of the hour, he was dressed in the same form-fitting charcoal-grey coat and tight buckskin breeches he'd been wearing when he'd visited her earlier, his shirt still unwrinkled and his cravat still immaculately tied. Good grief, did the man never relax? And did he have to look so irritatingly…*masculine*?

She placed her empty hand to her throat, trying her best not to look like somebody who'd recently been plotting escape. 'You startled me.'

'I noticed.' He moved a couple of steps closer, causing the wolfhound to unfurl itself from the floor, give a stretch, and then shuffle forward to greet him, tail wagging. 'Were you looking for something?'

'No-o.' She coughed, very aware of his proximity suddenly. 'I just couldn't sleep, so I was…following my feet.'

'Ah.' He glanced down at the appendages in question, his gaze lingering briefly on her bare ankles.

'I wanted to see where I was.' She pulled her shoulders back, hearing herself getting defensive. Up close, he was taller than she'd remembered, so that she had to tilt her head back to meet his gaze. 'You said that I wasn't a prisoner.'

'And I meant it.' He unfolded his arms to smooth a hand over the wolfhound's curly head. 'However, if you're curious, perhaps you'd allow me to give you a tour?'

'*No!*' She gasped, recoiling in horror at the very idea of being alone with him. No respectable woman would ever agree to an assignation with a strange man at night. No respectable man would ever suggest such a thing either! Only he wasn't a strange man, she remembered, a few seconds too late. He was her husband. Which meant that it wasn't scandalous at all, even if she still didn't much care for the prospect of his company. 'I mean, I'm happy to look around by myself. It's not necessary to accompany me.'

'Considering what happened earlier, I'm afraid it might be.' His expression didn't alter, although the tone of his voice suggested he wasn't particularly thrilled about the idea of spending time with her either. 'I wouldn't want you collapsing again, especially carrying a candle.'

'Oh.' She pursed her lips. It was a reasonable point, even if she suspected he was more concerned for the safety of his furniture than her well-being. Her legs *were* feeling somewhat more stable now, but she probably still ought to be careful.

'Very well.' She looked around, belatedly noticing two rows of alabaster busts, all of stern-faced men, confronting each other from red marble plinths on either side of the hall, like opposing teams on a chess board. 'This is very grand. I like the swan. Is there a reason for it?'

'My father liked birds.'

'Ah.' She glanced upwards. 'Well, that explains the cage.'

He nodded, following the direction of her gaze. 'That used to contain a pair of nightingales. The idea was that everyone who entered the house would be greeted by the sound of birdsong.'

'What a lovely idea.' She wrinkled her nose. 'Although not so nice for the birds.'

'I agree. That's why it's empty now.'

'Then maybe you should take it down?'

He gave her a sharp look, as if the idea had never occurred to him before. 'Maybe I should.'

'So…' She gestured past his shoulder as tension seemed to crackle in the air between them. 'What room is that?'

'Take a look.' He held a hand out for her candle. 'May I?'

She handed it over as she walked past him into a drawing room at least four times the size of her new, already sizeable bedchamber. Between the candle-light and the floor-to-ceiling paintings, it was hard to judge the colour scheme, but it looked like a shade of deep forest green with a pattern of…she peered closer…birds again. Golden eagles, by the look of it, engraved into the paper. The bird motif was evident all over the room, in porcelain figurines and ornate carved furniture with… Were those talons for feet?

She headed towards the fireplace, over which hung a gilt-framed painting of a large, stately-looking house. It was made of grey stone, with side wings that extended forward to form a courtyard, in which two external staircases led up to a terrace fronted by six massive stone pillars, themselves topped with a triangular-shaped pediment. The roof on either side, meanwhile, was flat, with a balustrade that ran the entire length of the house, giving the impression of medieval battlements. Clearly, it had been designed to look like a modern-day stronghold, a bastion of wealth and privilege.

She gasped as it occurred to her that there was only

one reason why such a painting would be given pride of place over the fireplace.

'Is that...*here*?' Suddenly she couldn't drag her gaze away.

'Yes.' Her husband answered from just behind her shoulder. 'That's Rainton Court.'

'You mean, we're inside...*there*?'

'We are.'

'So *that's* my home?'

There was a telling pause before he answered. 'Yes.'

'Oh.' She sank down onto a conveniently placed footstool.

'Are you feeling unwell?' His tone was completely neutral, as if he was neither surprised by, nor particularly interested in, her reaction. 'Do you not wish to continue our tour?'

'Yes. No. I don't...' She put her palms on either side of her head, as if she could somehow squeeze her thoughts back together. 'I just need a few moments.'

'Very well.' He placed her candle on the mantelpiece and braced his own hands against it, leaning forward to stare down into the fire, his posture rigid.

'How many rooms are there?' she asked at last, though her voice sounded small even to her. By contrast, the ticking of the clock on the mantel seemed almost deafening.

'Altogether?' He didn't move. 'I'm not certain.

Around one hundred, I should think, including the attics.'

'One hundred?' She gaped at him, watching as the firelight cast shadowy patterns over his face. It wasn't a house so much as a palace. What was *she* doing in a palace? Her family home consisted of only fourteen rooms in total!

'The original house was around half the size, I believe, but my father wanted something grander. He had it rebuilt forty years ago.'

'Well, it's certainly…impressive.' She cleared her throat, remembering something she'd heard over the breakfast table in London. 'I'm sorry about your father. Lady Wadlow said that you'd only come into your title recently.'

'Yes, he passed away earlier this year.' He turned his head to look at her finally, a speculative glint in his eyes. 'What else did Lady Wadlow tell you?'

'Oh, she wasn't telling me,' she clarified. 'I was only in town as Amabel's companion. I just overheard things.'

'Then what else did you overhear?'

She hesitated, though there seemed little point in hiding the truth, no matter how blunt it sounded.

'That you had thirty thousand acres, twenty thousand a year, and you'd come to London to find a wife.'

He made a faint huffing sound. 'Accurate on all counts.'

'Will you tell me what happened now?' she asked, sitting forward hopefully. 'How we were compromised?'

He shook his head. 'You only woke up this morning and the doctor said it's important for you to stay calm and avoid any mental distress.'

'Yes, he told me that too, only how he expects me to do it is another matter.' She rolled her eyes. 'I don't understand how anyone can expect me to be calm when I have so many unanswered questions.'

He pulled his head back at that, his expression penetrating as he stared down at her. With his mouth set in a grim line, there was something so cold and aristocratic about him, it was all she could do not to shiver.

'Please?' She tightened her shawl around her throat, willing her voice to remain steady as she held on to his gaze. 'I need to know.'

'Very well, then.' A muscle tightened in his jaw before he twisted his lips in a mirthless smile. 'Let's call it a bedtime story…'

Leo rested one arm on the mantelpiece and gazed dispassionately down at his wife. She looked as if she'd just fallen out of bed. Her hair had mostly escaped from its braid, hanging in wisps about her face, and although she'd changed into a new nightgown, it was already crumpled, albeit half hidden by a shawl wrapped around the top of her body. Despite that,

however, her appearance now was actually marginally better than it had been that morning, or at least
her nose wasn't quite so red and her eyes had lost their
panicked look. Obviously there was still a long way to
go before she was back to full health, but she made a
good point about her recovery. He doubted that he'd
be able to rest if he were in her position either. Losing her memory had to be a deeply disturbing experience. Maybe the best thing he could do for her was
try to jolt it.

Best or worst. He supposed he'd find out which
soon enough.

'Once upon a time,' he began, 'Lord and Lady Wadlow of Brampton decided to throw a ball on behalf of
their daughter, Miss Amabel Wadlow. It was at the
height of the London Season and I attended with the
intention of asking for that same daughter's hand in
matrimony. After broaching the subject with Lord
Wadlow early in the evening, I was in an optimistic
frame of mind. I danced twice with Miss Wadlow before asking if she would grant me the honour of a private audience in the library. Unfortunately, there was
a small tear in the hem of her gown which required
her to withdraw briefly to mend it, but she suggested
that I go ahead to the library and wait for her there.'
He drew in a deep breath, his voice hardening. 'That
was where you found me.'

'Me?' Her jaw dropped.

'Yes. You were standing close to Miss Wadlow when she made the suggestion, so I can only presume you overheard and decided to follow me.'

'But why would I—?'

'When you reached the library, you seemed curiously agitated.' He spoke over her, ignoring the question. Now that he'd started, he wanted to get the whole sordid story over with as quickly as possible. 'Naturally, I suggested we go somewhere more public before anyone came in and found us together, but you told me you had an important message from Miss Wadlow to communicate.'

'I see.' This time she was slow to respond, her expression perplexed. 'What was the message?'

'I have no idea.' He held on to her gaze, watching for any flash of recognition. 'When it came to it, you seemed rather at a loss for words.'

'That doesn't make any sense.' She drew her brows together. 'Why would I tell you I had a message and then not deliver it?'

'I remember thinking the same thing. Unfortunately, that was the moment the door opened and several members of the *ton* walked in, Miss Wadlow included.'

'You mean…?' She rocked backwards, a flush of red spreading up her neck and across her cheeks. 'But we were only talking.'

'We were still alone together. That was more than

enough to compromise us.' He couldn't keep the contempt from his voice. 'As you were no doubt well aware.'

She gave an audible intake of breath, holding her hands up as if to push the words away. 'You think I did it deliberately?'

He lifted an eyebrow. 'I admit, you made quite a good show of pretending to be as appalled as I was, but why else did you come to the library with some made-up story about a message? I might have applauded your cunning had it not made such a mess of my own plans.'

'But it's not true!' She shot to her feet, her eyes flashing like sapphires in the candlelight. 'Amabel is my best friend. I would never have betrayed her like that. Never! Why would I?'

He didn't bother to lower his eyebrow. 'You had no dowry or connections, whereas Miss Wadlow had both, as well as a number of suitors. Perhaps you were jealous?'

She reeled backwards again, seemingly outraged by the suggestion. 'I was *not* jealous!'

'And yet here you are, a marchioness, while your friend, as far as I know, remains unwed.'

'I'm also no fortune hunter.' She sounded as if she was speaking through gritted teeth.

'So you've been saying for the past month, but what other interpretation is there?'

'I don't know, I just know that that's not it! I came to London as Amabel's companion and I was perfectly content with my position! And if I've been saying so for the past month then it's the truth!' She put her hands on her hips, so that her shawl fell open. 'Didn't I tell you what the message was later?'

'No.' He fought the urge to glance downwards.

'What do you mean?'

'Interestingly enough, you said that you couldn't. Then, after our wedding, you persisted in saying there was an explanation for your behaviour, without actually telling me what it was. In that respect, not much has changed.' He gave a disgusted snort. 'You can understand my scepticism.'

'Oh.' She looked crestfallen before rallying again. 'Then what about Amabel? What did she say about the message?'

'Nothing. When I asked, she said she had no idea what I was talking about. She seemed as surprised as anyone. Anyone including the Earl and Countess of Malvern, Lady Lansbury, Baron Paltrow and Lord and Lady Wadlow.'

'Oh.' She dropped back down onto the footstool. 'So we truly had to marry?'

'We did.' He turned his gaze back to the fireplace. Technically, that part wasn't strictly true. He could have refused to go through with it. He'd certainly thought about doing so, but his sense of honour had compelled him. No matter how conniving she'd been, or the cost to his own status, considering her lack of family or connections, his conscience hadn't allowed him to ruin her.

'There just has to be some reasonable explanation for what happened.' She sounded genuinely at a loss.

'If there is, I'd be delighted to hear it.'

'What about an annulment?'

'What?' He turned his head again sharply.

'Why don't we have our marriage annulled?'

'On what grounds?'

'That we're not…you know…properly married.' A look of sudden panic flashed across her face. 'Are we?'

'We are not.' He felt a muscle twitch in his jaw. 'If you're asking whether or not we've shared a bed, the answer is most definitely no.'

'Thank goodness.' Her shoulders sagged with relief.

'Quite.'

'I didn't mean…' Her cheeks were so red now, he could see them glowing in the half-darkness. 'I only meant that if there was no wedding night, then there's still a way out of this marriage. I'll happily agree to an annulment.'

Happily? He let his gaze roam over her face for a few moments. Given what she'd done to trap him, the offer was…surprising. Unfortunately, it was also pointless.

'Overjoyed as I am to hear that, we've been living

together under the same roof for the past month. Even if a court believed us, the *ton* would not.'

'A divorce, then?'

'It's not quite so easy. A petition to parliament would be lengthy, expensive, and most likely unsuccessful.'

'Unlikely doesn't mean impossible.'

'No, but the scandal of a divorce would be even greater than that of our marriage.'

'I don't care about scandal!'

'You did on our wedding day. As I recall, your stated reason for going ahead was that you didn't want to bring any shame on your family.' He flexed his fingers. 'In any case, I won't allow my name to be tarnished any more than it has been already. I've had more than enough of being a laughing stock to the *ton*.'

Her posture went rigid. 'What's that supposed to mean?'

'I should think it was obvious. I'm the Marquess of Rainton. Your father is a gentleman farmer, is he not?'

'My parents are perfectly respectable.'

'I don't doubt it. However, I also doubt they ever expected to have a marchioness for a daughter.'

Her nostrils flared, as if she was restraining her temper with an effort. 'I still think there has to be a way out of this marriage.'

'There isn't.'

'So that's it?' She stared at him with an appalled expression. 'You're just going to give up?'

'Yes.' He sighed, feeling very tired all of a sudden. This whole argument seemed to have been revolving around his head for weeks. Ironically, tonight was the first time he'd involved her in the discussion, but every time he'd come to the same disheartening conclusion, that there was no way out. The marriage trap had well and truly closed around him. 'Now, I think that's enough of a tour for tonight. I suggest we both retire and get some sleep.'

'Well, that explains it.' She rose slowly to her feet, her gaze still fixed on his. 'That's why you look at me so coldly, like you despise me. It's because you do.'

'What else did you expect?' He didn't deny it. 'This marriage isn't what I wanted.'

'Me neither, no matter what you think.' She wrenched her shoulders back. 'All I know is that there has to be some explanation for what happened and I'm going to find out what it is.'

He looked her up and down, impressed despite himself. With her chin thrust outwards and a fierce glare on her face, she looked magnificently, almost regally defiant. If he weren't still so angry, he thought he might have been tempted to reach out and haul her against him, to stop her lips with his own. Desire rippled through him at the thought of how she would feel, what she might taste like…

'Then I wish you luck.' He turned away quickly, reaching for her candle and heading for the door. 'Come on, I'll show you the way.'

He didn't look back to see if she was following.

Chapter Five

'...And in here is the Print Room,' Mrs Fitch intoned solemnly as she led Florence into a wood-panelled room filled with mahogany cabinets. 'The former marquess was a great collector of engravings and paintings, particularly scenes of nature. He had a profound interest in the sublime.'

'How interesting.' Florence took a step forward and immediately bumped her hip against the corner of a table. 'Ouch. It's very dark.'

'Deliberately so, to prevent sun damage.' The housekeeper drew back some heavy damask curtains and lifted the blind a couple of inches, admitting the faintest influx of light. 'As you can see, the walls are also pasted with prints. The former marquess himself painted the borders to resemble picture frames. He was an extremely talented artist.'

Florence peered closer at the wall. Mrs Fitch was right, the brushwork was exquisite. The marquess had even gone to the effort of painting tiny picture hooks and chains. From a distance, the illusion would be very convincing. Only it was still so gloomy, the effect was somewhat wasted.

'Now, if you'd care to look in here, my lady...' The housekeeper slid open one of the cabinet drawers and pulled out an album. 'These Alpine scenes were His Lordship's favourites. He was a great traveller in his youth and purchased them while on his Grand Tour. He told me once that he felt a great affinity for mountains.'

'Mmm.' Florence smiled politely, inwardly bracing herself for the ten-minute lecture she knew was coming. Mrs Fitch had knocked on her bedroom door that morning just as she'd been finishing her breakfast, introducing herself as the housekeeper and offering a tour of the house, 'as per the marquess's instructions'. He might as well have sent a note saying that he didn't want to do it himself, Florence had thought, though in all honesty she'd been relieved. It had been two days since their midnight conversation, two days of enforced bed rest, fuming, and no progress at all with her memory. The fog in her mind was just as impenetrable as ever, no matter how hard she tried to push her way through.

She simply couldn't believe she was married to such a cold-hearted, close-minded, implacable man! Obviously, she'd only gone through with the wedding because she'd had no other choice. After being com-

promised, refusing him would have made her a social pariah, bringing shame on her entire family, so
how *dared* he accuse her of being a fortune hunter!
Admittedly, the circumstantial evidence seemed to
be against her, but there *had* to be some other, logical
explanation. All she had to do was figure out what it
was and then…well, then hopefully she could find a
way out of this marriage. He might have given up on
finding one, but she certainly hadn't. In the meantime, she didn't want to see him again for at least another day…a week…a month! In fact, why not make
it a full year?

But she *had* still wanted a tour of the house, which
was why she'd set her cup of hot chocolate aside and
clambered straight out of bed and into a dressing gown
when Mrs Fitch had arrived. With her leg muscles almost recovered and her nose feeling significantly less
blocked than before, she'd felt positively energised.

Unfortunately, she hadn't reckoned on the housekeeper's enthusiasm for her subject. Mrs Fitch seemed
determined to talk her through the entire history of
each room, including when it was last decorated,
which family members had favoured it, and the reason why the furniture was arranged 'just so', as well
as anecdotes about specific objects, of which there
were many. Florence had never seen so many porcelain birds in her life. It was like walking through a
giant aviary. Still, the tour *might* have been interesting,

if only the housekeeper's monologic delivery hadn't made her company as cold as any of the marble statues they'd passed in the sculpture gallery.

That had been Florence's least favourite room so far, reminding her of a cave her father had once taken her and her brothers to visit, a small opening in some rocks that had led down into a vast underground cavern filled with dripping water and strange-looking stalagmites and stalactites. Being there had given her an eerie sensation she hadn't felt again until today. In both cases, she hadn't been able to escape quickly enough.

But Mrs Fitch was still speaking…

'This entire drawer is filled with pictures of the Matterhorn, the former marquess's favourite mountain. And if we look in this drawer…'

'Is the current marquess a collector as well?' she interrupted, trying to distract the housekeeper before she could open yet another album.

There was a short pause, followed by a sniff. 'Not at the moment, but I'm certain he'll come to appreciate this room eventually. In the meantime, I shall maintain it, in accordance with his father's wishes. The former marquess left a list of extremely detailed, but kindly meant instructions regarding the management of both the house and estate.'

'Instructions?' Florence wrinkled her brow, struck by the word. 'Surely you mean suggestions?'

'No, I do not.' The housekeeper bristled. 'His Lordship's father was in charge of the estate for fifty years. He knew exactly how it ought to be run. His letter was addressed to his son, of course, but there were sections pertaining to both myself and Mr Sewell, the steward. We each received copies.' Another sniff. 'Mine is one of my most prized possessions.'

'Oh.' Florence pressed her lips together. It was only natural that the former marquess should have wanted to guide his son, she supposed, but the thought of him continuing to manage the estate from beyond the grave struck her as somewhat morbid. She had a sudden vision of a ghost floating around the hallways, issuing 'instructions'...

She blinked, pushing the image away. 'It just sounds a little restrictive. I mean, surely times change?'

'Times may. Rainton Court does not.'

'But shouldn't the new marquess manage the estate as *he* sees fit?'

Mrs Fitch drew herself up to her full height. 'The new marquess is aware that he has a great man to live up to. He keeps the letter on his desk for that reason. He would not, I am certain, wish to damage his father's legacy by making any unnecessary changes. Fortunately, however, despite one regrettable setback, for which he was blameless...' here she paused significantly '... I'm pleased to say that he's doing an admirable job of following in his father's footsteps.'

'If you say so.' Florence gritted her teeth. She was half tempted to keep on arguing, to say that, given the chance, maybe her husband might surpass his father, but she had a feeling there was no point. Besides, why should *she* stand up for him? Especially when she was obviously the 'regrettable setback' being referred to.

'Now, if you could direct your attention to this cabinet, my lady,' Mrs Fitch went on. 'It dates from the sixteenth century and was made in the Netherlands by Jozef van Stappen, a master craftsman from the Gelderland region. Note the brass handles...'

'Would you care to sit down, my lady?' a voice murmured.

Florence smiled over her shoulder, feeling a powerful urge to hug the speaker. Nurse McKay had insisted on joining the tour, a gesture that had irritated her at first, but now seemed like one of supreme self-sacrifice. It felt reassuring to have an ally beside her, somebody who not only had her well-being at heart, but, more importantly, was offering a route of escape.

'Actually, I think I might need a rest.' She interrupted the housekeeper. 'Perhaps we could have some tea?'

'Of course, my lady.' Mrs Fitch inclined her head.

'And then perhaps you could tell me all about the household?'

'The household?' For the first time, a flicker of

some emotion passed over the housekeeper's face, a look almost akin to panic.

'Yes, so I can learn how to manage it myself.' She forced a smile. Unappealing as the prospect of another lecture might be, this was one she needed to hear. If her husband wasn't prepared to consider either a divorce or an annulment then it was important for her to learn her new responsibilities, at least until she could find some way to change his mind.

'Forgive me, my lady, but as we discussed *before* your accident, my understanding is that I have been entrusted to run the household.' The housekeeper's tone was anything but apologetic. 'His Lordship certainly hasn't informed me otherwise.'

Florence sucked in a breath, her hands curling into fists at the insult. Because *of course* her husband didn't want her running his household. He probably thought her incapable of managing anything so grand. She wasn't the woman he'd wanted to marry. She wasn't even the type of woman he'd wanted to marry. His frigid manner the other night had made that abundantly clear. She was, or had been, a companion, little more than a servant to a man like him, and he already had a housekeeper, making *her* redundant.

A shiver rippled over her skin, as if a cold hand had just pushed its way into her chest and wrapped around her heart. Because if he didn't want her to manage the household, what did he expect her to do instead? Even if she hoped that her time as marchioness was temporary, she still needed some kind of role or she'd end up like one of the marble statues in the gallery, voiceless and frozen, with no purpose but to simply exist!

'Naturally I would be willing to listen to any suggestions Your Ladyship might have,' Mrs Fitch went on, her voice resuming its usual monotone.

'Would you?' Florence answered tightly. *Suggestions.* 'Or would you need to get His Lordship's approval first?'

There was a moment of silence before the housekeeper simply folded her long fingers over her waist. 'Well, now that's settled, if you'd care to follow me to the blue morning room, my lady, I'll ring for some tea.'

Florence didn't move, her mind spinning at the utter injustice of what she'd just learned. It was bad enough that her husband blamed *her* for their marriage, but now it seemed he intended to humiliate her as well, treating her as a marchioness in name only.

If only she could remember what had happened in London! Then she could defend herself properly. Or, failing that, if only she could speak to Jane again. If she'd told anyone about the events leading up to her marriage, surely it would have been her lady's maid, but her nurse was like a limpet stuck to the side of a ship. She absolutely refused to leave her alone, making private conversation impossible.

Although…it occurred to her suddenly that Jane had already told her something. *Look in the bag*, she'd said, as if that would explain everything. *Look in the bag.*

'On second thoughts…' she called out, just as Mrs Fitch reached the door, 'I think I'll go and lie down.'

'Of course, my lady. I'll have some tea sent up to your room.'

'That's not necessary.' She turned to the nurse, putting on her most ingratiating expression. 'Perhaps you'd be so kind as to make one of your special remedies? The last one was so invigorating.'

'Why, I'd be happy to, my lady.' The nurse positively beamed at the compliment. 'I'll just help you upstairs first.'

'Don't worry, I can manage by myself.' She was already heading out of the room, seized with a new sense of purpose. 'I'm perfectly steady now. And thank you so much for the tour, Mrs Fitch! It was very…educational.' She bit her lip and then couldn't resist adding. 'And don't forget to close the curtains!'

She hurried upstairs, possibly faster than was advisable, though thankfully without collapsing again, and closed her bedroom door firmly behind her. Based on previous trips to the kitchens, she estimated that she had approximately five minutes before the nurse appeared with a pot of some noxious brew, but hopefully that was long enough.

Quickly, she flung the wardrobe open, heaved

out the brown leather saddlebag and tipped the contents all over the floor, revealing two tightly folded cotton dresses, a petticoat, a woollen shawl, a hairbrush, some toiletries, a purse of money and a bundle of letters wrapped in pale blue ribbon. Then she crouched down on her haunches, examining the haul. The clothes and toiletries suggested that she'd been going on a journey, but where? And if that was the case, why had nobody else known about it? And why had she been alone? It didn't make any sense...

Unless she'd been running away.

Her breath stalled as she remembered the sudden fervour that had gripped her in the hall the other night, the powerful impulse she'd felt to run out of the front door and escape. Had her unconscious mind been spurring her on? Had some part of her been remembering? More importantly, that spoke of her innocence, didn't it? Because why, if she'd gone to such extreme lengths to compromise a marquess, would she have been running away within a month of her wedding? The rest of the items reinforced the theory because they were all hers, from Cumberland, not ones she'd obtained after her marriage, as if she hadn't wanted to take anything from her new life... And as for the letters...

The letters... She frowned. She had no idea about the letters.

She threw a swift look at the door before tearing the

ribbon away and unfolding the first piece of paper. It opened with a crackle to reveal unfamiliar handwriting addressed to… *Dearest?*

She gave a squeak of alarm as she carried on reading: *Every moment without you is an eternity... I yearn for the day when I can hold you in my arms... Seeing you with him when I ache for you... Signed, your devoted servant.*

Yearn, ache and devoted? She stared at the words for a few seconds, the back of her neck prickling with unease, then dropped the letter into her lap and opened another, only to find more of the same. They were all love letters, all unsigned and undated, all declaring their deep and abiding love for…*her*? But they couldn't be to her, could they? No one had written her a love letter in her whole life. She didn't have any suitors and they certainly wouldn't be from her husband. Yet they were in her possession, which left only one possibility…

No! She clamped a hand to her mouth at the idea. It was bad enough to find herself accused of deceiving a marquess into marriage, but to discover an illicit correspondence with another man as well, a man who called her darling and dearest, was even worse! What was going on? And how was it possible that absolutely nothing of any great import had happened for the first twenty-one years of her life and now two huge things were happening at once? And she'd somehow forgotten them both!

She racked her brains, trying to come up with some other plausible explanation for the letters. Perhaps they were unwanted? Perhaps she was being bothered by messages from some secret admirer? Although, in that case, why had she been carrying them in her saddlebag like some kind of precious cargo? Why hadn't she simply destroyed them?

No, whichever way she looked at it, they were incriminating. Just as everything she'd discovered since she'd woken up from her accident was incriminating. And now, as much as she didn't want to believe any of it, all of the evidence seemed to lead to the same horrible and inescapable conclusion: that not only was she the kind of person who would poach her best friend's future husband, but she was also the kind of person who would conduct a secret, adulterous liaison with another man within weeks of her marriage! It seemed incredible that her personality could have altered so much within one short month, but it must have. She *definitely* hadn't been corresponding with anyone before the Wadlows' ball, which meant the letters must have arrived after she was married, which further meant that the other items in her saddlebag were no defence at all. She might not have been escaping so much as running away with somebody else!

Her stomach lurched violently as she packed the

items away again, then hastily tucked the bag back into the wardrobe before throwing herself into the armchair by the window. Suddenly she no longer wanted to speak to Jane. She didn't want to talk to anyone, except possibly her mother, but she was three hundred miles away, probably still recovering from the shock of learning that her only daughter had somehow married a marquess…

'Here you go, my lady.' The nurse entered a few seconds later, placing a cup filled with some foul-smelling brown liquid on the table beside her. 'This will help to rebuild your strength. It's an old family recipe.'

'Thank you.' Florence wrinkled her nose before taking a mouthful. It tasted even worse than she remembered, but she was too guilt-ridden to care. Now that a seed of doubt had been planted, her mind was a swirling maelstrom of questions. What if her husband was right about her? *Could* she have deliberately trapped him on the night of the Wadlows' ball? Because if she was completely honest with herself, hadn't some deep-down part of her been intrigued by those thunderstorm eyes and scowling brows, despite his cold demeanour? Hadn't she felt a strange fluttering sensation in her chest every time he'd so much as glanced in her direction, and wondered, on occasion, how it would feel to be the recipient of his attention? Hadn't she even, to her own secret mortification, dreamed about it? And if all those things were true, then *could* she have been so powerfully jealous of Amabel that she'd seized an opportunity to take her place as the marchioness, destroying all of her friend's hopes and dreams in the process? Was that why she'd lost her memory? Because she'd done something so heinous that she didn't *want* to remember?

She squeezed her eyes shut, every fibre of her being screaming a denial. Amabel was her closest friend. They'd been enjoying the Season together, without even the tiniest hint of bad feeling! She'd never so much as thought about finding a husband for herself in London. *That* was the truth, she knew it! And yet something had happened, something that she couldn't remember, and the infinitely more frightening truth was that she had no idea who she was any more.

And if she didn't know that, then what else might she be capable of?

Chapter Six

This was his mother's fault, Leo thought, drumming his fingers on the tablecloth as he waited for Florence. The former Marchioness of Rainton was the parent from whom he'd inherited a conscience, one that had been gnawing at him ever since he'd parted ways with his new bride outside her bedroom door two nights ago. Yes, he'd told her the truth that she'd asked for, but he'd been rude—again—allowing his anger to govern his behaviour when he ought to have been sympathetic. And so, whilst he couldn't bring himself to apologise to a woman who'd manipulated and trapped him into marriage, he'd decided the least he could do, now that she was back on her feet, was invite her to join him for dinner, here in the cavernous dining room with its deep crimson walls, painted ceiling and twelve-foot mahogany table. It was a matter of honour, no matter how much he'd prefer to eat alone, as usual, at the desk in his study. And this time he was determined to behave in a polite and gentlemanly fashion.

The only slight flaw in his plan was that she didn't appear to be coming.

He spared a glance at his pocket watch, wondering how much longer to wait before telling his footmen to start serving. Five minutes, he decided. Five…or ten. He owed her—and his mother—that much.

Conscience aside, he was also curious to see how she would behave now that his words, the whole brutal truth about their marriage, had had a chance to sink in. As far as he could tell, their last conversation hadn't triggered any memories, but maybe by now? Despite his resentment, he'd been impressed by the strength of her conviction in her own innocence. Her blue eyes had seemed to shine with an even brighter lustre than usual. She'd actually offered him a divorce and pressed for an annulment! It made him wonder whether her actions on the evening of the Wadlows' ball had been less the result of pre-meditated calculation and more spur-of-the-moment opportunism. It didn't change the result, but the idea that she wasn't quite as conniving as he'd initially assumed made him feel marginally warmer towards her.

Of course there *was* another possibility… He took a sip of wine, pondering. Was it feasible that she'd been telling the truth all along and there really was some other explanation for their having been compromised?

Could she be a victim in this whole sorry mess too? In which case...*had* he been too harsh on her?

No. He set his glass down again, so roughly that wine almost sloshed over the rim. He'd witnessed her actions with his own eyes. She'd cornered him, lied to him and then trapped him. End of story.

So why did he feel as if he was missing something? Why did he still feel like the villain?

'Sorry I'm late.'

He jerked his head up at the sound of Florence's voice. He'd been so deep in thought, he hadn't noticed her enter the room, but it seemed she'd arrived just in time to catch him scowling. He'd become so used to seeing her in a nightgown, it was almost a shock to see her in a dress again, a pretty, pale blue evening gown with matching elbow-length gloves and a simple gold locket around her throat. Her hair was dressed too, pinned up at the back, with a few curls left free to frame and soften her face, accentuating the slender column of her neck in a way that made him want to reach out and stroke the delicate skin there.

He blinked, mentally comparing her appearance now with that of the wild-eyed wraith he'd found in the entrance hall just two nights before. Thankfully, the bruise on her forehead had faded and her nose had returned to an almost normal colour, and yet despite that, she seemed diminished somehow, like a shadow of the woman who'd argued with him so vociferously.

Her shoulders were slumped, her brows were drawn, and her mouth was turned downwards at the corners. As for her eyes, all the brightness he'd admired had faded completely away. Something about that caused an unwonted pang in his chest.

'Good evening.' He stood up and bowed. 'I was starting to think you weren't hungry.'

'My lady's maid wanted to try out a new hairstyle, but it was more complicated than she expected.' Her voice sounded different, almost listless, as she gestured vaguely at her head. 'Eventually, we settled for this.'

'Ah. Well, it looks…nice.' He cleared his throat as a footman pulled out a chair for her. 'Mrs Fitch tells me we're having cream of asparagus soup, followed by salmon with broccoli and beef a la mode. I trust that's acceptable?'

She paused halfway into her seat. 'Of course. I'm sure that whatever Mrs Fitch chooses is fitting.'

'Good.' He sat down again, perplexed by the sudden edge to her voice. 'How are you feeling today? Any headaches?'

'Yes.' She pressed her brows together. 'But not from the accident, I think. More from everything else, the things you told me.' She paused, a pained expression passing over her features. 'I wish I could stop thinking, even for five minutes, but it all keeps going round and round my mind.'

He felt a pang of guilt. 'I'm sorry. I shouldn't have spoken so bluntly the other evening. I should have waited to tell you.'

'No. I was the one who insisted on hearing the whole story. The consequences are my own fault.' She hunched forward, as if her body was curling in on itself. 'I just never imagined it would be anything like that.'

'Well…' He reached for his spoon as soup bowls were set before them. 'Perhaps some food will help.'

'Perhaps,' she murmured, staring at her cutlery for several seconds before turning her head to meet his gaze full-on. 'Can I ask you a question?'

He grimaced. 'Considering how the last one went, perhaps we ought to wait until after dinner?'

'It's not about what happened. It's just… Why am I here?'

'Here?'

'Why did you invite me to dine with you this evening?'

'You're my wife.'

'But you don't like me. You admitted as much the other night.'

'I didn't…' He stopped, shifting awkwardly in his chair. She was right, he *had*. 'None the less, it's fitting that we dine together.'

'Have we ever done so before?'

He paused before answering. 'No.'

'Then why invite me now?'

'Because…' He faltered again. *Because things are different now*, he almost said, except that they weren't, not really. She might have banged her head and lost her memory, but she was still the same person underneath. As was he. Nothing fundamental had changed. It was only his conscience that was now compelling him to spend some time with her.

'The reason doesn't matter,' he said finally. 'The fact is, we've been married for almost a full month and it's time we shared a meal, don't you think?'

'I suppose so.' She held on to his gaze, her own narrowing, as if she was trying to see past the words into his mind.

'Do you have another question?' He supposed he might as well get it over with.

'Yes. How should I address you? As Rainton? Or should I say *my lord* every time?'

'Leo.' He inclined his head. 'You may call me Leo.'

'Leo.' She gave him another long look before dipping her spoon into her bowl and moving it around slowly.

'What about you?'

'Mmm?' She blinked, as if her thoughts had been elsewhere.

'What should I call you? I mean, obviously your name is Florence, but is there a shortened form you prefer? Or perhaps a middle name?'

She shook her head. 'My brothers call me Florrie when they want to annoy me, so not that. As for my middle name...definitely not.'

He quirked an eyebrow. Did he know her middle name? It must have been read out during their wedding ceremony, only for the life of him, he couldn't remember.

'It's Patience,' she admitted, noticing his expression. 'After my grandmother. I loved her dearly, but as a name, it's always felt like a lot to live up to.'

'I understand. I have five names, my own and those of the former marquesses, all the way back to my great-great-grandfather. As you say, it's a lot.' He lifted his eyes to the clouds painted on the ceiling before dropping them back to his soup, struck with the feeling he'd just revealed too much.

He cleared his throat again. 'I understand that Mrs Fitch continued our tour?'

'Yes.' Her spoon scraped loudly against the edge of her bowl, though she didn't eat anything, he noticed.

'I hope it was illuminating?'

'Oh, yes, I learned a great deal.' The edge was back in her voice. 'She was very thorough.'

'She always is.'

'I think she hopes you're going to start collecting prints of mountains soon.'

'I know.' He grimaced, then nodded towards her

bowl. 'Don't you care for the soup? Would you prefer something else?'

'No… I mean, yes.' Her expression wavered before shifting to one of sudden resolve. 'I want to go back to London.'

He blinked. 'I'm sorry?'

'I want to go back to London.'

'For dinner?'

'As soon as possible.'

'That's quite a request.' He put his spoon down and pushed his bowl away.

'I know.'

'Especially since we left less than a month ago.'

'Not to me.' She tossed her head, a flicker of defiance returning to her face. 'For me, it's like I was picked up in my sleep and deposited one hundred and fifty miles away overnight.'

'I still don't think…'

'Please.' She clenched her fists on the table. 'Everything you told me…it all feels so unreal. I can't… I just *can't* accept it. I need to go back and see if I can remember anything for myself.'

'I told you what happened.'

'I know, but…' a shadow of something like guilt flickered in her eyes '… I have other questions too, and maybe if I can get the answers to those then I can find some way out of this marriage for us.'

'There's no way out.'

Her face blanched. 'Maybe not, but familiar surroundings might help to jolt my memory.'

'Well, that's possible, I suppose...' He reached for his wine glass again. 'But you're still recovering and London is a three-day journey away.'

'I've been in bed for a week.' She thrust her chin higher. 'It may not be the wisest course of action, but I don't care. I have to know if I'm really the monster you say I am.'

'I have never called you a monster.'

'A manipulative fortune hunter, then.' She gave a brittle laugh. 'What's the difference?'

'I have never used those words either.'

'They were implied.' She pursed her lips before continuing. 'Look, I can understand why you hate me. Somehow I ruined your proposal to Amabel and forced you into a marriage you didn't want. But I have to find out if I truly deserve your hatred or I'll go mad.' Her voice cracked. 'And I need to see Amabel. With any luck, the Wadlows will still be staying in Grosvenor Square. The Season doesn't finish until the end of the month, does it?'

'No,' he admitted. 'But I told you how Miss Wadlow reacted when she found us together in the library. Admittedly, I don't know what transpired between you afterwards, but there's a chance she may not wish to speak with you.'

'I know.' She flinched at the admission. 'But I still

have to try. She's the only one who can explain about the message. If I'm telling the truth and she sent me to speak with you, then she must have had a reason for denying it afterwards, and if I'm lying then I need to hear it from her own mouth. And surely it's better to visit her in London than travel all the way to Cumberland?'

'Shall I discuss that idea with my coachman or will you?'

'All I'm saying is that London would be easier.' She dropped her gaze and her voice at the same time. 'It's not that I don't believe what you told me. I just wonder if there was some important detail that you missed. And you said that a group of people found us in the library, didn't you? If Amabel won't see me then maybe I could talk to some of the others, see if they noticed anything unusual, something that might offer a different explanation.'

He swilled the wine in his glass. 'So you intend to traipse around London, visiting peers of the realm, asking them for their recollections of a ball over a month ago?'

'If necessary, yes. You don't have to come with me, and I don't need to bring a maid or anyone else, but I need to do this.' She paused, clenching her jaw before adding, 'With your permission, that is.'

Leo leaned back in his chair, considering the idea while their soup dishes were cleared away and two plates of salmon were placed in front of them. Maybe a return to London *would* jolt her memory. She seemed so anguished, how could he deny her that? And once the other witnesses corroborated his story, she would have no choice but to stop protesting her innocence. Given the circumstances, he wouldn't get a great deal of pleasure from saying, *I told you so,* but some was better than none.

Considering her condition, however, he couldn't in all conscience let her travel alone. And although he had absolutely no desire to mingle with the *ton* again, having provided quite enough gossip for one season, so long as they avoided any social events, he had no personal objection. It would get him away from Rainton, which was always a good thing, and if they only went for a few days, just the two of them, it would be a good excuse to stay with his sister rather than open up his own townhouse again. Unlike him, Cassandra was genuinely warm-hearted. She would be able to help Florence deal with whatever emotional turmoil she was currently experiencing. It was certainly a better scenario than his attempting to do it.

'Very well.' He nodded at last. 'If you really want to go that badly, we'll go. On condition that—'

'Thank you!' She broke into a relieved-looking smile.

'You're welcome. However—'

'Tomorrow?' Her eyes widened.

'*Not* tomorrow.' He held a hand up to pre-empt any more interruptions, though her enthusiasm was strangely endearing. 'And only if Dr Pritchard approves the plan. I'll speak with him when he visits in the morning.'

'Oh.' She sounded as if she was about to argue some more before changing her mind. 'Very well.'

'In which case, you might wish to eat something.' He looked pointedly at her untouched dinner. 'You wouldn't want him to think that you've lost your appetite.'

'You're right.' She grabbed at her cutlery.

'And no matter what happens in London, we'll need to be back in time for the summer fair at the start of August.'

'Of course.' She nodded vigorously. 'That's plenty of time.'

'Good. My London house is currently shut up, so if we go, we'll stay with my sister and her family, if you have no objection?'

'None at all.' She paused with her fork in mid-air. 'Do I know your sister? Have we met?'

'Briefly.' A wry smile tugged at the corner of his mouth. 'And if it's information you're after, Cassie's certainly the right person to speak to.'

'What do you mean?'

'You'll see.' He turned his attention back to his plate. 'In the meantime, let's enjoy our dinner.'

Chapter Seven

Mayfair! Florence caught her breath as the carriage in which she and Leo had been trapped for what felt like an eternity turned a corner and she caught a glimpse of familiar territory. A wave of relief and excitement swept through her as she wriggled forward to the edge of her seat. Dr Pritchard had made her wait five days before finally dismissing the nurse and letting her attempt the journey to London, but here she was at last, amidst streets and buildings she remembered. There was Hyde Park, then Oxford Street, followed by New Bond Street, then Grafton Street, all leading to Albemarle Street, where Leo's older sister, Cassandra, lived with her young family. It felt so good to know where she was again!

'I sent a messenger ahead to say we'd be arriving early, so they'll be expecting us,' Leo commented from the other side of the bench.

'I hope your sister won't mind the intrusion.' She sat back again, smoothing her hands over the soft leather seat. The carriage was surprisingly comfortable; well-sprung, with a sizeable footwell, silk-lined walls and velvet cushions finer than the ones in her parents' parlour at home. It was a good thing, since they'd travelled faster than even the coachman had anticipated, neither of them wanting to stop more often, nor be confined in each other's company for any longer than necessary. Judging by the speed of their journey, a casual observer might have assumed they were eloping to Gretna Green, not travelling to London in the hope of finding a way to end their marriage.

'She won't.' He sounded confident. 'Cassandra's always saying she doesn't see enough of me.'

'Are you close?'

'We are, but she married George the summer she turned eighteen and they spend most of their time on his estate in Kent or in London.' He shrugged. 'Growing up, I was either at home or school or Oxford and then...' He paused and then shook his head. 'I always seem to be in a different part of the country, that's all.'

She nodded and turned back to the window. It hadn't exactly been a conversation-filled journey. She'd tried talking to him on several occasions, simply to alleviate the boredom of travel, but he hadn't asked any questions himself or volunteered any more information than was necessary, as if, like just now, he was reluctant to share certain aspects of his life. There had been a few times when she'd felt as though his eyes were on her, but every time she'd turned her head to confirm it, he'd been looking in another direction. Still, she was too grateful to him for bringing her to find fault, and his manner in general had been different since the evening they'd dined together. It still couldn't exactly be described as warm, but it had thawed slightly. That was probably the best she could hope for.

Now that she was back in London, however, it was time to focus on the task in hand. She needed to start looking for answers, not just about the events leading up to their marriage, but about…well…the letters. As usual, her mind shied away from thinking about them, but with any luck she'd find some completely innocent explanation for their presence in her saddlebag. She really and truly hoped so, because otherwise…

Fortunately, their carriage slowed before her thoughts could start spiralling again, coming to a halt outside a honey-stone townhouse. It was tall and elegant, much like the woman who came to greet them as they crossed the threshold, dressed in an elaborate peach and white striped day gown, her round face wreathed in smiles. It had to be Cassandra, Leo's sister, Florence thought, although they looked nothing alike. Instead of dark hair, hers was a reddish shade of blonde, arranged in a tower of intricate plaits on top of her head that threatened to topple over as she sprang forward to embrace him.

'There you are!' The woman kissed him on both cheeks. 'I was so surprised when I got your message. We didn't expect you until tomorrow at the earliest.'

'We made good time.'

'And Florence.' The woman turned to her with a concerned expression. 'Leo mentioned your accident in his letter. What a dreadful experience for you. How are you feeling now? Has your memory returned at all?'

'Um…' Florence blinked uncertainly, taken aback by the woman's familiar tone. 'No, not yet.'

'Then I ought to reintroduce myself. I'm Lady Brooke. Cassandra to my friends. Cassie to my family, which now includes you.'

'It does?' She blinked again. 'I mean, yes, I suppose it does. Thank you.'

'I just hope that your poor head hasn't been jolted around too much by the journey. I can't imagine what Leo was thinking, making you travel this far so soon after such a terrible accident.'

'Oh, it was my idea.' She interjected quickly. 'I insisted. I thought that coming back to London might help me to remember.'

'Well then, I shan't scold him too severely, not about that anyway.' Cassie smiled kindly. 'Now come through to the drawing room and have some tea. My husband's out at present, so it's just me and—'

'Uncle Leo!'

They'd barely gone a step before two identical small shapes came barrelling down a staircase, hurling themselves against Leo so violently, Florence was amazed the impact didn't knock him off his feet.

'Anthony! Patrick!' Cassie clucked her tongue. 'Honestly, anyone would think you were a pair of puppies, not young gentlemen. Let go of your uncle at once!'

'Too late.' Leo wrapped an arm around each of the boys' waists, lifting them up into the air on either side of him. 'I've got them now.'

'Oh, for pity's sake, you're all as bad as each other.' Cassie rolled her eyes before hooking a hand around Florence's arm and drawing her onwards. 'Those are my twins. They're perfect monsters, always pretending to be each other to try and get out of trouble, so don't let them fool you. Patrick has a small mark on his chin from when he fell down a step as an infant and Anthony can't keep a straight face for more than five seconds at a time. I love them dearly, of course, but it's a wonder my hair hasn't turned white trying to keep them in line. Now, here we are. Make yourself comfortable.' She stopped in the middle of a large, airy drawing room, decorated in assorted shades of blue, with a table in the centre holding a teapot and an impressive assortment of cakes. 'As you can see, I ordered tea the moment I saw your carriage arrive. Do you care for milk or sugar?'

'Both, please.' Florence sat down on a turquoise sofa, her head spinning with bemusement. She'd spent the latter part of the journey growing increasingly anxious about the kind of reception she was going to receive from Leo's family, anticipating hard stares and recriminations. Never in her wildest dreams had she expected cake, but Cassie seemed so warm and welcoming, so completely unlike her brother.

'Why are you being so nice to me?' she asked, blurting out the words before she could stop herself.

'Why, what a funny question!' Cassie picked up the teapot with a laugh. 'You're my new sister. Why wouldn't I be nice?'

'Because I'm not one of you.' She jutted her chin out. 'One of the *ton*, I mean. My father is a gentleman farmer.'

'And mine was a marquess.' Cassie handed her a cup. 'As well as a thoroughly unpleasant man. Believe me, I gave up caring about that sort of thing a long time ago.'

'You did?' Florence lowered her chin again. 'Then what about what Leo says about me tricking him into marriage?'

'Oh, yes, he told us about that on your wedding day, but it was all such a rush, I didn't have a chance to question him properly.' Cassie took a seat opposite. 'We heard about the scandal at the Wadlows' ball, of course, but he wouldn't speak to anyone about it, just hid himself away afterwards. Then I was in the middle of eating breakfast one morning when he simply marched in and announced that he was getting married that morning. I barely had time to change my dress before we had to leave.'

'So you came to our wedding?'

'Of course. He's my only brother.'

'What was it like?' Florence tilted her head quizzically. Somehow it had never occurred to her to be curious about it before.

'Well...' Cassie scrunched her mouth up for a moment, as if she was searching for the right words. 'It was a little unusual, what with there only being the four of us: you, me, Leo and George.'

'Oh.' Florence dropped her gaze with a pang of dismay. She hadn't expected Amabel to be there, but she'd thought the Wadlows might have been, if only for appearances' sake.

'But never mind that now.' Cassie reached across to pat her knee. 'I'm just so glad you're back in London. You and Leo left so soon after the ceremony, we barely had a chance to exchange pleasantries. Now we can get to know each other properly.' She gestured towards the table. 'Let me recommend the Savoy cake. It's absolutely delicious. My cook is worth her weight in gold.'

'Thank you.' Florence accepted a slice. She wasn't particularly hungry, but Cassandra's manner was so kind and sisterly, she couldn't bring herself to say no. Even if thinking about sisterly behaviour made her think of Amabel again… The pang in her chest dug deeper.

'Now, tell me.' Cassie looked serious suddenly. 'How are you and Leo getting along? I know that things between you were a little awkward at first, but are they any better?'

'Um…' She took a bite of cake to hide her expression.

'Oh, dear.' Cassie's face fell. 'It's that bad? I was afraid it might be. He was so angry when…well, when he told us the circumstances of your betrothal. I told him not to jump to conclusions, that sometimes there's more to things than meets the eye, but…'

Florence jerked her head up. 'You mean, you think I'm innocent?'

'Oh, I've absolutely no idea.' Cassie lifted her shoulders, as if it didn't matter either way. 'All I know is that sometimes people have good reasons for doing bad things. I should know that better than anyone.' She threw a quick glance at the door. 'Has Leo told you anything about our upbringing?'

'No-o.' Florence knitted her brows. Now that she thought about it, she knew very little at all about her husband.

'Well, it was perfectly awful.' Cassie sighed heavily. 'As I said, our father didn't have a caring bone in his entire body. Leo and I were summoned to his study every evening for him to lecture us. It was the only time we ever saw him and it was always about the same subject, the history of our family and the estate. It was so boring, it was an effort just to stay awake. Even now, when I can't sleep, I think back to it and then I'm snoring within minutes. Anyway, when he was done, he would test us, and if we got an answer wrong he would send us to bed without any dinner, or worse. And of course, being the son, Leo took the brunt of the questioning.' She shook her head. 'Of course, it all had the opposite effect to the one our father intended. We both utterly despise the place now.'

'You do?' Florence sat back in surprise. 'What about your mother? What did she think?'

'Oh, there wasn't much she could have done to stop it. Our father never cared for anyone else's opinions. Then she died of the putrid throat when Leo was six.'

'I'm so sorry. That's tragic.' Florence shook her head sadly. Somehow she'd gone from knowing almost nothing about Leo to knowing a great deal in the space of a minute. Now she couldn't help but wonder what it must have been like for him to grow up in such a cold environment.

'It was.' Cassie sighed again. 'I was twelve, so I have some memories of her, but Leo was so young, I don't think he remembers a great deal. Then once he reached ten, Father became obsessed with moulding him into the perfect heir, which in his mind meant being a younger version of himself. He wanted to control everything. To be honest, I was amazed he hadn't already selected a bride for Leo before he died, but then, his illness was rather sudden. No doubt he would have arranged it otherwise. Anyway, my point is that our father was a very domineering personality, which is why I resolved to escape as soon as I could.'

'Escape?'

Cassie grinned. 'When I came to London to stay with my aunt for my first season, I promised myself that I would never go back to Rainton, at least not as a resident. I decided to marry before the month was out.' She laughed. 'Oh, I know what you're thinking, that it could all have gone terribly wrong, and you're right, of course, but I was young and foolish and my life had been so desperately dull. It wasn't that I had such a high opinion of my charms either. I just knew that my dowry meant I wouldn't want for suitors. I might have thrown myself away on the very first person who asked me, but luckily I met and fell in love with George. My only regret was leaving Leo behind, but by then he was going to school anyway. Still…' A shadow of some remembered pain flickered in her eyes before she banished it with a sip of tea. 'I suppose what I'm trying to say is that if I hadn't had money, I can only imagine what I might have done to escape.

Maybe I would have thought that my only option was to trick somebody into marrying me.'

'But I didn't want to escape anything,' Florence protested. 'I love my home and I'm very close to my family. That's why the idea of me trapping Leo doesn't make any sense.'

'Well, all I'm saying is that I don't judge, especially not other women. Our lives are difficult enough, given how little control we're allowed over them. Besides, I'm old enough to know there's no point in endlessly raking over the coals. You and Leo are married, which makes us sisters, and I'm determined that we shall get along famously. In fact, I insist upon it, especially when I'm surrounded by so many males. Did Leo tell you, my youngest is a boy too? Edgar. He's still in the cradle, so he doesn't treat his uncle like a climbing frame yet, but I'm sure it's only a matter of time. Ah, there you are.' She twisted in her seat as the uncle in question entered the room, one boy on his shoulders, the other clinging to his waist. 'Don't worry, there's still plenty of cake. Have they broken any of your bones yet?'

'Not yet.' Leo looked between them, his gaze faintly suspicious. 'What are the two of you talking about?'

'The weather,' Cassie answered placidly. 'We're English, after all. We think it might rain later.'

'Rain?' He glanced sceptically towards the windows. Sunshine was practically pouring through, drenching the room in golden rays.

'Yes.' Florence found herself sharing a quick smile with Cassie. 'In fact, I think I just heard some thunder.'

'Well, it all sounds dashed strange to me,' George, Leo's brother-in-law, declared as he shunted a red ball into the corner pocket of the billiards table.

'That's one word for it,' Leo agreed, finally beginning to relax after the journey. Two days in a carriage with his wife had been a somewhat strained and uncomfortable experience; strained because, despite her occasional attempts to talk to him, he still couldn't allow himself to forget what she'd done, uncomfortable because the floral scent emanating from her side of the carriage had been damned distracting. She hadn't smelt that way on their journey *from* London; he would have noticed. The fact that she smelled so enticing now had made him painfully aware that they were alone in a closed carriage. Somehow the scent had heightened his other senses too, causing a sharp, craving sensation every time he'd caught her soft exhalations of breath or cast even the slightest glance towards her. His only respite had come in the coaching inn where they'd spent the night in separate bedrooms.

Thankfully, however, they were here now and he

was glad to be back. Despite being only six years his senior, Cassie was in some ways more like a mother than a sister, while George, with his booming voice and open, cheerful manner, was one of his most trusted friends. Until he'd seen them again, he hadn't realised how much he'd needed to talk.

'Are you certain she's not faking her memory loss?' George asked as a ball ricocheted off the side pocket.

'I'm certain.' Leo reached for his own cue. 'She was unconscious for three days.'

'Three days?' George gave a low whistle. 'It was that serious, then?'

Leo gave a murmur of assent as he leaned over to line up a shot. Yes, it really had been that serious, more than he'd let himself acknowledge at the time. If the branch had hit her any harder, or if she hadn't been discovered before nightfall... The very idea of it made him shudder now.

'Of course she's not faking anything!' Cassie swept into the room just as his ball slammed into a pocket. 'Don't be preposterous.'

'I just said she wasn't.' Leo straightened up, looking at her quizzically. 'But how are you so certain?'

'Because she clearly had no idea who I was when she arrived. And if that was a pretence then she's the best actress I've ever come across, and I've seen Dorothy Jordan.'

'Well, I still think the whole thing's dashed odd,

especially forgetting such a specific period of time.' George leaned on his cue. 'But I bow to your wisdom, my dear.'

'Thank you, darling. The mind can do strange things, especially when it's a period a person might wish to forget.' Cassie looked accusingly at Leo. 'Judging by your behaviour at the wedding, I can easily believe that she's had a perfectly wretched month.'

He lined up another shot, feeling his hackles start to rise. 'You make it sound like I'm some kind of wicked husband. I haven't laid a finger on her.'

'There are other ways to be cruel. You can hurt a person with words, or the lack of them, just as much as with deeds.'

'How did you expect me to behave? She tricked me into marriage!'

'So you keep saying.'

'So I *know*. I was there, remember?'

'Yes, well…' Cassie reached for her husband's whisky and took a large mouthful. 'I fancy myself a good judge of character and *I* like her.'

'Father wouldn't have approved.'

'Exactly!'

'Cassie, you've had *one* conversation with her.' Leo rammed his cue forward again. 'And I very much doubt that she got many words in.'

'I say, steady on.' George thrust his chest out.

Cassie held a hand up to her husband. 'I may *only*

have had one conversation with her, and I may be seeing what I wish to see, but the woman I met today is nothing like the one you described when you told us you were getting married. She's no more conniving than I am.' She narrowed her eyes. 'And I advise you to be extremely careful about what you say next.'

'Then I won't say anything. We'll just have to agree to differ.'

'For pity's sake, don't be so hard. You're behaving just like—'

'Who?' He arched an eyebrow when she stopped talking.

'Nobody.'

'Who?'

'Oh, very well. If you must know, you remind me of Father. I thought it the last time you were in town, but I hoped I was imagining things. Now I can see that I'm not.'

'That's not so extraordinary, is it?' He clenched his jaw, aware of a muscle twitching there. 'He was my father, after all.'

'And mine, but I seem to remember us promising each other that we'd never turn into him.'

He tensed as the memory leapt into his brain. It had been after one of his father's beatings, when he'd been too slow to answer a question. Afterwards Cassie had come up to his room and wrapped her arms around him, telling him that it wasn't his fault, that their father was wrong, and they should make a pact, just the two of them, but it had been easier for her. She'd always been so much more like their mother. And then she'd left soon after, going to London for the Season, and never coming back…

'That was a long time ago.' He potted the last ball on the table, pushing the memory out of his mind.

'Not so long.' Cassie's voice softened. 'Just give the poor woman a chance, that's all I'm asking.'

'Why?' The last thread of his temper snapped. 'Why should *I* be the one to forgive and forget? I'm not the villain. She is!'

'Ahem.' George cleared his throat.

Damn it. He closed his eyes briefly before turning around to find that his wife was standing in the doorway. If her flushed cheeks and clenched fists were any indication, she'd arrived just in time to hear him launch into yet another attack on her character.

And now he had no idea what to say, though fortunately his sister did.

'Florence.' Cassie swung into action, smiling as brightly as if they'd just been discussing some pleasure outing. 'How lovely you look this evening. Doesn't she, Leo?'

He made a harrumphing sound that might, just about, be construed as agreement as he put his cue down. In fact, his wife *did* look remarkably pretty, despite the scowl she was currently aiming in his direction. He hadn't seen her for a couple of hours, since, in a rare display of tact, his sister had allotted them separate, albeit adjacent, bedrooms, and it hadn't occurred to him to see how she was settling in, but now she looked completely refreshed from the journey, dressed in a pale green, round-necked gown, with the same gold locket he'd noticed around her neck a week ago.

'Come and meet George.' Cassie gave her husband's arm a none-too-gentle tug. 'You met him before at the wedding, but…well, here he is again.'

'Lord Brooke.' Florence curtseyed.

'An honour, Lady Rainton.' George dutifully bowed over her hand. 'I'm delighted to make your acquaintance.'

'Excellent.' Cassie beamed between them. 'Now, I don't know about anybody else, but I'm famished. Shall we go into dinner? George, take my arm.'

Leo aimed a glare in his sister's direction. Now there was no way he could avoid offering the same attention to his wife, no matter how tempted he was to march out of the house and dine at his club instead.

'Shall we?' Reluctantly he extended an arm, though apparently the gesture was more shocking than he'd realised. Florence's facial muscles went completely rigid, as though he'd just drawn some kind of weapon on her. Now that he thought about it, however, aside from their wedding day, when he'd slid a ring over her finger, and that time she'd collapsed against him in her bedroom, he'd managed to successfully avoid *all* forms of physical contact with her. He hadn't even helped her into or out of the carriage on their journey.

Well, this was awkward.

'I said, shall we?' He lifted his arm higher. Not very gallant, but he wasn't going to beg.

'Very well.' She thrust her chin into the air as she slipped a hand tentatively around his elbow, sending an inconvenient tingle of sensation shooting straight up his arm, just as the scent of her perfume collided with his nostrils again. The combination made him feel a little unsteady on his feet.

'So what are your plans now that you're in town?' Cassie asked as they took their seats at the dinner table. 'Leo's letter was typically vague. The Season is winding down, of course, but there are still a few events left to attend. The Jenners have already sent you an invitation to their ball on Friday evening.'

'The Jenners?' Leo frowned, trying to ignore the way his arm was still tingling. 'How do they know we're back in town?'

'Because I told them.'

'Cassie.' He exchanged a swift look with George. 'I specifically asked you not to tell anyone.'

'Did you?' Cassie placed a hand on her chest with a look of surprise. 'Well, if you did, you must have written it in very small letters. Although I do have an appalling memory on occasion.'

'Appalling or selective?'

'I've no idea what you mean. In any case, Lady Jenner was absolutely thrilled to hear you were back in town. It was very cruel of you, leaving without giving anyone so much as a glimpse of the pair of you together, and it would be such a coup for her if you were to attend. Your wedding was so private. Everyone's desperate to see the new Marquess and Marchioness of Rainton together.'

'I'm sure they are.' George snorted. 'You two were the biggest topic of conversation for at least a fortnight. No one's known what to talk about since.'

'Pshaw. The surest way to stop any more talk is to show yourselves. If you're seen behaving normally then all the gossip will be put to bed once and for all. Then the next time you come to London it will be old news.' Cassie batted her eyelashes. 'Surely one ball isn't so much to ask? Especially when George and I will be there for moral support.'

'We'll think about it.' Leo rolled his eyes. 'But we have other matters to attend to.'

'What matters?'

'I came to visit a friend.' Florence spoke up this time. 'Miss Amabel Wadlow. She's staying in Grosvenor Square.'

'Amabel Wadlow...' Cassie repeated thoughtfully. 'Why do I know that name? I'm certain I've come across it recently. Oh, yes, I remember now. It was in the Society pages. She got married a few days ago, didn't she?'

'She…what?' Florence's jaw dropped so far, it looked in danger of hitting the table. 'Who did she marry?'

'Oh, goodness, who was it? Somebody with a name beginning with V, I think.' Cassie tapped a finger against her chin. 'Or was it a W? No, definitely a V. Vaughan, that was it. Major James Vaughan. His father was the second son of the old Earl of Bewholme and he's a second son himself. The family has an estate in Norfolk and his older brother is engaged to Miss Serena Wilcox. Major Vaughan himself fought at Vitoria, although he's sold his commission now.' She spread her hands out. 'That's all I can remember.'

'Is that all?' George chuckled. 'Honestly, darling, you need to try harder.'

'Major Vaughan?' Florence's brow creased. 'I remember him. He called on Amabel a few times. She thought he was…' She bit her lip mid-sentence, her expression conflicted.

'There's no need to stop on my account.' Leo raised an eyebrow as she glanced towards him. 'Tell us. What did Miss Wadlow think he was?'

She hesitated for another moment before looking down at the terrine set in front of her. 'She said that he was charming, that's all.'

'Oh, gracious, I completely forgot. She was the one you were going to…' For once, Cassie looked embarrassed. 'Well, never mind. That's all water under the bridge now.'

'Quite.' Leo kept his gaze fixed on Florence, watching as she lifted her fork to her lips. He was mildly surprised at how little he cared about the news of Miss Wadlow's marriage. Considering how close he'd come to proposing to the woman, he would have thought he might feel some jealousy, but he couldn't pretend to feel anything. In all honesty, he was having a hard time remembering what exactly she looked like. And he was still staring at his wife's mouth, he realised…

'In any case, I'm afraid you're too late,' Cassie continued. 'The announcement said they were travelling to Ireland straight after the wedding. His family has land there, on his mother's side.'

'Amabel's left London?' Florence's voice sounded strangled.

'I believe so.'

'But… I have questions.' Her eyes locked back onto Leo's, the expression in them the same as when she'd first woken up. Panicked. Lost. Stricken.

'Oh, dear.' Cassie looked between them. 'Have I said the wrong thing?'

'It's not your fault. I just thought…hoped…' Florence's voice trailed away.

'We were hoping that Miss—that is, Mrs Vaughan might be able to cast some more light on what happened on the night of her parents' ball,' Leo finished when she seemed unable to continue. 'There was some confusion regarding a message.'

'Oh, I see. Well, isn't there anyone else you could ask?'

'I don't know. Maybe…but I really wanted…' Florence gulped, sounding on the verge of tears. 'Forgive me, but I'm feeling a little unwell. Would you mind if I go to bed?'

'Of course not, my dear.' Cassie tilted her head sympathetically. 'You do look very pale. Would you like me to send a plate up?'

'No. Thank you, but I think I just need to sleep.'

'Very well, then. We'll see you in the morning.'

Leo got to his feet as Florence pushed her chair back and fled the room. Briefly, he thought about following her before immediately dismissing the idea. What could he, of all people, say?

'Not a word.' He looked pointedly at his sister as he sat down again. 'Not one word.'

Chapter Eight

Florence took a deep breath as she grasped the brass lion knocker of the Wadlows' Grosvenor Square townhouse and rapped it sharply against the door. Despite her eagerness to return to London, she hadn't anticipated just how strange and disorienting it would feel to be back here. Part of her wanted to dispense with formalities, to simply walk straight in and charge up the staircase to her bedroom the way she always had with Amabel, but if what Cassie had told them at dinner was true, then Amabel was no longer here and she no longer had a bedroom. Because she was no longer welcome. A knot of tension lodged itself in her chest at the thought. This was the last place she remembered being before she'd woken up at Rainton Court, and yet somehow her whole life had irrevocably changed since she'd last stood on this spot.

An early night had done nothing to assuage her shock at the news of Amabel's marriage and departure from London. She'd been so fixated on the idea of seeing her, of appealing to her for help and establishing the truth about what had happened at the ball together, it had never occurred to Florence that she might not be there. The prospect of facing her parents instead was a daunting one, but it had to be faced if she was going to get any answers to her questions.

She'd lain awake, tossing and turning until the small hours, trying to decide what to say to them. Half of her thought she ought to start by apologising, only that would sound like an admission of guilt, and how could she apologise for something she couldn't remember doing? She'd eventually given up trying to sleep and risen early, walking around Mayfair until it was a reasonable hour to pay a call, deliberately skipping breakfast to avoid bumping into her husband. The way he'd spoken about her last night wasn't exactly new, but it still hurt. She wasn't a villain—or at least she hoped not anyway—and in an hour or two, if everything went well, she'd be able to prove it!

So here she was. And she'd already used the knocker, which meant that it was too late now to lose her nerve and run away. She only hoped the Wadlows didn't hate her too much.

Grover, the Wadlows' grey-haired butler, opened the door after a few moments, his eyes widening slightly at the sight of her. 'Lady Rainton. This is a surprise.'

'Good morning, Grover.' She smiled, relieved to see a friendly face. Unlike Rimmer, who seemed to live in perpetual terror of Mrs Fitch, the Wadlows' butler was a cheerful presence in the household. 'How is your back?'

'My back?' He sounded confused.

'Yes. You injured it, did you not?' She pushed her smile wider. 'Of course, that must be over a month ago now, but I recall you were in some pain?'

'Oh, yes. Much better, thank you, my lady.'

'Good.' She paused, shifting her weight from one foot to the other. 'I expect you're wondering why I'm here. I'd like to speak with Lady Wadlow, if it's convenient?'

'Ah.' Grover's eyes darted from side to side before fixing straight ahead, on a point just beyond her shoulder. 'I'm afraid that Lady Wadlow is not at home.'

'She's not?' Florence blinked in surprise. Lady Wadlow was nothing if not a creature of habit. She ate breakfast in bed at eight o'clock every morning, rose promptly at nine, spent the morning attending to correspondence and never left the house before luncheon. Unless… A wave of panic gripped her… Unless she'd missed her opportunity to see Amabel's parents too? 'Has she left London?'

'No, my lady.'

'Oh, thank goodness.' She exhaled with relief. 'What time do you think she'll be back?'

'I'm afraid I'm not at liberty to divulge that information, my lady.'

'I can wait.' She gestured to the hallway behind him. 'I don't mind.'

'Unfortunately, that isn't possible. She's simply... not at home.'

'You mean...? Oh.' She stiffened as a hot flush flooded over her cheeks. If Lady Wadlow wasn't at home in perpetuity, then it meant she had no desire to see *her*. Ever. But she'd come this far...

She coughed, swallowing the last of her pride. 'Would you mind making sure? Please?'

'I'm afraid it won't do any good, my lady. She was most explicit about her...at-home status.'

In other words, she was banished, Florence realised, pressing a hand to her empty stomach, suddenly glad that she hadn't eaten anything that morning, or last night, come to think of it. It was probably the only thing stopping her from being sick.

'The thing is, my lady,' Grover went on, lowering his voice, 'this whole situation has been a terrible shock for her nerves.'

'Yes, I suppose it must have been.' She lowered her own voice to match. 'But the "situation" is why I'm here. You see, I don't know what it is exactly. I've lost my memory. All I've been told is that I was found in a compromising situation with Lord Rainton, and something about a message, but I can't understand how it happened.' She moved a step closer. 'I don't suppose you know anything?'

'Only the rumours, my lady.' Grover threw a swift look over his shoulder. 'None of us staff saw what happened. We only heard the commotion.'

'Commotion?'

'Her Ladyship had proper hysterics. She wanted to throw you out of the house that night, only Lord Wadlow said it would cause an even bigger scandal, so in the end she settled for locking you in your room.' He checked behind him again. 'We were sorry to do it, especially since she only allowed you bread and water, but she was so angry. It was more than our jobs were worth to go against her.'

'What about Amabel? How did she react to what happened?'

Grover's expression wavered, as if he wasn't sure what to say. 'She was…also upset.'

'Was I able to speak to her after the ball?'

'No. Lady Wadlow didn't let anyone visit you.'

'But did she want to?'

'I'm afraid I don't know, my lady. We had orders not to let her into your room if she asked, but as far as I know, she didn't.'

'I see.' Florence looked past him again, making one last attempt to get inside. 'The thing is, I only want to ask Lady Wadlow a few questions. I know she must think I betrayed her trust, but I'm certain there must have been some kind of misunderstanding. If I could only talk to her for five minutes. Or Lord Wadlow—'

'I'd put that idea out of your head, my lady.' Grover sounded sympathetic. 'But I wouldn't worry about what they think if I were you. You're a marchioness now. You don't need the approval of the Wadlows of this world any more, and good luck to you, I say. Now I'd better get back inside.'

'Wait.' Florence placed a hand on the door as it started to close. 'Just one more thing. It's about Amabel's marriage. Was she happy about it?'

'I believe so, my lady. *Them* not so much.' Grover jerked his eyes upwards, to the room where Lord and Lady Wadlow were, presumably, 'not at home'. 'But Miss Amabel herself was in high spirits when she left for her honeymoon. That's some good news, I suppose.'

'Yes,' Florence murmured as the door finally shut in front of her. 'I suppose it is.'

'It's outrageous!' Cassie's furious voice echoed through the downstairs of the house as Leo walked through the front door. He'd spent the morning at Tattersalls, looking at a pair of bay geldings, and had fully intended to eat luncheon at his club, until a sudden impulse had brought him back to Albemarle Street instead. Florence had already gone out when he'd come down for breakfast that morning, and making sure she was all right, especially after the way she'd run out of the dining room so abruptly last night, seemed like the husbandly thing to do.

'What's outrageous?' He handed his hat to the butler on his way into the drawing room.

'The Wadlows!' Cassie was clearly on the warpath, waving her arms around like windmill blades as she marched up and down the room. 'They refused to see Florence.'

'You went to visit the Wadlows?' He turned to his wife. She was sitting in the window seat, her hands folded neatly in her lap as if she were perfectly calm. Only the absolute stillness of her features, combined with the silvery sheen of her clenched knuckles, gave her away. Something about that stillness, the obvious pent-up emotion, caused an unexpected tug in his chest.

'Yes.' She gave a jerky nod. 'I was told they weren't at home.'

'Perhaps they weren't?'

'They were.' A muscle twitched in her cheek. 'Their butler is a kind man, but he made the situation very clear. And even if he hadn't, I saw Lady Wadlow's face at one of the windows as I walked back across the square. She wanted me to see her, I think.'

'How dare they?' Cassie was still raging. 'I'll ruin them for this. I'll make sure all of their invitations are revoked! I'll speak to Mrs Wheeler. She's one of the patronesses of Almack's. I'll have them banished for life!'

'Please don't.' Florence winced. 'Not on my account.'

'Yes, on your account. You're a Claridge now and they had no right to treat you so rudely. Who do they think they are? You're a marchioness!'

'If I did what they think I did, it doesn't matter who I am. I can understand their reaction.' Florence dropped her gaze to her hands, her shoulders drooping. 'Besides, to them, I'm still just their daughter's companion.'

'May I?' Leo gestured to the opposite side of the window seat.

'Mmm?' She looked up, her eyes widening as if she was surprised by the request. 'Yes, of course.'

'Thank you.' He sat down beside her. 'Are you all right?'

'Honestly?' She dug her teeth into her bottom lip. 'No. I've known them since I was a child. Maybe I was tolerated rather than welcomed for Amabel's sake, but it's upsetting to think they hate me so much now. I thought they'd at least give me an audience.'

'I'd like to give *them* an audience!'

'Cassie.' Leo shot his sister a warning look. 'You're not helping.'

'Because I'm furious! And not just about them not seeing her. Tell him what else they did!'

Leo tilted his head. 'What else did they do?'

'It doesn't matter.'

'Yes, it does!' Cassie put her hands on her hips. 'Well, if you won't tell him, I will! After their ball, they locked her in her bedroom like an animal, with only bread and water. She wasn't allowed to see or speak to anyone until your wedding day.'

'Is that true?' He clamped his brows together.

Florence gave a jerky nod without looking at him. 'So their butler told me.'

'For the whole time?'

'I think so, although I don't know how long that was.'

'Four days.'

'Four?' A look of hurt flashed across her face.

'I'm afraid so.' He ground his teeth at the admission. In his defence, obtaining a special licence had taken a little longer than he'd expected, but he hadn't exactly been in a rush. He hadn't made any attempt to visit her either. He'd spent most of the time brooding over a bottle of brandy, trying to think of some way to escape the marriage. And all the while she'd been trapped alone in a room with only bread and water for sustenance. It was a good thing it hadn't been winter or Lady Wadlow would probably have deprived her of a fire too, although it would have been partly his fault if she had. A stab of guilt pierced him at the realisation.

'Could you be a little more outraged?' Cassie threw

her hands up again. 'You're the Marquess of Rainton and those people mistreated your wife! And now they've insulted her! Aren't you angry at all?'

'Just because I'm not storming around the room doesn't mean I'm not angry.'

'Then do something!'

'There's no need.' Florence shook her head. 'Truly.'

'Yes, there is.' He waited for her to meet his gaze again before standing up and holding a hand out. 'Cassie's right. Come on.'

'What do you mean?' She looked at his outstretched fingers dubiously.

'I mean that they may have refused to see you, but they won't refuse to see me. If you want answers, let's go and get them.'

'Oh, good!' Cassie gave a small bounce. 'I'll get my bonnet.'

'Just Florence and I.' He clarified. 'This is between us and the Wadlows.'

'But—'

'We can manage perfectly well on our own.' He lifted an eyebrow. 'Can't we?'

'You'd really help me?' Florence gave him a long, evaluating look.

'I will. I should have offered last night, but I hope you'll accept my help now. This is our marriage and our problem, is it not?'

'Yes.' Slowly, she lifted a hand and placed her fingers in his. 'Yes, it is.'

* * *

'Would you care for some tea, my lord?' Lady Wadlow, sitting ramrod-straight beside her husband on a green velvet sofa, gave a pointed cough. 'My *lady*?'

Florence, sitting beside her own husband on the opposite sofa, looked down at the assortment of cups and saucers set out on the drawing-room table and wondered if the contents of the teapot might be poisoned.

As it turned out, Leo had been right. The Wadlows *had* been at home for a marquess, although the atmosphere in the room was so horrible, her skin was actually crawling. She'd never understood that expression before, but now it struck her as the exact right phrase. She couldn't have felt any more uncomfortable if an entire swarm of ants were wriggling their way over her body. Both Lord and Lady Wadlow looked like two people biting their tongues so hard, they were in danger of spitting blood, their obsequious attitude towards Leo obviously warring with their blatant fury towards her. Every time their eyes so much as drifted in her direction, they ripped them away again as if she were somehow contagious. She'd never experienced such a visceral degree of loathing before and the effect was chilling. Half of her wanted to run from the room, the other half needed answers. Either way, her lips appeared to be frozen.

'No.' Fortunately, Leo answered for both of them.

'Thank you, but this isn't a social call. We're here because we have some questions.'

'What questions?' Lord Wadlow sounded suspicious.

Leo tipped his head towards Florence, as if prompting her to begin, which was nice of him, she thought, just as it was nice of him to use the word 'we', though frustratingly her voice still seemed to be trapped.

To her relief, however, he appeared to understand the problem, giving a small cough before turning back to the Wadlows. 'You may have heard that Lady Rainton recently suffered a head injury that resulted in some memory loss. Since she has no recollection of our engagement, we—'

'Harrumph.' Lady Wadlow made a disparaging sound.

'I beg your pardon?' Leo tipped his head sideways again.

'Nothing. Do go on, my lord.'

'Very well. As I was saying, Lady Rainton has no memory of your ball last month. Naturally, I've told her my own recollections, but she believes there may have been some kind of misunderstanding regarding what happened in the library. We therefore came to London to speak with your daughter, but, as Mrs Vaughan is no longer here, it seemed prudent to visit you instead. In short, we'd like to ask whether you think it's possible there was some innocent explanation for our being compromised?'

'Ha!' Lady Wadlow sounded like a woman who'd been holding her 'ha!' in for a very long time. It was so loud, it seemed to echo around the walls.

'That would be a no, I take it?'

'There was no misunderstanding.' Lady Wadlow's eyes flashed daggers. 'You arranged to speak with my daughter in the library and *she* went with the express intention of compromising you, using some ridiculous story about a message to keep you there. It was simply a ploy.'

'But not a very good one.' Florence protested, finding her voice finally. 'That's one of the things that doesn't make sense to me. I mean, if I'd really wanted to compromise the marquess, surely I would have needed some more effective means of keeping him with me? Otherwise, how could I have been sure anyone would find us together?'

'It's true, we were discovered surprisingly quickly,' Leo mused. 'We can't have been alone together for more than thirty seconds.'

'She was lucky!'

'It could have been chance, I suppose, but that would have been risky.' Florence looked straight at Lady Wadlow. 'What was it that made you come to the library that evening?'

'I've no idea.' Lady Wadlow twisted her face to the

side, as if she resented being spoken to directly. 'It was over a month ago.'

'Still, there must have been some reason. For the Earl and Countess of Malvern too. And Baron Paltrow and Lady Lansbury. What made so many people suddenly decide to visit the library during a ball?'

'Are you thinking that somebody might have sent them to find us?' Leo sounded thoughtful.

'It's possible.'

'Yes, but why?'

Florence opened her mouth and then closed it again, unable to think of an answer. She was the only person who'd stood to gain from their being caught together.

'I don't know,' she admitted. 'I just thought it might be significant. I mean, if we only knew who suggested going to the library in the first place, that might tell us something.'

'It was me,' Lord Wadlow intoned sombrely. 'I was the one who suggested it. I wanted to show the Malverns my rare edition of Fielding.'

'Oh.' Her stomach dropped.

'There you go.' Lady Wadlow's tone was gloating. 'Not so significant, after all.'

'What about Amabel?' Florence lifted her chin. 'Did she mention anything about the message?'

'She told you at the time, there was *no* message!'

'But maybe she remembered one afterwards? Something she hadn't thought was a message, but actually...

was?' She faltered, realising how ridiculous the words sounded. 'Or did she mention something else? Anything that might explain what happened? Even if it's a tiny detail, it could be helpful.'

'My daughter was so shocked, she could barely speak at all.' Lady Wadlow pressed a hand to her throat. 'I'll never forget the look on her face. To witness her so-called best friend stealing her suitor! And to think that we were the ones who brought you to London, who fed and clothed you and provided a roof over your head, little realising that all the while we were cherishing a viper in our nest!'

'Perhaps you ought to go and lie down, my dear?' Lord Wadlow put a restraining hand on his wife's shoulder, his gaze flicking nervously towards Leo.

'Ha!' Lady Wadlow's exclamations were getting louder. She was beginning to resemble Cassie, pushing her husband's hand away, her own practically shaking with fury as she pointed a finger towards Florence. 'Why shouldn't I speak my mind? This was your nasty little plan all along, wasn't it? And if your parents think they can lord it over us when we return to Cumberland, they can think again!'

'They wouldn't!' Florence gasped, shocked by the other woman's venom. 'My parents would never do anything like that.'

'Your parents raised an ungrateful, back-stabbing, conniving little—'

'That's enough.' Leo's voice was like flint.

'Why? *You* didn't want to marry her!' Lady Wadlow was clearly unable to stop. 'You would have found a way out of the marriage if you could. You wanted Amabel! Or do you deny it?'

'I don't believe I'm obliged to confirm or deny anything. My thoughts are my own business. I would, however, remind you that Florence *is* now my wife.'

'She's still a—'

'My *wife*,' Leo pushed himself to his feet so abruptly, everyone jumped, 'not to mention the Marchioness of Rainton, and I refuse to stand by while she is insulted.' He tipped his head back, looking down his nose at the Wadlows. 'And should I hear any reports of her being maligned in such terms again, or of her parents being slandered, then I shall make it my personal business to have you blackballed by the *ton*. Is that understood?'

'I say!' Lord Wadlow spluttered.

'Similarly, should Her *Ladyship* choose to call on you in the future, unlikely though that prospect may be, I suggest that you be at home.' He turned towards Florence. 'Do you have anything to add?'

'Um…no.' She shook her head, gaping with bafflement and disbelief, as she rose to her feet beside him. Was he really standing up for her? Sounding genuinely angry too? Even if it was only his family name that he was defending, it made her feel better, as if not everyone in the room hated her.

'Then I believe that concludes our business.' Leo placed a hand on the small of her back, not even glancing at the Wadlows as they headed for the door. 'Good day.'

Chapter Nine

'That was…' Florence stopped on the pavement outside the Wadlows' house, unable to finish the sentence, as she stared at Leo. It was hard to explain quite how his defence of her had made her feel. Relieved? Grateful? Flabbergasted? It was all three at once and more. 'I don't know what, but thank you.'

'You're welcome.' He was still frowning, though for once not at her. 'I'm sorry you didn't get what you came for.'

'It's not your fault. You tried to warn me.'

'I'm still sorry that they upset you.'

'Maybe I needed to hear it.'

'So what now?' He rubbed a hand across his chin, his voice softening slightly. 'Is there anyone else you wish to visit?'

She hesitated, feeling a tightness in her chest at the question. The Wadlows hadn't just corroborated Leo's story. They'd confirmed her worst fears about herself too. Because all the evidence still pointed towards her. And unless she wanted to make a complete fool of herself by going all around London, begging members of the *ton* for some alternative version of events, maybe it was time for her to accept the truth about what she'd done, time to acknowledge her guilt and the fact that there was no way out of this marriage. She really was the villain, after all. It wasn't an easy truth to accept.

'I don't think so.' She wrapped her arms around her waist, as if she could somehow shield herself from a sharp pang of self-loathing. 'I don't suppose anyone else's story will be any different. We can leave London as soon as you wish.'

'Are you certain?'

'Yes, but first I owe you an apology. It seems you were right about me trapping you. There's no other feasible explanation.' She sucked in a deep breath and then exhaled again slowly. 'I still don't know why I did it. I've racked my brains, but all I can think is that I acted on impulse and it was a moment of madness. It's not an excuse, but I *know* I never thought of trapping you before that. If I could go back and change things, or find a way out of this, I'd do it, but I can't. All I can do is accept the truth and say how sorry I am.'

He didn't answer for a long moment, some new emotion flashing over his face, one she'd never seen there before, something like understanding, before he nodded slowly. 'Then apology accepted, especially since it's possible you did me a favour. I'm not sure I would have liked having the Wadlows as my in-laws.'

She gave a startled laugh. With his stern, upright demeanour, she hadn't thought him capable of humour, but now, for the first time in their acquaintance, his eyes held a hint of warmth. 'You shouldn't blame them for what they said. They're disappointed and lashing out. It's understandable.'

'But still unacceptable.' He moved a step closer. 'I believe that I owe you an apology too. More than one, in fact. Firstly, for what I said about you last night.'

'Even though it turned out to be true?'

'I still shouldn't have said it. Secondly, for not speaking to the Wadlows before our wedding. It was thoughtless of me. I should have found a way to prevent any gossip. Now I'm afraid it's possible they've already spread rumours around town.'

'I'm certain they have.' She gave him a wry look. 'But hopefully you've made them think twice about doing so when they return to Cumberland, and that's more important. I don't want my parents to suffer because of all this.'

'Then I'm glad I could help.' He threw a glance at their waiting carriage and then up at the sky. 'Shall we take a walk? It's a pleasant afternoon. It might be calming.' His lips curved infinitesimally. 'Certainly more than going home and being interrogated by Cassie.'

'That's true.' She laughed again. 'A walk sounds nice.'

'Good.' He made a gesture to the coachman and then offered an arm.

Florence slipped her hand around his elbow in surprise. *More* surprise. It wasn't the first time he'd offered his arm. That had been last night, when he'd been forced into it by Cassie. It had felt strange to touch him, not unpleasant exactly, but...odd, as if all her nerves had been twitching. Then he'd offered it again this morning, when he'd escorted her to the Wadlows', but that had only been a gesture of support, surely? The fact that he was offering it again now, of his own free will, not to mention suggesting that they spend *more* time together, was enough to render her momentarily speechless.

And that was before she remembered the way his fingers had skimmed across her lower back earlier, sending a skitter of sensation all the way down to her toes. Honestly, she wasn't sure how many more surprises she could take in one day...

'Tell me about your family,' he said abruptly as they started off down the street.

'My family?' She gave him a sidelong look. 'Haven't I told you about them before?'

'No. I didn't ask before.'

'Then you don't have to now. I appreciate you trying to take my mind off what just happened, but I'm happy to walk in silence.'

'But I'd like to know.' His arm tightened against hers. 'It seems like I ought to, especially now that you've met mine.'

'Very well, then.' She paused, wondering where to begin. It occurred to her that this was the first time she'd felt even remotely comfortable in his company, as if some of the tension between them had finally dissipated. His usual forbidding expression had softened into something almost sympathetic. That was one thing to thank the Wadlows for, she supposed… 'Well, I have five brothers.'

His step faltered. 'Five?'

'Samuel, Thomas, Ellis, Cyrus and Jude. Two older, three younger.'

'You're the only girl?'

She nodded. 'I think that's part of the reason Amabel and I were always so close. We were neighbours and she only had brothers too. We used to pretend we were sisters.'

'And your home is in Cumberland?'

'Yes. We have fifty acres, east of Brampton. The terrain is quite wild and rugged, with a cold wind a lot of the time, but it's very beautiful. I miss it. I miss them all.' She felt a lump in her throat. 'I was horribly homesick when I left, but it was only supposed to be for ten weeks.'

'Then you didn't anticipate finding a husband in London?'

'No.' She felt a pulse of anger at the question. 'I told you, I didn't come to London to find a husband. My parents have land, but they're not wealthy and my dowry, as you presumably already know, was not large. My sole purpose was to be a companion for Amabel. She was afraid that she was too old to be a debutante, so she brought me for moral support.'

'And you didn't consider the possibility of a love match?'

'Not with one of the *ton*, no.' She snorted. 'I was well aware of my position and I certainly knew better than to let any foolish romantic notions go to my...' She stopped, her whole body tensing as a new and horrifying thought suddenly occurred to her. What if he was asking because *he'd* wanted a love match? He'd never given any overt sign of a romantic attachment to Amabel, but maybe she'd simply misread him, assuming he didn't have feelings because he didn't put them on display. That would explain why he'd been so angry with her for what had happened, because she'd come between him and the woman he loved!

'Is something the matter?' Obviously, she'd tensed too much, because now he was looking at her with a concerned expression, she realised.

'Were you in love with Amabel?' she asked, pulling her arm away from his. 'I didn't think of it before, but hearing about her marriage last night… It must have upset you too.' She stopped and pressed her hands to her cheeks. 'This is all such a mess. If I'd known, I'm sure I would never—'

'Florence,' he interrupted, reaching for her hands and pulling them gently away from her face, 'it wasn't a love match. Miss Wadlow had many exemplary qualities and I thought she would make an exemplary marchioness, but my heart isn't broken, if that's what you're worried about. I wish her every happiness with Major Vaughan.'

'Truly?' She pinched her brows suspiciously. 'You're not just saying that?'

'I never just say things. I would have thought you'd learnt that by now.' His lips quirked as he offered his arm again. 'Shall we continue?'

'Um…yes.' Her feet started to move while her mind continued to spin. What was happening? Not only had he defended her reputation and offered her not one, but *two* apologies, but he'd also voluntarily asked her to walk with him, and he hadn't been in love with Amabel! That was definitely enough surprises to take in for one day.

The moment they got back to Albemarle Street, she was going to need a lie-down.

Leo stared into the distance, admiring the way the sunlight bounced off the red and brown brickwork of the terrace ahead, as he and Florence continued their walk through the streets of Mayfair. The weather was fine, her gloved hand was resting on his arm, he could smell something floral again and, despite the unpleasantness of their interview with the Wadlows, he felt, for the first time in a long time…content?

His brows rose in surprise. A month ago, he would never have conceived of feeling this way in his wife's company. He could never have imagined defending her either. On the contrary, he might have taken some secret, shameful pleasure in hearing her belittled and insulted by the Wadlows, and yet today he'd only felt anger. Defiance too, because the person they'd described, the person he might himself have described until recently, wasn't the person he was married to. 'Ungrateful, traitorous and conniving'? No. She might have trapped him into marriage, but he'd spent enough time with her now to know she was none of those things.

He glanced sideways. Arguing with the Wadlows seemed to have unravelled something inside him, some knot of tension, making him feel looser and lighter. He couldn't even bring himself to dislike Florence any more. Not once had she behaved like the fortune hunter he'd presumed her to be. In the face of her accident and amnesia, she'd been brave and determined and impressively stubborn, so convinced of her innocence that he actually believed what she'd said, that her behaviour must have been a moment of madness, one for which she'd apologised and offered to make amends for by leaving him. What more could he reasonably ask? And maybe, without her memory, she wasn't the same person who'd trapped him. Maybe she was the person she'd been before her moment of madness. In which case, maybe it was time to set his pride and prejudices aside, stop punishing her, and try to see her as a wife rather than a usurper...

'Select a bride whose fortune will enhance the estate, whose temper will benefit your domestic harmony, and whose bloodline is worthy of our illustrious family...'

The words flashed into his mind, but he was tired of feeling bitter and resentful. What was it Cassie had said last night? That he'd sounded just like their father. The idea had sent a glacial chill down his spine. He'd respected his father, he'd admired his accomplishments, but despite the myriads of lectures he'd sat through, he'd never wanted to *be* like him. He'd promised himself, and Cassie, that he wouldn't. He wanted this...this feeling of...whatever it was instead.

And they were entering Berkeley Square, he realised, on one side of which stood Gunter's Tea Shop. He could see a large array of carriages and barouches up ahead, as the *ton* gathered to eat ices in the open air. And Florence hadn't eaten breakfast. Or dinner. She had to be ravenous by now. Their appearance would attract stares and gossip, of course, but he was heartily sick of caring what the *ton* thought too.

'You're right.' He stopped walking in the shade of a lime tree.

'I am?' She sounded taken aback. 'What about?'

'What you said about accepting the truth.' He shifted to stand in front of her. 'And the truth is, we're married. There's no way out of it, so all we can do is make the best of the situation. The past is the past.'

'You mean forgive and forget?' She arched an eyebrow, quoting his words from the previous night.

'I suppose so, yes. I don't know if I can, but I want to try. At the very least I don't want us to be enemies.'

'Neither do I,' she answered solemnly.

'Otherwise it somewhat defeats the purpose I had for marrying in the first place.' He gave her a strained look. 'I'm the Marquess of Rainton. I need an heir.'

Her eyes widened. 'You mean…?'

'Yes. One day. Not yet. Or soon even. But once we know each other better.' He coughed, dropping his gaze to her throat as a tide of red flushed over her skin. 'So maybe we don't have to leave London straight away? We've travelled all this distance and the summer fair isn't until next week. Maybe we could stay and get to know each other a little better before we go back to Rainton.'

'Oh.' She blinked several times, as if she didn't know what to say. 'I mean…yes, if you wish.'

'Then why don't we start with an ice?' He gestured towards Gunter's. Aside from anything else, it might help to cool her flaming cheeks.

She looked from him to the collected carriages, her expression suddenly wary. 'It looks busy. What if everyone stares at us?'

'I'm sure they will, but we can ignore them together. The chocolate ice is your favourite, is it not?'

'Yes.' She jerked her gaze back to his. 'How do you know that?'

'Because I accompanied you and Miss Wadlow here once and I remember you saying so.' He was faintly amazed at the memory himself, especially since he had no recollection of what Amabel had ordered.

'So you did. In that case, an ice sounds like a wonderful idea.' Her own lips curved in reply. They were plump and bow-shaped, he noticed. Strangely beguiling when she smiled, too, so much so that he felt a powerful impulse to trace a finger along them, to press his thumb to the dip in her bottom lip, maybe even slip it inside…

Damn it. He jolted himself back to the present. Maybe he needed a little cooling down as well.

Chapter Ten

'Oh, dear.'

'What's the matter?' Leo stopped as the curtain swung closed over the doorway behind them. After their trip to Gunter's the day before, where he and Florence had indeed attracted a marked degree of attention—though the ices had been delicious—he'd suggested a different kind of expedition today, one in which they could mingle with the *ton*, but where their faces would be half-concealed in shadow.

'I don't want to alarm you…' Florence twisted to look up at him with a serious expression, though if he wasn't mistaken, there was a hint of mischief in her eyes too '…but there aren't any mountains.'

He scanned his eyes over the dimly lit panorama before them, then threw back his head and laughed. She was right, there wasn't a single mountain in sight. Instead, the entire interior of the building, a cylindrical structure temporarily erected in the centre of

Leicester Square, was covered from floor-to-ceiling with a vast painting of the Trojan War.

'Perhaps we should we go to the Royal Academy instead.' She was grinning outright now, her eyes sparkling in a way that lit up her whole face. 'They probably have *lots* of mountains. I'm just not certain it counts as art without them.'

'I'm sure that's what my father would have thought, but I think I'll manage for one day.' He chuckled as they stepped down into the room, where several other people were gathered in groups, admiring the vista.

'Good, because this is very impressive.' Florence twirled around as she walked beside him. 'It's like we're actually in Ancient Greece.'

'I saw a panorama last year of the Battle of Trafalgar, but this is even better.' Leo peered closer at the wall. On one side of the room was the huge walled city of Troy, on the other, the Greek camp and the sea behind it, illuminated by narrow, half-concealed windows in the ceiling. To add to the mood, a group of musicians sat on one side of the room, playing harps and flutes.

'Look.' Leo pointed to two small figures standing on top of the city walls. 'That must be Helen and Paris on the battlements.'

'Or Hector and Andromache.' Florence moved a step closer, bringing her face alongside his. 'I always felt sorry for them. They didn't do anything wrong, yet they suffered the consequences of Helen and Paris's actions anyway.'

He half turned his head, surreptitiously admiring the soft curve of her cheek and her small, slightly pointed chin. It made it somewhat difficult to concentrate on the painting. 'Maybe they thought Helen was worth it?'

'Maybe.' She sounded dubious. 'But don't you think Helen must have known what would happen when she ran away with Paris? Yet she wreaked all that destruction just to be with him.'

'It was a great love story.'

'What about Hector and Andromache's love story?' She sounded indignant. 'I wonder if either Helen or Paris ever considered the effect on them.'

'How about a different love story, then?' He waved towards two other figures, half hidden in a cluster of trees a few feet from the great walls of Troy. 'There are Troilus and Cressida.'

She seemed to freeze beside him, her tone turning hard before she turned away abruptly. 'Cressida betrayed Troilus, did she not? Hardly a great love story.'

He furrowed his brow, surprised by the sudden shift in her mood, following her towards the Greek camp.

'Look, there are Agamemnon and Menelaus, storming about in front of their tents.' Florence pointed, her tone lighter again. 'And there's Odysseus, building his wooden horse.' She shook her head with an expression of wonderment. 'It's a magnificent painting. I've never seen anything like it before. Amabel and I wanted to come earlier in the Season, but we never got round to it.'

'Then I'm glad we have the opportunity now.' He gestured towards some wooden chairs set in the centre of the room. 'Shall we sit and take it in for a while?'

'Good idea.' She took a seat beside him, innocently arranging her skirts in a way that drew his attention straight to her thighs.

'So…' He wrenched his gaze upwards again. 'Is there anywhere else you'd like to visit while we're in London? The British Museum? Astley's Amphitheatre?'

'Actually I've always wanted to visit the Tower, but Lady Wadlow said it was too educational.'

'How shocking.' He laughed. 'But I'm sure we can manage that.'

She twisted in her chair, fixing him with a speculative look.

'What is it?' He arched an eyebrow.

'I just don't think I've ever heard you laugh before. It makes you look like Cassie.'

'Really?' Heat radiated through his chest at the words. 'She looks like our mother.'

Her expression shifted. 'Cassie told me a little about her, about how young you were when she died. I'm sorry.'

'Thank you.'

'She told me about your childhood too, and how much you both dislike Rainton Court because of it.'

'Dislike?' He made a sceptical sound. 'That sounds like an understatement for my sister.'

'You're right. She said you both despise it.'

'That's true.'

'Even though it's yours now?'

'Is it?' The words of his father's letter flashed into his mind before he pushed them aside. 'I've nothing against the estate itself. When I was a boy, the only freedom I had was riding about the fields, pretending I was running away, but the house itself has always felt like a prison. There's no joy or happiness there. I hate it even more than Cassie does, which is saying something.' He gave her a sideways look. 'She's told you about her great escape, I take it?'

'Yes. She said she left as soon as she could.'

'We both did. After I finished at Oxford, I moved into my own house in Cornwall.'

She gave a small jolt of surprise. 'Cornwall?'

'Yes. It was where my mother's family came from. The house had been a part of her dowry and she left it to me.' He smiled, thinking about the white house on the edge of Truro. 'It wasn't large. You could probably fit the whole place into the drawing room at Rainton Court, but it was big enough for me. The gardens were beautiful too, filled with magnolias and camellias and rhododendrons.'

'It sounds lovely. What did your father think about you moving there?'

'I think he was relieved. Rainton was always his great love, not his family, and he would never have allowed me to help run the place, not while he could do it. We weren't estranged exactly, but I couldn't bear the idea of living under the same roof as him again and he had no interest in me beyond as his heir. As long as I knew what my duty would be when the time came, he let me do what I wanted. And the house in Cornwall was all mine. I could do as I pleased and be independent.'

'So you were happy there?'

'Very. For the first time in my life, I felt like I could breathe properly. My friends from university visited often, and…' he paused, clearing his throat at the memory of a certain widow with whom he'd enjoyed an occasional, casual dalliance '… I enjoyed my life,' he concluded.

'How long were you there?'

'About three years.' He stretched an arm out, draping it along the back of her chair, surprised to hear himself still talking. 'I still had family in the area, so I got to learn more about my mother too. Just being there made me feel closer to her.'

She smiled sympathetically, her posture softening

until her back was almost, but not quite, touching his arm. 'What was she like?'

'A lot like Cassie. Kind-hearted. Generous. Loving. Everything my father was not. From what I've heard, they led separate lives.' He clenched his jaw, swallowing the lump in his throat. 'That's one benefit of Rainton Court. It's easy to avoid people if you wish.'

'Yes.' A shadow passed over her face. 'I suppose it is.'

He winced, remembering how he'd successfully avoided her for two whole weeks before her accident. 'In any case, I knew that my freedom couldn't last forever and that I'd have to go back to Rainton eventually, but I enjoyed my life for a while.'

'That must have made it very hard to leave.'

'It was, but I knew my duty. I couldn't shirk it.' He was aware of a sudden heaviness in his chest. It didn't help that a group of ladies had gathered close by and were now paying more attention to them than they were to the painting. 'Once I inherited the title, I had no choice.'

'What about your house in Cornwall?' Thankfully, Florence seemed oblivious to their audience. 'Have you been back since?'

'No. I gave it away.'

'You...' She sat upright again. 'You what?'

'Like I said, I had family in the area. Some of them were quite distantly related, but they were all good, kind people. One of my cousins was in love with the local doctor, but their income wasn't sufficient for them to marry.'

'So you gave them your house?'

'I knew I wasn't going back.'

'That's very generous.'

'Not really, when you consider the size of Rainton Court.' He tilted his head. 'You sound surprised.'

'Actually…no. It just seems like Cassie isn't the only one who takes after your mother.'

He smiled, feeling the warm glow again, despite the openly curious looks of the ladies. If he wasn't mistaken, they were moving slowly but steadily closer too, obviously attempting to eavesdrop.

'You know, speaking of Cassie, maybe she's right and we ought to show ourselves at the Jenners' ball,' he said, directing a glower at the ladies that stopped them abruptly in their tracks. 'It would help to counteract whatever stories the Wadlows have been spreading about us.'

Florence followed the direction of his gaze, a look of surprise, followed by understanding, passing over her face. 'Do you think?' She dipped her chin, lowering her voice to a near-whisper. 'What about being laughing stocks?'

'You're my wife.' He let his fingers brush gently against her shoulder. 'Like I told the Wadlows, I won't let anyone insult you.'

She held on to his gaze for a long moment, her own doubtful, before she gave a small nod. 'Very well. If you think it will help, I suppose one ball can't hurt so much.' She threw a defiant look at the ladies and then pushed herself to her feet. 'Now, I think it's getting a little crowded on this side of the room. Let's try the other side, shall we?'

Chapter Eleven

It was one thing, Florence reflected, agreeing to attend a ball when the event was still two days away. It was another thing entirely on the evening of said ball, when the moment of departure was growing steadily and terrifyingly closer. And it wasn't going to be like Gunter's or the panorama, where there had been no requirement to mingle and she'd been able to hide her face behind either a large bowl of chocolate ice or in the semi-darkness. This was a social event. With people! Worse, the *ton*!

She ran her hands over her hips, studying her reflection in the mirror. Cassie had been so thrilled by their change of heart that she'd insisted on taking Florence straight to the modiste for a new dress in creamy organza, with a low neckline, fashionably short peak sleeves and a dusky pink overskirt. A row of tiny flowers had even been embroidered around the hem, so that it looked as though she was walking through a meadow. It was incredible that such a gorgeous item could have been produced so quickly, although she had a worrying suspicion that bribery was involved and that somewhere, some poor debutante was missing a gown. None the less, with her hair twisted into a sophisticated bun and a selection of gorgeous accessories, including her gold locket and a pair of ruby earrings, a pair of kid gloves and impractically white silk slippers, she felt that, no matter what happened that evening, at least she looked like a marchioness.

'Because that's what you are!' Cassie laughed when she voiced the idea aloud. 'You and Leo are going to look splendid together.'

'Mmm.' Florence dropped her gaze, pretending to adjust her gloves. The time she and Leo had spent together over the past few days had certainly been an improvement on their time at Rainton Court. As promised, he'd taken her to the Tower of London, as well as for several walks around Mayfair and in Hyde Park in an attempt to jolt her memory. She was grateful to him for that, as well as for what he'd said about putting the past behind them. He'd been polite and open and attentive, as if he was genuinely trying to make the best of things. Which was good, she supposed, since she wanted to as well, and yet, despite admitting her guilt after their meeting with the Wadlows, some part of her still resisted the idea. Every night she woke with the same questions spinning around her mind. *Why* had she deliberately trapped herself into marriage with a man who'd wanted her best friend, not her? The *ton* might marry for position and power, but was that really the kind of marriage she'd impetuously decided she wanted? Something about it just didn't feel right, as if her head was telling her one thing about what had happened and her heart another. And there was still the matter of the love letters…

Fortunately, the more she thought about those, the more convinced she became that they must have been written to somebody else. Because firstly, how would she ever have met another man in Dorset? Especially right under the nose of her new husband? And secondly, if there *had* been another man, surely he would have found some way to contact her by now?

'There's absolutely no reason to feel intimidated,' Cassie linked arms with her as they descended the staircase, 'except for the obvious. It's the *ton*, after all. Collectively, they're quite terrifying, but you'll have Leo and George and me to support you. And remember, you'll outrank most of the people there. You could stand on your head and they'd still have to defer to you.'

'I don't want anyone to defer to me,' Florence protested. 'I'd rather blend in with the wallpaper.'

'Well, you can't. You look far too pretty for a start. Doesn't she?' Cassie demanded of the two men waiting in the hallway below.

'Doesn't she what?' George was busy putting on a topcoat.

'Look pretty?'

'You do indeed.' He made Florence a courteous bow before kissing his wife's hand. 'As do you, my love, as always.'

'Thank you, darling. Leo?' Cassie's tone sharpened. 'What do *you* think?'

Florence turned her eyes nervously in her husband's direction. Unlike George, who was wearing sage-green and white to match Cassie's emerald ballgown, he was dressed in monochrome black and white, with only a single sapphire pin in his cravat for embellishment. As usual, he looked perfectly polished and pristine, only tonight there seemed to be something new about him, an intense, arrested gleam in his eye that made her breath catch in a whole new way too. There was no time to interpret what it meant, however, before his, and everyone else's, attention was distracted by a loud crash somewhere in the vicinity of the dining room. It sounded a lot like pottery breaking, closely followed by shrieks and running footsteps. Seconds later a pair of small figures wearing matching guilty expressions skidded to a halt in the doorway.

'Boys?' George folded his arms. 'Going somewhere?'

'It was an accident!'

'He did it!'

'*Don't!*' Cassie lifted a hand. 'Whatever it is, tell me in the morning. I'm in a good temper and I don't want it ruined. O'Neil?'

'My lady?' A butler appeared out of nowhere.

'Could you please escort my sons to the nursery and then find somebody to clear up whatever it is they've broken?'

'I'll see to it myself, my lady.'

'Thank you. And please tell Nurse to send them straight to bed. They'll need the rest so they can enjoy a bracing two-mile walk before breakfast tomorrow. Clearly they need to work off their excess energy with more exercise.'

'Mama!'

'*Three* miles!' Cassie thrust her chin into the air. 'Now I suggest the rest of us go and enjoy ourselves.'

'We'd better do as we're told,' Leo muttered to Florence, throwing a sympathetic glance at his nephews. 'Are you ready?'

'As I'll ever be.' She turned around, letting him drape a red velvet cloak around her shoulders. If she wasn't mistaken, his fingers lingered there for a few seconds, as though he were wrapping her in his arms.

'We can do this,' he murmured softly, his breath skimming her neck in a way that sent a rash of goose-pimples shooting across her skin.

'Are you certain?' She half turned her head, feeling unaccountably dizzy all of a sudden.

'Positive.' He inhaled, as if he was breathing in her scent, freshly washed with a new floral soap that Jane had given her, before moving back to her side, his eyes seeming even darker than usual. 'Now let's go to the ball.'

Lord and Lady Octavian Jenners' Summer Rose Ball was an annual event, and notorious crush, hosted in their Mount Street townhouse. It was attended, as Cassie had repeatedly commented, by everyone who was anyone, and marked the beginning of the final week of the Season, after which members of the *ton* gradually dispersed to their country estates for the rest of the summer, either to celebrate their successes or lick their wounds, as the case depended.

It was not, Florence reflected, as she climbed down from the carriage, the kind of event at which she would ever have been the focus of attention before. On the contrary, she would have walked in behind the Wadlows, then sat patiently with the chaperones on the sidelines, ready to fetch drinks or keep Amabel company whenever she didn't have a partner. She might occasionally have danced, if an acquaintance had asked her, but she would have been perfectly happy as an observer too. Frankly, the idea of being noticed would have terrified her.

It still did, so much so that she was seriously considering expelling the contents of her stomach onto the pavement.

'Are you feeling all right?' Leo sounded worried.

'Yes.' She pulled her spine straighter, putting on a look of bravado. 'Why wouldn't I be?'

'No reason, except that your hand is shaking and you're as white as a sheet.' He moved a step closer, blocking her from the view of those people gathered in front of the house. 'We can still change our minds, if you wish?'

'No.' She gulped. 'We've come this far. We should at least show our faces. Then it'll be done.'

'Very well. In that case, let's get it over with.'

'Oh, for pity's sake, stop looking so glum, the pair of you!' Cassie thrust her face between them. 'It's a ball, not a public hanging. We're going to have a wonderful evening, I've already decided.'

'Well, in that case, how can we argue?' Leo gave Florence a teasing smile.

She tried to smile back, but it was impossible. The very moment they entered the crowded vestibule she was aware of a low murmur running around the room, closely followed by a sea of heads turning in their direction. She swallowed hard, feeling as if she were being pierced by hundreds of stares, as she handed her cloak to a waiting attendant. Leo, on the other hand, exuded total calm, keeping his own eyes fixed straight ahead, seemingly unperturbed by all the attention. Of course, the combination of his dark good looks and title meant that he was used to it, she thought with a degree of jealousy, but it was a whole new experience for her. And yet this was what she'd agreed to, a fitting punishment for what she'd done, allowing herself to be gaped at and judged by the very people whose ranks she'd tricked her way into. Her only consolation was that, after this, facing them would never be so terrible again. Hopefully.

By the time their names were announced at the entrance to the ballroom, her legs were trembling so violently, she wished that a hole would open up in the floor so she could jump through it. Everywhere she looked, people were staring and murmuring, some behind their fans, some openly. Thankfully, she was briefly distracted by the splendour of the ballroom itself, a huge, high-ceilinged space shimmering with the light from hundreds of candles. A twelve-piece orchestra was also arranged in one corner, behind a three-foot wall of pink and white roses, the scent of which filled the air, overpowering the other, less pleasant smells of pomade and perspiration. There were flowers all around the room too, filling each sconce and table, so many that every hothouse and garden in London had to be empty. Despite the beauty around her, however, it was impossible to completely ignore the whispers, as every word Lady Wadlow had spat erupted back into her brain and began spiralling, like a tornado of insults. No doubt that was what the *ton* thought of her too. If she listened closely, she could probably hear them. *Ungrateful, back-stabbing, conniving fortune hunter...*

'You're doing well.' Leo's voice, accompanied by the gentle touch of his fingers on her elbow, gave her mind the jolt it needed.

'I don't feel like I am.' She exhaled heavily as they stopped beside a large potted plant. 'It's all right for you. You were born to this. People admire you.'

'If they admire anything, it's my title, not me.' His tone was clipped. 'I personally have very little to do with it.'

She lifted her eyebrows, surprised by the edge in his voice. It had never occurred to her that someone like him could feel as if he didn't belong, but maybe that was why he always looked so stern and severe, because deep down he felt uncomfortable too. The idea made her feel a little less conspicuous, as if it was the two of them against the rest of the ballroom.

'I didn't mean to accuse you.' She tightened her fingers around his arm. 'It's just hard, knowing what they all must think of me. Everyone's looking at us.'

'Not true.' He tilted his head towards some chairs at the far corner of the room. 'There's an elderly gentleman over there who appears to be studying the backs of his eyelids.'

'Very well, then, everyone who's awake is staring at us.'

'I don't blame them. Cassie was right. You look beautiful.'

She blinked in surprise. To her recollection, it was the first compliment he'd ever given her and her still shaking knees almost gave way in response. 'Thank you. I've never worn anything this exquisite before.'

'I wasn't referring to your dress.' His gaze swept downwards, lingering briefly over her hips. 'Although it looks lovely too.'

'Oh.' She wasn't certain what to say to that, except... 'Well, you look very nice as well.'

'Thank you.' His lips twitched. 'I appreciate the compliment.'

'Gracious, it's so crowded in here, I can barely breathe.' Cassie swept down on them suddenly, thankfully preventing her from making the situation any more awkward. 'Now, Florence, come with me and I'll introduce you to a few people.'

'Not yet.' Leo shook his head, obviously catching her horrified expression. 'We were just about to dance.' He bowed, a sardonic glint in his eyes. 'Ordinarily it's considered bad form for a gentleman to dance with his own wife, but under the circumstances... Shall we?'

She threw him a grateful look. 'I'd be honoured.

Although…' she tensed as the music started '…it's a waltz.'

'Yes.' One of his eyebrows quirked upwards. 'Don't you know the steps?'

'I do, but Lady Wadlow always said it wasn't respectable for young ladies. She forbade Amabel and me from dancing it, even after we got permission from Almack's.'

'Ah.' He swept a hand behind her back and leaned closer, bringing his lips to her ear. 'I think we can agree to disregard anything Lady Wadlow says.'

She gave a startled laugh, aware of a strange, fluttering sensation in her stomach as she placed one hand in his, the other on his shoulder, and they swung away from Cassie into the dance. And it was nice…at least, to begin with. The music and the setting were beautiful, only nobody had ever held her so intimately before, and the fact that it was *him*, of all people, and there were still so many eyes watching and judging… She swallowed, acutely aware of every small detail of the dance, the warmth of his fingertips against her back, the rise and fall of his chest, the sound of their shoes sliding over the floor. She could feel herself becoming flustered, her cheeks heating as though she were some innocent debutante, not a woman who was supposed to have been married for over a month. It was the exact opposite of the calm and composed image she wished to convey to the *ton*!

'You dance well,' Leo murmured after a few minutes.

'Amabel and I used to practise together when she came to our house.' She seized on the words, glad of the distraction. 'My brother Thomas would play the pianoforte for us.'

'Indeed? Did Miss Wadlow often visit your house?'

'Sometimes, although she had to bring her governess, of course.'

'And the governess allowed waltzing?'

'She wasn't supposed to, but Miss Thompkins was sweet on one of my other brothers, Samuel, so she was easily distracted.' She smiled at the memory, beginning to relax. If Leo was trying to set her at ease, it was working. 'Of course, she isn't Miss Thompkins any longer. She's Mrs Lowrie now. They're expecting their first baby in the autumn.'

'Ah.' His expression turned questioning. 'What about you? I know you said you didn't come to London for a husband, but weren't there any eligible suitors in Cumberland? A tutor perhaps?'

'I suppose there were a few gentlemen.' She pursed her lips thoughtfully. One advantage of having so many brothers was that she'd often been thrown into the company of their friends. And she had never been short of dance partners at the local assembly rooms. Still, there was nobody who'd ever touched her heart, not yet anyway. 'I suppose the closest I ever came to marriage was with Mr Archer.'

'Mr Archer?' His fingers flexed against her back.

'Yes. Lord Wadlow's land agent. I liked him very much. He was pleasant and amusing and very handsome.'

'Indeed?' There was a new tension in his voice suddenly. 'Did he make you an offer?'

'Oh, yes, and he wrote me a poem with it. He was a very good poet.'

She thought she heard him mutter something under his breath, but when he spoke again his tone was neutral. 'A love poem, I take it?'

'An ode.' She sucked her cheeks in and sighed. 'I was very impressed for the first few lines, but then he compared me to a daisy.'

'And that's bad?'

'Not inherently. I like daisies. They're dainty and pretty. Only his imagery made it clear that he considered them to be something else.'

'Dare I ask?'

'He made them sound strong and self-sufficient, neither of which are negative qualities, of course. In fact, they're very good, only his point was that they don't need to be nurtured. They're just *there*, surviving whether you pay them any attention or not.' She tipped her head to one side. 'He was a widower with two young children. I believe that he wanted a new mother for them more than he wanted me. It was understandable, but not very romantic, so I refused him.'

She sighed again. 'I felt quite bad about it, until he made some unflattering comments about my age and appearance, all of which made me quite sure I'd made the right decision. I might not be a rose like Amabel, but I'd like to be more than a flower that just exists, if that makes sense?'

'Perfectly.'

'I suppose I always thought that if I ever married, it would be for love.' She paused, remembering how she'd apparently trapped him. 'At least, that's what I used to think.'

'Whereas I always anticipated a purely practical arrangement.'

'So neither of us got what we expected?'

'It seems not.' His eyes sparked with some indefinable emotion. 'However, if I ever feel inspired to write you a poem, I'll be sure to compare you to something other than a daisy.'

'Thank you.' She laughed at the idea. As if *he* would ever write her a poem... 'That would be lovely.'

An hour later, Leo stood at the side of the ballroom, drinking a glass of champagne while Florence danced a quadrille with George. To his relief, she was looking visibly more relaxed and animated than she had earlier in the evening. The buzz that had greeted their arrival had taken a good half-hour to fade away, but eventually eyes and conversations had moved on. Only some male attention lingered on her, his own most of all.

He watched as she danced, his gaze roaming from the swell of her breasts above the top of her bodice down to her hips as they swayed with the music, feeling his stomach tighten every time he caught the shapely outline of her legs through the fabric of her gown. Now that he'd made the decision to put the past behind them, he couldn't seem to take his eyes off her, as if by setting his resentment aside, he'd left the door open for attraction to sneak back in. Her hair, which he'd previously thought of as simply light brown, now struck him as a lustrous and vibrant shade of walnut, shot through with threads of honey and gold, while her eyes, even from the other side of the dance floor, were surely the most vibrant and luminous shade of blue he'd ever seen.

As if she sensed his gaze on her, she glanced in his direction and smiled, her face lighting up in a way that made him feel as if he'd had too much to drink.

'Rainton!' A loud voice boomed in his ear before he could reciprocate. 'I didn't expect to see you in London again this season.'

'Archibald.' He turned to shake his old school friend's hand. 'Neither did I, but it was a last-minute decision.'

'How are you?' Archibald lowered his voice, a mass of shaggy blond hair falling forward into his eyes. 'I never got a chance to say how sorry I was about what happened. Damned shame to be caught like that.'

'Caught?' Leo feigned an expression of surprise, as a new idea occurred to him. Since there were obviously plenty of rumours already circulating about him and Florence, why not start another? There was nothing Archibald enjoyed more than spreading gossip.

'Yes. You and that companion in the library. I heard she lured you there with some story about a message.'

'You've been listening to the Wadlows.' He took a casual sip of champagne. 'There was no trap and if there was any luring, it was entirely my idea. Their daughter might have been the sensible choice, but when it came to it, my heart overruled my head.'

'What?' Archibald gave him a double look. 'You mean, you and the companion…?'

'I admit, I behaved badly, playing court to one woman whilst conducting a secret liaison with the other, but I couldn't resist. Only things had gone so far with Miss Wadlow…' He lowered his voice, as if he was sharing a confidence. 'Causing a scandal seemed the only way out.'

'Why, you old cad, I didn't think you had it in you!' Archibald sounded gleeful. 'They said you were trapped by a scheming fortune hunter. Paltrow and the Malverns and Lady Lansbury as well. They witnessed the whole thing, didn't they?'

Leo snorted, adopting a cynical expression. 'No

doubt the Wadlows resented the fact that I preferred the companion to their daughter. As for the others… perhaps they simply misunderstood the situation?'

'Well, I have to say I'm relieved. I've been afraid to go anywhere near a library for weeks in case any other ladies get ideas.' Archibald grinned. 'Married life isn't so bad, then?'

'Not at all. I'm perfectly content with my choice of bride, thank you.' Leo took another sip of champagne, surprised by how true the words felt.

'Then perhaps you'll do me the honour of an introduction?' Archibald nudged him with his elbow as the dance ended and George escorted Florence over to join them.

'Of course.' Leo advanced to meet them, reaching for her hand and pressing a lingering kiss to her knuckles. 'Florence, this is Mr Archibald Thornton, an old friend. Archibald, my wife, Lady Rainton.'

'Oh.' Her eyes widened at the attention, though she recovered quickly. 'Good evening, Mr Thornton.'

'Delighted to meet you.' Archibald managed to bow and tap the side of his nose at the same time. 'Your husband's just been setting me straight about a few things. Well played.'

'I'm sorry?'

'I'll explain later.' Leo tightened his grip on her fingers, reluctant to share her with any other man a moment longer. 'I believe the next dance is a cotillion. Shall we?'

'Dancing twice with your own wife?' Archibald waggled his eyebrows. 'You really have fallen hard. Lady Rainton, good evening.'

'What was all that about?' Florence watched him go with a quizzical expression.

'More gossip, I'm afraid, although it should work in our favour this time.' Leo repressed a smile. If he wasn't mistaken, Archibald had already found a group of people to share his news with. Whether they believed it or not, at least he'd added an element of doubt.

'I'd say tonight was a triumph, wouldn't you?' Cassie declared as they climbed into their carriage at four o'clock the next morning. 'I had a marvellous time. And I made a point of telling everyone how wonderfully happy you are, so hopefully that should put a stop to any more rumours.'

'Thank you.' Florence smiled. 'We could never have done it without you.'

'Well, obviously, but it's nice to hear.' Cassie twisted her gaze towards Leo. 'Some people might say I was right and that attending a ball was the smart thing to do.'

'Some people might.' He paused. 'And I would have to agree with them.'

'Good!'

He chuckled as his sister laid her head on George's shoulder and gave a self-satisfied sigh. The whole evening had gone much better than he'd anticipated. There had only been one strange moment, when he'd caught sight of Hugh Vaughan, Major Vaughan's older brother, during supper. He didn't know the man well, only from his club, but from the way his expression had shifted, turning to one of mild panic, shortly before he'd made his excuses to leave, anyone would have thought he'd been afraid of being challenged to a duel. As if Leo might object to his brother marrying Miss Wadlow. As if he cared in the slightest...

'Speaking of rumours, I heard a new one tonight.' George commented, yawning widely.

'Oh, really?' Leo lifted an eyebrow.

'Yes. From what I gather, the two of you are a love match.'

Florence inhaled sharply. 'What?'

'According to someone, the whole scene in the Wadlows' library was staged to get Leo out of an engagement with their daughter. Several people assured me they'd known all along.'

'George, what on earth are you talking about?' Cassie lifted her head again.

'It would appear that somebody besides you has been spreading counter rumours, my dear.' George smirked. 'Can't think who.'

'Quite.' Leo turned his head to look out of the window, acutely aware of Florence's gaze on his face as he smiled.

Chapter Twelve

He should go to bed, Leo told himself as he stood at his bedroom window, watching dawn rise over the city. A gibbous moon was still high in the sky, which was itself a magnificent swirl of orange and purple. He ought to feel tired. He'd suffered through an entire night with the *ton*, at a ball of all places. He ought to be closing his eyes with relief that it was finally over. Instead he felt strangely energised, as if, unbelievably, he'd actually enjoyed himself.

Strange as *that* was, he was aware of an undercurrent of some other emotion too, one that had reared its head the moment Florence had told him about the Wadlows' land agent, *Mr Archer*. The very name made him grit his teeth. Which was ridiculous. She hadn't sounded remotely regretful about the man. On the contrary, she'd taken exception to his poetry and rejected his proposal. Still, just the idea that somebody else had written a poem for her made him feel irrationally…jealous? Yes, definitely jealous.

It didn't help that she'd been wearing her locket again tonight. Now that he thought of it, aside from during her convalescence, he'd never seen her without it. Now he couldn't help but wonder whose portrait was inside.

He glanced over his shoulder at the door that separated their two bedchambers. Would Florence be asleep already? Probably. It must have been an hour since their return from the ball. By now one of Cassie's maids would have removed all the pins from her hair, then helped her out of her gown and into a nightdress. Imagining it stirred his blood, making him feel even less like sleeping. *He* wanted to be the one to strip away her clothes, to unfasten her stays and roll down each stocking. Then he wanted to gather her to him, beneath him, on top of him. His breeches were straining almost painfully tightly just thinking about it.

He turned back to the window, focusing his attention on the garden in the middle of the square. Maybe he ought to go down there. The cold morning air might do something to quell the desire now raging inside him. Damn it, he should have asked Cassie to put him in a different room, one on the other side of the house, because the idea that his wife was so close, on just the other side of a wall, lying in bed, crying out… Wait… He whipped his head round… Crying out?

He snapped his brows together, wondering if he was

imagining things. But there it was again, a faint cry, as though she was in pain.

He didn't hesitate any longer, flinging the door open, crossing her room in three strides, and wrenching the bed-curtains apart to find her writhing on the bed, thrashing from side to side, a sheen of sweat on her forehead as she muttered words he couldn't understand.

'Florence?' He bent over, putting his hands on her shoulders to steady her. 'Wake up!'

'What?' She pushed back against him, before opening her eyes and giving a startled jolt. 'Leo?'

'Yes. You were having a bad dream.' He pulled his hands away quickly, in case his presence there frightened her even more. 'You were crying out. I was worried.'

'Oh.' She pushed herself up onto her elbows, panting heavily, her face a mask of distress. 'I'm sorry for waking you.'

'You didn't.' He made a conscious effort not to look to at her breasts, heaving beneath her nightgown. 'And even if you had, it doesn't matter. We all have nightmares sometimes.'

'Really?' She gave a ragged laugh. 'You?'

'Yes. Why wouldn't I?'

'I don't know.' She shook her head. 'I don't know why I said that. You just always seem so confident, I suppose.'

'Appearances can be deceptive.' He gestured at the edge of the bed. 'May I sit? Or would you rather be alone?'

'No.' She shifted sideways to give him some room. 'Some company would be nice, if you don't mind?'

'Not at all. It might be a good idea to talk about your dream. Was it a memory perhaps?'

'Perhaps.' Her face took on a far-off expression as he sat down beside her. 'I was in a forest, or at least there were trees. Lots of them.' She gulped. 'I think I was lost.'

'That would make sense. You were found in the woods close to the village.'

'I was?' She sagged back against the headboard. 'It never occurred to me to ask.'

'I should have told you. Anything else?'

'No, I don't think so.'

She shuddered and he felt a pang in his chest, fighting the urge to wrap his arms around her. It had nothing to do with desire now, only comfort. Slowly, he reached for her hand, brushing his thumb lightly against her wrist where her pulse was still thumping.

'Maybe it was just my imagination,' she said after a few moments, looking down at their joined hands. 'I was so nervous before the ball. Maybe this was just a reaction to it.'

'Perhaps.' He moved his thumb slowly back and forth. 'But I hope you enjoyed this evening a little. In case Cassie didn't mention it enough times, you were the perfect marchioness.'

'Not perfect, but I did enjoy myself. Everyone was much nicer than I expected, especially towards the end of the evening.' She slid her tongue between her lips. 'I suppose that was after someone started those rumours about us being a love match.'

He didn't say anything. Now that her panic had eased, he found his mind drifting towards how smooth and silky her skin felt beneath his fingertips, sending fiery sparks shooting along his nerves. He could smell that floral scent again too, jasmine and honeysuckle and rose. The confined space of her bed seemed far too small suddenly, as if the air between them was getting thinner. He ought to go back to his own room, he told himself, only he couldn't quite bring himself to get up. Sitting together in the semi-darkness, while the rest of the house slept, reminded him of the night he'd found her in the hallway at Rainton Court. Only their relationship had changed since then.

He coughed. 'How are you feeling now?'

'Much better.' She took a deep breath, her breasts heaving again. 'Thank you for coming to help me.'

'Do you think you can sleep?'

Her gaze flickered uncertainly. 'I might read for a little bit, but you should go. I'll be all right.'

He hesitated, looking towards the door and then back again. 'You know, after my mother died I had nightmares every night for months. Cassie used to sleep in my room to comfort me. Whenever I woke, we would play games. Cards mostly. Vingt-Un is still my favourite.' He tilted his head. 'What do you say?'

'You mean now?' A shy smile crept across her lips. 'I'd like that.'

'So would I.' He let go of her hand reluctantly. 'Let me fetch a pack of cards and a candle.'

It was almost noon by the time Florence found herself at the breakfast table the next morning, blowing air over a cup of steaming hot chocolate, while she listened to her husband and sister-in-law bicker. It was, she reflected, a lot like listening to her brothers back home in Cumberland. The whole scene felt strangely comforting, as if she was part of a family again.

'Surely a couple more days won't make so much difference?' Cassie implored Leo. 'You've barely arrived.'

'We've been here for five days.' He bit into his toast with a loud crunch.

'Exactly. Scarcely time to unpack. Oh, do say you'll reconsider. The Ives are holding a Venetian picnic by the river tomorrow afternoon.'

'And?'

'And you and Florence were such a success at the Jenners' ball, it seems a shame not to capitalise on it.

I'm sure the whole *ton* is still talking about you this morning.'

'Do you really think that's going to encourage me to do it again?' He reached for his tea. 'Have we met? Do you know me at all? Because I could have sworn we were related in some way...'

'Pooh!' Cassie rolled her eyes. 'All I'm saying is that it's unfair to deny people further opportunities to see and discuss you, especially when the Season finishes so soon. Besides, *I'd* like to spend some more time with you. That's not so terrible, is it?'

'Not at all. You're welcome to visit Rainton Court whenever you wish.'

'Oh, don't be so difficult. You know I can't stand the place *and* I hate to travel.' Cassie waved a hand dismissively. 'I only married George because his estate is in Kent.'

'I thought you said you loved me?' George peered over the top of his newspaper.

'I do, darling. But I only agreed to marry you once I discovered how close your property was to London.'

'Ah.' The paper lifted again. 'Fair enough.'

'In any case,' Leo went on, 'we have commitments back at Rainton.'

'Rearrange them!' Cassie pouted. 'Have you asked your wife what she thinks?'

'Yes, he has,' Florence answered, lifting her cup to hide her amusement.

'And you want to leave me too?' Cassie sounded dismayed.

'No, but it's the summer fair. We need to be back for it.'

'Oh, good grief, you're as bad as he is.' Cassie abandoned her perfect posture in order to fling herself back in her chair. 'Who cares about the blasted fair?'

'Our tenants, our staff, the tradespeople who supply it...' Leo started to list on his fingers.

'Well, all right, yes, they probably all do, but they could still hold it without you.'

'The marquess is always in attendance. It's tradition.'

'That's exactly the sort of thing Father would have said.'

'I am *not* Father.' Leo's tone hardened. 'However, on this particular subject, I happen to agree with him.'

'You're right, that was uncalled-for.' Cassie hauled herself upright again. 'Very well, if you've made up your minds, I suppose I'll just have to make the most of you both today. Will you at least accompany me to Hyde Park this afternoon?'

'Of course.' Florence answered before Leo could refuse. 'It would be our pleasure.'

'Thank you.' Cassie threw him a superior look before pushing her chair back. 'Now I suppose I ought to go and see what havoc my boys are wreaking in the nursery.'

'I'll come with you.' George folded his newspaper. 'We'd better find out what it was they broke in the dining room too.'

'Hyde Park?' Leo arched an eyebrow at Florence once they were alone.

'Yes. It's the least we can do after she's been so welcoming and generous.' She smiled unrepentantly. 'Besides, you can't blame her for wanting to keep you here. She really does care for you.'

He made a harrumphing sound.

'What does that mean?'

'Nothing.' He sighed. 'I know she loves me and that she feels guilty for leaving me behind at Rainton when she married George. I've told her a hundred times that she had her own life to lead, but she's not the best listener.' He rubbed a hand over his forehead. 'Sometimes all this just feels like a lot of fuss.'

Florence nodded slowly, choosing her words with care. 'She told me a little about your upbringing. Maybe she's afraid that the way your father treated you still affects you?'

'Perhaps.' He held her gaze for a moment, his own unfathomable, before looking away and changing the subject. 'How did you sleep after I left last night? No more nightmares? I left the door ajar just in case.'

'I noticed.' She smiled. She didn't remember his leaving. She only had a vague memory of drifting to sleep mid-game and waking hours later to find herself neatly tucked into bed, with only a stack of cards on the cabinet beside her to prove it hadn't been another dream. 'And I slept very well, thank you.'

'Good.' There was a flicker of heat in his eyes. 'Perhaps we should play cards more often?'

'Perhaps.' She cleared her throat, aware of a ripple of something warm and liquid spreading through her body. The way he'd comforted her during the night had caught her entirely off guard. She'd assumed that his attentive behaviour at the ball had been an act for the *ton*, but when he'd rubbed his thumb across the inside of her wrist, it had been only the two of them. Then her own body's response had surprised her as well. Even now, just thinking about it made her toes curl, making her extremely conscious of the fact that they were alone again, with only a breakfast table between them. She felt a sudden urge to stretch those same toes out, to move them closer to his, maybe even to slide her slipper across his thigh…

'You know, you don't have to agree with me.' He sounded serious all of a sudden. 'I'd like to be back for the fair, but if you want to stay in London for a while longer…?'

'I don't.' She answered quickly, jolted out of her reverie. 'I've done what I came to do and the fair is important. Besides…' she knitted her brows '…even though I enjoyed last night, I can't help thinking about how we must have appeared to the Wadlows. I don't know if they were there, but I wouldn't want them to think I was gloating, especially if they hear this new rumour.'

'Does it really matter what they think?'

'Yes,' she answered emphatically. 'They were kind enough to bring me to London in the first place. I don't want to hurt them any more than I already have. Or Amabel.'

'Very well, then.' His gaze softened. 'We'll stick to our plan of leaving tomorrow.'

'Good.' She leaned forward over the table. '*After* a promenade in Hyde Park with your sister this afternoon?'

He groaned aloud. 'If I must.'

'Oh, I think you must.' She couldn't stop herself from smirking. 'You'll never hear the end of it otherwise.'

Chapter Thirteen

Florence jolted awake as the rhythm of the carriage shifted, though it took her a few moments to come back to herself. Despite Cassie's loud protestations, they'd decided to make the most of the good weather by leaving London early in the morning, intending to make the journey back to Dorset as quickly as possible, but she hadn't the faintest idea what time it was now. They'd been travelling for so long that her internal clock, never mind her sense of geography, was a complete mess.

Groggily she glanced out of the window, careful not to disturb the sleeping figure of her husband, just in time to catch a glimpse of twilight before the carriage turned into the lantern-lit yard of a coaching inn. They must have both dozed off after the last time they'd stopped to change horses, and then slept all the way through until evening. She wasn't entirely surprised. They'd been up until the early hours the night before, Leo with George, she with Cassie, and this afternoon had been so hot, and the carriage so well-sprung and comfortable, that it had proved impossible to stay awake. At some point Leo's head had slipped sideways too, so that his dark hair now tickled her chin where it rested on her shoulder. Feeling him there was a somewhat confusing sensation. It made her feel pleasantly cosy and yet curiously restless too, as if her whole body was tingling. Part of her didn't want to disturb him, but she supposed it was better for her to do it than wait for the carriage to lurch to a stop.

'Leo?' She gave his shoulder a gentle shake, but his only response was to make a sound of protest and then shuffle his body sideways, wrapping an arm around her.

Oh… She sucked in a breath as the weight of him pressed against her breasts, pinning her against the seat and making her feel even more confused. Heat flared to life in her chest. And her stomach. And lower, between her thighs, in her very core, where her heartbeat seemed to be beating in a heavy, frenetic rhythm…

Carefully she unpeeled his arm, sliding herself away along the bench, before shaking him more forcefully. 'Leo? Wake up.'

'Mmm?' He opened his eyes, looking so rumpled and disoriented, she felt a strong urge to reach out and stroke his hair away from his forehead.

'We're here.' She moved a little further away to be safe.

'Already?' He sat up and rubbed a hand around the back of his neck, apparently oblivious to where his head had just been resting. 'Ow. I must have been sleeping at a strange angle. My neck is stiff.'

'I wouldn't know.' She twisted her face away quickly, peering out of the window as the carriage came to a halt outside a large coaching inn, its weathered stone half hidden behind huge swathes of ivy. 'This looks pleasant. Is it the same place we stayed on the way to London?'

'Yes.' Leo gave her a double look as a boy stepped forward to open the carriage door. 'Don't you remember?'

'Not really.' She caught his worried expression and smiled. 'But don't worry, I'm not forgetting anything else. I was just preoccupied at the time.'

'I think we both were.' He climbed out and then reached a hand back to help her down. 'Hopefully tonight will be more memorable. Are you hungry?'

'Famished.' She dropped her gaze as she descended the steps. The idea of a memorable night implied something other than what he surely intended, but it made her heart start to race again.

'Then we'll eat as soon as possible. I sent a man ahead yesterday to reserve a suite, so we should be able to go straight up.'

'That sounds perfect.' She pulled her shoulders back and lifted her eyes again, waiting for him to release her hand. Only apparently he had no intention of doing so. Instead, he gave it a quick squeeze before draping it across his arm.

She blinked, taken aback by the gesture. She might not have paid much attention the last time they were here, but he definitely hadn't done anything like *that*.

Their suite was really quite cosy, Florence thought, half an hour later, as she looked around the private drawing room that separated their two bedrooms. There wasn't a great deal of furniture, just an oak table and two dining chairs, as well as a wooden settle by the fireplace, but what there was looked clean and comfortable, not that she wanted to sit down again just yet. She'd changed out of her heavy cambric carriage dress into a lighter calico day gown, but her shoulders were so knotted and tight, she was happy to stand for a while.

'Dinner, my lady.' A maid came into the room, carrying a large tray, just as Florence finished stretching her arms over her head.

'Wonderful.' She rapped her knuckles on the door to Leo's bedroom while the maid arranged everything on the table, but there was no answer. How odd. Surely he would have told her if he was going out?

'Will that be all, my lady?' the maid asked.

'I think so, thank you.' She smiled over her shoulder, already savouring the aroma of the food. 'I'll ring when we're finished.'

She waited a few seconds until the maid had gone before turning back to Leo's door, pushing it open a crack and peering through. The light inside was dim, but it was impossible to miss the large male lying flat on his back on the bed, his leather boots discarded on the floor, while his coat, shirt, waistcoat and cravat hung casually over a chair. Only his breeches remained, as if he'd started to change out of his travelling clothes and then been overwhelmed by the urge to sleep instead.

She took a step forward, biting her lip as she let her gaze roam over his chest. He was more powerfully built than she'd realised, his stomach firm and corded with muscle, with a dusting of dark hair that tapered downwards like an arrow towards his breeches. Something about the sight of it made her muscles clench. Briefly she contemplated leaning over and shaking him awake the way she had in the carriage, but this situation was different. One, because he wouldn't expect to find her there and two, because…well…it was a bedroom and he was very nearly naked.

And, no matter what he'd said about requiring an heir, she wasn't quite ready for that. No matter how intriguing that arrow of hair might look…

Carefully, she backed out of the room, closed the door and then raised her voice. 'Dinner is here!'

'What the—?' There was a muffled exclamation, closely followed by a thump and the sound of feet on floorboards. 'I'll be there in a moment!'

Stifling a laugh, she went across to the table and took a seat, her stomach rumbling at the sight of their dinner. It looked and smelled delicious: partridge, potatoes, gravy and carrots, with a bottle of claret to wash it all down.

'My apologies.' Leo emerged from his room a minute or so later, looking noticeably more dishevelled than usual. 'I must have dozed off again. I only intended to lie down for five minutes.'

'It's your own fault.' She gave him a teasing look. 'I was up late enough talking to Cassie, but what time did you and George finish playing billiards?'

'Too late. It turned into a tournament.'

'Who won?'

'Me, obviously.' He threw her a quick smile and then rubbed his brows. 'Although I didn't sleep much afterwards either. I received a letter yesterday from my steward, Sewell, and I spent the rest of the night thinking about it.'

'Is something the matter at Rainton?'

'Very much so, according to him.' He rolled his eyes. 'But it's a farming matter. I wouldn't want to bore you with the details.'

'Why would it bore me?' She passed him the gravy

jug. 'My father is a gentleman farmer. Maybe I can help?'

'I'd be delighted if you could.' He looked at her thoughtfully. 'I don't suppose your father kept cows?'

'Yes. Galloways mostly, with a few Ayrshires for milk.'

'Really?' He put down the knife and fork that he'd just picked up. 'Well, in that case, I recently bought a herd of Red Devons. They were supposed to be delivered at the end of August, but it seems there was a misunderstanding and they arrived early, just after we arrived in London, in fact. It's caused some disruption. We've never had cattle at Rainton before and Sewell seems to think they're going to ruin the whole estate. He hasn't specified how, but his letter suggests we'll be lucky if the house is still standing when we get back.'

'That sounds a little over-dramatic. In my experience, cows prefer to live outdoors, and they certainly prefer eating grass to tapestries.' Florence speared a piece of roast potato and waved it at him. 'Why does he object? Red Devons are a very resilient breed, and cattle farming is good for the land. Their dung is very useful for healthy soil.'

'Is that so?' Leo's lips twitched. 'I don't believe I've ever heard a young lady use the word *dung* before.'

'Sorry.' She shrugged. 'I suppose I probably shouldn't

mention it at the dinner table, but I couldn't think of another way to phrase it. Besides, it's the truth.'

'And good to know.' He raised his wine glass.

'As for them potentially ruining your estate, it's your estate, therefore it's your decision, is it not?'

'Not in Sewell's eyes. He and I don't see eye-to-eye on a number of things. Change is anathema to him. It makes me wonder if it wouldn't just be better to give in and keep everything as it was when my father was alive, at least for a few years.' He sighed. 'I could always sell the herd on.'

'Or you could get a new steward?' She clicked her tongue. 'No offence to Mr Sewell.'

'I've thought the same thing, believe me. I'd be thrilled if he'd retire, but my father left specific instructions stating that he should remain in his job. Mrs Fitch too.'

'Oh, yes, Mrs Fitch…' Florence gritted her teeth at the mention of the housekeeper, the woman who'd so smugly relayed her husband's wishes regarding the management of the household. That had been before she and Leo had decided to put the past behind them, of course, but the subject still rankled… 'She mentioned something about your father leaving a letter of instructions. Then she took umbrage when I suggested they might simply be guidelines.'

He gave a laugh, though there was no humour in it. 'It's obvious you never met my father. He had very strong views on how the house and estate ought to be run, even after his death. His instructions aren't legally binding, of course, but the estate thrived under his care. It would be foolish of me to completely ignore his instructions just because I have a few ideas of my own.'

'Maybe your ideas are good too?'

'Maybe they are. Or maybe they would prove to be dismal failures, in which case Sewell and Fitch would be waiting in the wings ready to say "I told you so".'

'But at least you would know if your ideas worked.'

He looked pensive for a moment, before shaking his head. 'I wish I could do more, but it's been hard enough making any changes, like introducing the herd, and not just because I've had to argue with Sewell every step of the way. Going against my father's instructions makes me feel guilty too, like I'm letting him down, even though the rational part of my brain tells me I'm the marquess now.'

'That must be difficult.' She nodded sympathetically, remembering what Cassie had told her about how their father had tried to mould him into another version of himself. She had a sudden mental image of a motherless twelve-year-old boy, whose sister had just left for her first Season, being forced to endure that kind of domineering influence alone. Just the idea of it made her want to get up, walk around the table and wrap her arms around him.

'It could be worse.' Leo tucked back into his dinner. 'He could have left the estate in debt. Then I'd have much bigger problems to deal with.'

'I suppose so, although that doesn't mean this isn't a problem too.' She tipped her head to one side. 'But since the new herd is already at Rainton, you might as well see how that particular change goes, no matter how much Mr Sewell complains.'

'You're right, I will. Thank you.' His gaze warmed as he smiled across the table at her. 'For both the support and the advice.'

'You're welcome.' She smiled back. 'So did your father mention anything about marriage in his letter?'

'Mmm?' Leo's fork seemed to freeze in mid-air.

'It's just that Cassie thought he would have chosen a bride for you himself if he'd had time, so I wondered if his letter gave you any instructions about marriage?'

There was a moment of hesitation before Leo started eating again. 'No.'

Which meant yes, she thought, biting into a carrot. Almost certainly, his father had told him to marry somebody refined and well-bred like Amabel, and instead he'd found himself trapped with her. No wonder he'd been so angry about their marriage. It wasn't just that she'd made him a laughing stock, it was the fact that she'd caused him to fail his father too. He must have felt so guilty. And the fact that he wasn't flinging the accusation in her face now was profoundly touching, even if her food didn't taste quite so delicious any more.

And what else was in the letter? she wondered, watching her husband out of the corner of her eye while they chewed in companionable silence. Some kind of stipulation about Mrs Fitch continuing to run the household perhaps, as there was with Sewell and the estate? If there was, then at least that meant it wasn't the personal attack that she'd thought, although it still didn't seem entirely fair. Not fair at all, in fact...

'I want to manage the household,' she announced abruptly, hurrying on before he could say anything back. 'If we're making the best of our marriage then I want to make the best of my new position too. I might not have been trained to run such a large house, but I'm not completely ignorant or incompetent, and I'm a fast learner. Mrs Fitch said that you wanted her to keep doing it, but I don't see why I should necessarily be constrained by your father's instructions as well. No offence.'

Leo stared at her, his expression inscrutable as he took another sip of his wine. 'You're right,' he answered finally. 'You shouldn't be constrained by them. To be honest, I've never given the subject of housekeeping much thought, but it was remiss of me. You're the marchioness now and you should manage the household as you see fit.'

'Oh.' She opened her mouth and then closed it again. 'Right. Good.'

'Mrs Fitch really told you I asked her to keep managing everything?' A shadow passed over his face.

'Yes, during our tour of the house.' She frowned. 'Or at least she said something about being entrusted to do it and you not telling her otherwise.'

He muttered something under his breath. 'Yes, that sounds like her.'

'Will she mind very much if I take over?'

'*When* you take over, and yes, definitely. She's been running the house without a mistress for almost twenty years now, ever since my mother died. She won't find it easy to cede control but it's your house, not hers. I'll speak to her as soon as we get back.'

'Thank you.'

'Now, if that's settled, I have my own request to make.' He leaned back in his chair, his eyes darkening as he looked at her.

'Oh?' She felt the hairs rise on the nape of her neck. Whatever his request was, her mind was already veering towards *yes*.

'I'd like you to tell me some more about cows.'

'Cows?' She gave a shaky exhale, then tipped her head back and laughed. 'Very well. What do you wish to know?'

Chapter Fourteen

Thanks to an overturned cart blocking one of the roads close to Southampton, it was another whole day of travel before their carriage finally rumbled down the drive of Rainton Court, just as the orange sun dipped over the edge of the horizon.

'My lord, my lady. Welcome home.' Rimmer was waiting at the front door to greet them.

'Thank you, Rimmer.' Leo nodded to his butler, then stopped in the doorway and turned towards Florence, lifting her hand slowly to his lips. It was a marked contrast to the first time they'd entered the house together, when he'd stormed ahead by himself, but he wanted this time to be different, and for everyone to know it too. It wasn't quite carrying her over the threshold, but it was certainly an improvement.

'Rimmer.' There was a breathless quality to his wife's voice as she turned to the butler, her cheeks tinged with pink. 'It's good to see you.'

'You too, my lady.' The butler's gaze, Leo noticed, was approving. 'How was your journey?'

'Long. I don't want to see the inside of another carriage for a good six months.'

'At least.' Leo found himself reluctant to let go of her hand again, though it was unfortunately necessary to remove his greatcoat. 'Any news to report?'

'Not in the house, my lord, although I understand the arrival of the herd has caused some consternation in the steward's office.'

'So I gather. Sewell wrote to me.' Leo made a wry face. 'I'm already bracing myself for our next interview. You may need to refill the brandy decanter.'

'Already done, my lord.'

'Ahem.'

All three of them jumped at the sound of a pointed cough, as the slim figure of Mrs Fitch suddenly detached itself from the wall, where she'd been doing an excellent job of camouflaging herself in the shadows, and walked towards them, lips pursed with disapproval.

'I beg your pardon, my lord, but Mr Sewell only has the well-being of the estate at heart.' Her voice was as monotone as always.

'Of course he does.' Leo removed his hat. 'Good evening, Mrs Fitch. How are you?'

'Quite well, my lord, thank you for asking. I took the opportunity of your absence to have the maids clean the carpets and curtains in all the receiving rooms. The time has been spent most productively.'

'I'm glad to hear it.'

'My lady.' Mrs Fitch inclined her head towards Florence. 'Would you care for something to eat?'

'No, thank you, we had some refreshments at our last stop.' Florence smiled a greeting. 'Although I'd love a cup of tea if you wouldn't mind sending one up to my bedroom?'

'Of course, my lady.'

'And I'd like for us to sit down and have tea together as well some time soon. I think we have a great deal to talk about.'

'Indeed, my lady?'

'Yes.' Florence paused, throwing a quick glance at Leo before continuing. 'His Lordship and I have discussed it and, now that we're back, I'm going to take over the running of the household. With your assistance, of course.'

There was an audible gasp from the butler, though when Leo looked, Rimmer was staring intently at his shoes.

A prolonged moment of silence followed before Mrs Fitch turned her gaze towards him. 'Is that what Your Lordship wishes?'

'It is.' Leo lifted an eyebrow at the implication.

'I see.' The housekeeper's expression was so sour,

it might have turned milk. 'Then you should know, there is a great deal to learn.'

'I'm certain there is.' Florence's tone was conciliatory. 'And I'd be very grateful for any advice you could give me. I'd like for us to work together.'

There was another long pause. 'As you wish, my lady.'

'Wonderful. Then how about we meet tomorrow afternoon? That should give me a chance to gather my thoughts. I have so many ideas.' Florence beamed at each of them in turn. 'Now, if you'll excuse me, I need to bathe before bed. I'm sure I smell like a horse!'

'Goodnight.' Leo smiled after her as she headed for the staircase, waiting until she was out of hearing distance before clearing his throat. 'Rimmer, perhaps you could send Her Ladyship's maid up to her?'

'Of course, my lord.' The butler scurried away.

'Mrs Fitch…' Leo turned slowly back towards the housekeeper '…as the new marchioness, Her Ladyship has the right to make any decisions relating to the household, wouldn't you say?'

'In principle, my lord.' Mrs Fitch lifted her chin imperiously. 'However, your father's instructions—'

'My father is no longer here.' He spoke over her. 'As for his instructions, they were written before I was married. Therefore, they do not apply to my wife.'

'But by her own admission, she has no experience of managing a household this size.'

'She can learn.'

'What about the mistakes she might make in the meantime? The reputation of Rainton is far too important for it to be imperilled by some…farmer's daughter.'

'That farmer's daughter is my wife.' Leo's tone was cutting. 'Mrs Fitch, I'll let today pass because I admit my own poor behaviour in the past might have encouraged yours, but from now on you will treat Her Ladyship with the respect she deserves, is that understood?'

A series of expressions seemed to dart across the housekeeper's face before she made a stiff curtsey. 'Of course, my lord.'

'Good.' He inclined his head. 'Now, before anything else happens, there's one other matter I should like to be dealt with as quickly as possible.' He pointed upwards. '*That* needs to come down.'

Mrs Fitch gasped. 'You father's birdcage?'

'Yes. I don't want to set eyes on the damn thing ever again.'

'It's good to have you back, my lady,' Jane commented, holding up a linen towel a short while later. 'You look much better than when you left, if I may say so.'

'Thank you.' Florence climbed out of the bath, drying herself off before pulling on a white lace nightgown. 'I feel much better.'

'Mr Rimmer says that His Lordship seems to be in a much better mood too.' Jane gave her a sly smile.

'I think so. I believe we both found the trip helpful.' She sat down at her dressing-table, meeting her maid's eye in the mirror. 'Don't look at me like that!'

'Like what?' Jane batted her lashes, feigning innocence. 'I'm sure I don't know what you mean. I'm just glad it was *helpful.*'

'It's not like that. His Lordship and I have come to an understanding, that's all. Our marriage may have begun under difficult circumstances, but we've resolved to make the best of it. We're getting to know each other.'

'Mmm.' Jane sounded sceptical. 'Well, if you want to carry on *helping* His Lordship, I think that nightgown ought to do it. You look very *helpful.*'

'Stop it!' Florence couldn't help but laugh, although, looking at her reflection in the mirror, she could see what her maid meant. The nightgown had been a gift from Cassie and was so thin as to be almost transparent, not to mention cut quite shockingly low. Whatever else she'd achieved in London, it seemed that her marriage had her new sister-in-law's approval.

'Anyway, I hope you got the answers you were looking for in London.' Jane winked, reaching for a hairbrush.

'Some of them.' Florence twisted around on the stool, remembering one answer she still hadn't found.

'Can I ask you a question? It might sound a little odd, but when I first came here, were you aware of me receiving any correspondence?'

'I don't think so.' Jane tapped the brush against her hand. 'But I could check with Mr Rimmer, if you like?'

'No!' She shook her head quickly. 'That's all right. I just wondered.'

She swivelled back round to her mirror, hardly knowing whether to feel relieved or frustrated. Surely Jane would have remembered her receiving so many love letters? The fact that she didn't made them even more mysterious. Now it wasn't just a question of *who'd* sent them. It was also a question of *how* they'd been delivered.

'Now that you mention it, though, a letter did arrive while you were away,' Jane said, starting to draw the brush through her hair. 'All the way from Cumberland, the man said.'

'It must be from my parents.' Florence sat up eagerly.

'I'll go and fetch it once I've finished your hair.' Jane smiled. 'And I can't tell you how glad we all are that His Lordship's finally put that old harridan Mrs Fitch in her place. Mr Rimmer told us what he said. Everyone in the servants' hall was thrilled.'

'Really?' Florence blinked in surprise. 'What did he say?'

'Just that you were in charge now and she was to start showing you some proper respect. I would have cheered if I'd been there.' Jane grinned and then bit her lip. 'Only please don't tell His Lordship that any of us know. Mr Rimmer was supposed to have left, but he couldn't resist eavesdropping.'

'Isn't Mrs Fitch popular downstairs?'

'Urgh, no.' Jane rolled her eyes. 'She's a tyrant. She dismissed Jemima, one of the scullery maids, last month just for *talking* about her beau, saying it reflected poor moral character, and she talks to everyone except Mr Sewell like she thinks she's the marchioness. She even demands to know what we're doing on our days off so she can tell us whether or not it reflects well on the family.'

'Gracious.' Florence made a face. 'How does she think *I* reflect on the family?'

'Oh…um…' Jane's attention seemed very focused on one particular hair knot suddenly. 'I can't say as I know for certain.'

'Yes, you do. It's all right, she hasn't exactly hidden her opinion. You can say it.'

'I'd rather not.'

'That I'm an upstart farmer's daughter?'

'Something like that.' Jane sounded embarrassed. 'But on the plus side, it got me this job. I would never have been promoted to Lady's Maid otherwise.'

'In other words, she didn't think me enough of a *lady* to warrant an experienced lady's maid?'

'Oh, dear.' Jane looked crestfallen. 'It sounds bad when you put it like that.'

'Well, the joke's on her, because I think it's all worked out perfectly.' Florence smiled. 'You're an excellent lady's maid, no matter what Mrs Fitch thinks, and now that I'm managing the household there are going to be some changes around here.' She straightened her shoulders, reevaluating her nightdress. Yes, it was a little shocking at first, but it was also quite pretty, with dainty sleeves and buttons all the way down to her waist. She couldn't help wondering what Leo would think of it.

'That sounds like fighting talk.' Jane grinned. 'I knew there was a reason I liked you.'

'I like you too.' She laughed. 'And my first change is that everyone may treat their private time as their own. No one will be dismissed simply for talking about their beau. What else?'

'Well…' Jane twisted her mouth to one side. 'There's the summer fair.'

'Oh, yes. That's in two days, isn't it? What should I expect?'

'Plenty. It's a big event. There are stalls, of course, as well as contests for the children, sack races and such like. Then there are competitions too, like embroidery, baking, wood carving, flower arranging, all

that kind of thing. Then everyone sits down to a picnic on the lawn.'

'It sounds lovely.'

'It is, only…' Jane paused, as if she was trying to
be tactful. 'No offence to the marquess, but it can be
a little uncomfortable. Everyone feels like they have
to be on their best behaviour in case you-know-who
tells tales on them.'

'No!'

'Yes! A couple of tenants almost lost their farms
last year because their sons drank a little too much
ale and got into a brawl over Agnes Tanner. Fitch re-
ported it and the poor fathers had to come cap in hand
to the steward's office. The old marquess made them
grovel for half an hour and then gave them a lecture on
raising children. As if he had any idea.' She snorted.
'Begging your pardon.'

'It's all right. I met the marquess's sister, Lady
Brooke, in London and she told me something similar.
She said she got away from him as soon as she could.'

'I don't blame her.'

'Well, there won't be any tale-telling this year.' Florence nodded at her reflection in the mirror. 'Or if there
is, I'll make sure the new marquess ignores it. Now
what else can we do for the fair?'

'Some music would be nice. Everyone would love
some dancing.'

'You haven't had music before?' She hoisted her eyebrows towards her hairline. 'At a fair?'

'Mrs Fitch says it leads to debauchery.'

'Then we'll definitely have some this year. Music, that is, not debauchery. Although we might have trouble finding musicians at such short notice.'

'Leave that to me. My brother and his friends play their fiddles in the local tavern.' Jane leaned forward eagerly. 'They're not an orchestra, but they're pretty good.'

'Perfect. Could you ask them?'

'I'll send one of the kitchen boys tonight with a message.'

'Wonderful.' Florence heaved a deep, gratified sigh. 'We're going to make this the best fair Rainton has ever had.'

Chapter Fifteen

'I understand what you're saying...' Florence clenched her teeth as she looked across the tea table at the housekeeper. It had only been twenty minutes since they'd sat down together and she was already reaching the end of her tether '...but I really don't think one day of holiday a month is sufficient. Everyone deserves some free time, don't you think? At least an additional evening per week.'

'In my experience, my lady, free time is a temptation to vice, especially in the evenings.' Mrs Fitch made a show of folding her hands in her lap. 'I would be far more amenable to the idea of allowing staff a morning's holiday each week, but there's far too much to be done.'

'That's hardly the staff's fault. And surely what people choose to do with their spare time is their own business?'

'I disagree. The behaviour of the staff reflects upon this house and its family. As housekeeper, I demand

and expect the highest standards. Anyone unable to meet them is welcome to leave.'

'But we should also provide as pleasant a working environment as possible, don't you think?'

'Who says it's unpleasant?' The housekeeper's eyes narrowed. 'The honour of working at Rainton ought to be *pleasure* enough.'

Florence poured a second cup of tea, wishing it were something stronger. She was feeling unsettled enough, after reading her parents' letter the previous night. Their kind words, in which they'd expressed their surprise at her marriage but assured her of their belief in her innocence, had made her feel so guilty that she'd found it hard to sleep afterwards. Apparently she'd lied to them about her behaviour too.

'I'm afraid we'll have to agree to disagree,' she answered finally. 'From now on, I insist that all members of staff are permitted one day of holiday *and* an evening free each week, as well as half-days on Sundays.'

'Absurd.' Mrs Fitch sniffed, as she had at least half a dozen times already. 'I warn you, such lax rules will make this house a...a...den of iniquity!'

'Well, that would certainly be interesting, but let's see how it goes, shall we?' Florence cleared her throat. 'And on that subject, I understand there was some kind of misunderstanding with one of the maids last month. Jemima, I think?'

'There was a scullery maid by that name, but there

was no misunderstanding. She was spreading impure thoughts amongst the other maids.'

'From what I've heard, she was only talking about a beau.'

'Which she knew was forbidden. You may think it draconian, my lady, but in time, she would have corrupted them all.'

'None the less, I should like her to be rehired, perhaps with a warning not to discuss such matters during working hours again?'

There was a long pause before Mrs Fitch turned her face aside. 'On your head be it.'

'Good, and I think it would be a wise idea to increase everyone's wages too.'

'Everyone's?'

'Yes, yourself included, of course. Now, about the fair.'

Mrs Fitch's head whipped back again. 'What about the fair? The arrangements are already in place.'

'And I'm sure they're all excellent. I'd just like to make a few additions to the programme. Music and dancing, for example.'

'There's a maypole.'

'For the children, yes, but I'm sure a lot of adults would appreciate the chance to—'

'I must protest!' The housekeeper sounded appalled. 'The fair is a sober and dignified occasion, exactly as the former marquess wished. There has never been any dancing, nor has anyone ever complained about it to me.'

'Perhaps they've been worried about how you might react?' Florence cleared her throat. 'Just because nobody's said anything doesn't mean they wouldn't enjoy a little music. But if you're worried, it could be in the evening, once all the picnicking and prize-giving is over.'

'That would be even worse. Once it gets dark, who knows what depravity it might lead to? Next you'll be telling me the staff should be allowed to attend.'

'Well, yes, actually, once the picnic is over, I can't see why they shouldn't—'

'My lady,' Mrs Fitch rose to her feet, 'might I have your permission to withdraw?'

'If you wish.' Florence sighed. 'If you need some time to think about it all, I completely understand.'

'I do not require time to think. You and your ideas are *exactly* what my former master warned me of.'

'He warned you about me?'

'This entire situation!' The housekeeper tossed her head. 'And I know exactly what he would have expected me to do about it!'

'Sewell, Mrs Fitch…what is this about?' Leo set his ledger and quill aside as his steward and housekeeper came to stand in front of his desk. Rimmer had just been in to inform him, with a particularly pointed look, that the pair of them were requesting a meeting, but whatever the matter was he hoped they'd make it quick. The dinner bell would be ringing soon, and he was impatient to see Florence again. After spending two days alone together in a carriage, it had felt strange to spend so much time apart, but he'd had so many practical matters to catch up on, he hadn't even stopped for lunch. Most of his day had actually been spent with Sewell, a fact that made his steward's reappearance now even stranger.

'We've come to speak with you about a sensitive matter, my lord.' Sewell tipped his head so far back, Leo could practically see up his nostrils. 'In fact, we believe it is our duty to do so.'

'Indeed?' He leaned back in his chair, bracing himself. 'Go on.'

'Since your return from London, there have been some alarming developments.'

'You mean, my return from London yesterday? Less than twenty-four hours ago, in fact?'

'Yes, my lord. Although really, it began before that, with the arrival of the herd.'

'Sewell, didn't we discuss that this morning?' Leo pressed a hand to his forehead. 'You've made your feelings about the new cattle very clear, so if you're here to denounce them again—'

'It's not just about that, my lord. I've also recently

been told about some new and extremely alarming developments.'

'Her Ladyship is out of control!' Mrs Fitch burst out.

Leo lifted an eyebrow in surprise. In one moment, his housekeeper had just demonstrated more emotion than she had in the entire rest of the time he'd known her. 'That's quite a charge. What exactly has she done?'

'It's more a question of what she hasn't done. She wants to destroy my entire life's work!'

'How so?'

'She wishes to hire undesirables, to increase the staff's wages and holidays, and to allow dancing at the fair!' The housekeeper's face was turning an alarming shade of puce.

'Those items being your life's work?'

'It's the ethos behind them. Your father's ethos.' Mrs Fitch's gaze slid, as usual, to the letter on his desk. 'Everything that Mr Sewell and I have strived to maintain since his passing, as he asked us to do. If she has her way, she'll drag us all down to her level.'

'I see,' Leo answered softly, keeping his voice deliberately calm. 'And what level would that be exactly?'

There was another pause. 'That's not for me to say, my lord.'

'Ahem.' Sewell coughed. 'I believe that what Mrs Fitch is trying to say is that we feel it is our duty to speak out when we see your father's legacy being threatened, whether that be in regard to the estate or the management of the household. The new cottages and cattle were bad enough, but the rest of these changes…' He hung his head, as if he couldn't bear to go on. 'We're sorry that it's come to this, my lord, but we cannot in good conscience stand back and say nothing. We've discussed it and we would rather resign.'

'You would?' Leo sat up straighter. 'Both of you?'

'I'm afraid so, my lord.'

'Very well.'

'I'm sorry?' Sewell looked startled.

'I said, very well.' Leo pushed himself to his feet and clasped his hands behind his back. 'If you both feel so strongly about the situation then I accept your resignations.'

'But, my lord, surely you can see what a mistake—'

'What I can see are two people who believe that my father is still the marquess.' Leo looked between them. 'I can understand the confusion. You worked with him for a long time and you both did excellent jobs. However, the estate is now mine and I shall run it as I see fit. Therefore, I accept your resignations and thank you for all your hard work over the years. Sewell, you may of course keep your house, and Mrs Fitch, a cottage will be provided for you on the estate. On top of that, you will also both receive an annual stipend.'

'This is monstrous!' Mrs Fitch's face resembled an overripe tomato in danger of bursting at any moment. 'If that's your decision then I shan't stay here a day longer. I shall go to my sister's house until my cottage is ready.'

'If that's what you wish. Sewell?'

'I...' The steward exchanged an uncertain look with the housekeeper. 'I shall also go, my lord.'

'Then I thank you both again and wish you the best for the future. Good evening.'

He stood there, waiting until they'd both departed before heaving a long sigh, one that he felt as if he'd been holding in for months. A fortnight ago, if someone had told him he was about to lose both his steward and housekeeper in one evening, he might have experienced some degree of alarm, but now he felt as if a giant boulder had just been lifted from his shoulders. Relief swept through him like a cool breeze. And the best part of it was that they'd made the decision to go themselves, excusing him from any sense of obligation and leaving him free to be himself, his own man, more than just a dutiful son. He glanced briefly at the letter on his desk and then placed his ledger on top of it.

Yes, that was much better.

Florence hurried across the hall, following the sound of a cue hitting a ball into the billiards room.

After what Jane had just told her, she'd run straight out of her bedroom in search of Leo, dressed for dinner in a simple blue muslin evening gown, but with her hair still unbound, half-brushed and hanging loose over her shoulders. She didn't care. She needed to speak with him as soon as possible.

'Is it true?' She burst into the room and stopped breathlessly in the doorway. 'You've dismissed Sewell and Mrs Fitch?'

'News travels fast.' He looked up and smiled. 'Although not entirely accurately. They resigned.'

'What?' She gasped. 'Was it because of my meeting with her? Because I tried to be polite—'

'I'm sure you were perfectly reasonable.' He laid his cue on the table and walked towards her. 'If you'd asked her to move a single chair in the drawing room, she would have found fault. Sewell too. They both wanted to manage the house and estate as my father did or not do it at all, so they gave me an ultimatum. It might have been a bluff, but I found that I didn't wish to find out. I accepted their resignations at once.'

'Leo…' she didn't break his gaze '…are you telling me that we have no steward and no housekeeper for a house with a hundred rooms and an estate of thirty thousand acres?'

'That's pretty much the long and short of it, yes.'

'How can you be so calm about that?'

'I don't know, but I am.' He lifted a hand to her

head, sliding his fingers around a tendril of hair. 'It feels like a fresh start.'

She swallowed as the backs of his fingers skimmed her cheekbone. It felt like such an intimate gesture, definitely more than just making the best of things, although she wondered if he was simply in shock from losing his two most important members of staff... 'You know, she said something very strange, about how your father warned her about this situation, although I got the feeling she meant me specifically. Do you know what she meant?'

A flicker of some emotion passed over his face, though so quickly she thought she might have imagined it. 'She was often quoting my father. I shouldn't worry about it.'

'Oh...' She pressed her brows together, struck with the distinct impression there was something else he wasn't telling her, something he didn't want to tell her. 'What will happen to them?'

'They'll each have a pension and a house on the estate. I'm not throwing them onto the street, but this has been a long time coming.' He lowered his hand again. 'It's quite a strange feeling, to be honest, having free rein over my own property.'

'I suppose it must be.' She tilted her head. Now that his hand was gone, she found she wanted it back again. 'But, just between us, it seems you've made the rest of the staff very happy, especially Mrs Hotham, the cook. Apparently she and Mrs Fitch have been arch enemies for the past decade.'

'Then I shall expect a feast fit for a king tonight. And don't worry. I'll send word to my man of business in London for a new steward and housekeeper tomorrow.'

'Good idea.' She reached for the cue and leaned forward, taking aim at a red ball. 'You know, I'm sorry it's come to this, but I can't help feeling glad too. Trying to have a conversation with Mrs Fitch was impossible. She disagreed with everything.'

'Sewell too. They must have given each other tips on how to be obstructive.' He nodded at the billiards table as her ball slammed into a pocket. 'That was impressive. You've never told me you played.'

'You've never asked.' She was already lining up another shot. 'Amabel and I used to sneak into her father's billiards room to play. It was just far enough away from the parlour that her mother couldn't hear us.' She potted the second ball with a snap and then straightened up, aware of a sudden pang of sadness. 'I still miss her.'

'Amabel?'

'Yes. Sometimes I think about writing to her, but I still wouldn't know how to explain. And I wouldn't know where to send the letter.'

'I'm sorry.'

'It's my own fault. I was the one who betrayed her.'

'Still…' He lifted a shoulder, wanting to make her feel better somehow. 'Maybe we should go out to-morrow?'

She blinked at the change of subject. 'Out?'

'Yes. It's about time I gave you a tour of the estate. Then perhaps we can come up with some more ideas for improvements together?'

'But the fair's the day after tomorrow. Don't we have things to organise?'

'I doubt it. Knowing Mrs Fitch, everything's already been taken care of.'

'Oh.' She smiled. 'Well, in that case, I'd love to.'

'Good.' He wrapped his hand around the top of the cue, still clutched in her hand. 'Now, let's have a real game, shall we?'

Chapter Sixteen

It was a beautiful day, Florence thought, tilting her face up to the sunshine as she and Leo cantered through the park, much better than the weather had promised when she'd got out of bed that morning and seen a ridge of towering grey clouds on the horizon. To her amazement, however, by the time she'd finished her breakfast, the clouds had already moved on, thankfully without depositing a single drop of rain, leaving a swathe of crystal-blue sky behind them.

It was like a metaphor for their marriage, she reflected as they spurred their horses into a gallop. Stormy at first, becoming brighter over time. She only hoped the sunshine didn't fade away, but for today, at least, the forecast seemed good. Unlike with his tour of the house, Leo actually seemed enthusiastic about showing her the estate.

Their first stop was the site of some half-constructed cottages. The old ones, about half a mile away, were still lived in, Leo told her, but they were old and damp and unlikely to last another winter. He'd tried for several years to convince his father to build new ones, to no avail, and after his death Sewell had repeatedly thrown obstacles in the way of finding a builder. It had taken the threat of Leo's hiring somebody himself for the steward to finally take action. The whole saga made her own issues with Mrs Fitch sound comparatively easy.

Now they were on their way to see the new herd, something else that Sewell had tried to obstruct. If she'd had any doubts about the wisdom of letting both steward and housekeeper go at once, Leo's many stories about their attempts to thwart even the tiniest change would have convinced her it was for the best. And in case *he* had any doubts, she also took the opportunity to relay parts of her recent conversation with Jane.

'Are you saying that, all this time, our tenants have been attending the summer fair under sufferance?' Leo asked, his expression appalled.

'I wouldn't go *that* far.' She tried to sound reassuring. 'Obviously people were happy to attend the picnic and win prizes, but it sounds as though everyone was quite tense, worrying about saying or doing the wrong thing.'

'Good grief, I thought I was the only one who felt that way.' He shook his head. 'Well, this year will be different. If people want dancing, they can dance all night for all I care. And they can behave in whatever manner they wish. There won't be any repercussions.'

'That might depend on the behaviour.' She laughed. 'I mean, we should probably draw the line at murder and mayhem. But perhaps we should make ourselves scarce in the evening? Then people won't feel like they're being watched.'

'Good idea.'

'It's just a pity that I can't participate in some of the contests too...' she threw him an arch look '...since I'm on *such* a winning streak with both cards and billiards.'

'As I recall, we both beat each other at billiards.'

'Yes, but I won three games and you only won two. Therefore, the overall winner would be me.' She gave him a superior smile. 'Don't feel too bad. I beat my brothers in most games. Oddly enough, they always object too. It must be a male trait.'

'I don't object at all. On the contrary, I'm glad to have a new opponent. Clearly, I just need to up my game.'

'Then would you care for a rematch tonight?'

'I'd be delighted.'

'Excellent.' She smiled and then bit her lip. 'Although we'll also need an early night. I want everything to go well tomorrow.'

'I'm sure it will. And if it doesn't, it's only a fair.'

'But it's my first fair as the marchioness. I'd like

for it to be a success.' She glanced nervously up at the sky. 'I just hope the weather stays nice. Those clouds this morning were a little alarming.'

'Don't worry. It never rains on fair day.'

She swivelled towards him. 'Never?'

'So my father told me. There was some mild alarm in 1784 when a single grey cloud was spotted on the horizon, but other than that, it's taken place in glorious sunshine for the past eighty-five years.'

'"A single grey cloud in 1784"?' She lifted her eyebrows incredulously. 'Are you making that up?'

'As strange as it sounds, no.' He chuckled. 'So the odds are, it'll be another beautiful day. And speaking of beautiful...' he drew rein as they crested a hill '...there they are. Red Devons.'

'Oh, they're magnificent,' Florence breathed, sitting back in her saddle as she took in the view of rolling green fields and deep ruby-red cattle. 'They look like a fine herd.'

'I'm glad you think so. As I recall, Sewell warned me they might cause ladies to swoon.'

'To be fair, they are rather large. I suppose they could be a little intimidating for anyone who wasn't raised around them, although I don't see why the statement only applies to ladies.' She drew in a deep breath and then let it out again slowly. 'It really is beautiful here. The view from the house is so flat, it still looks strange to me, but this is much better. It makes me feel less homesick.'

'You've been homesick?' He moved his horse a little closer, his voice edged with concern.

'A little. My family are so far away.' She rubbed a hand quickly across her cheek, wiping away a stray tear. 'I know it sounds odd, considering what I apparently did in order to come here, but I suppose I didn't appreciate just how much I'd miss them until it was too late.'

'I'm sorry.' He rubbed a hand over his chin. 'I'm also afraid I can't do anything about the flat views from the house, but maybe I can offer you something else. You said that your farm was near Brampton, did you not? In the middle of the country?'

'Yes.'

'In that case, I think I can show you a view your home doesn't provide.'

'It's not a Roman wall, is it?' She managed a sidelong smile. 'Because we have one of those.'

'It's not a wall.' He picked up his reins again. 'Quite the opposite. Follow me.'

'It's spectacular.' Florence stood on the beach, gazing out at the wide expanse of water before twisting her head to take in the white chalk cliffs behind them. 'I haven't been to the seaside for years.'

'As views go, it's still quite flat, at the moment anyway.' Leo couldn't keep the gloating expression off his face. 'But it's not bad.'

'It's not bad at all.' She grinned at him. 'I can't believe we have the entire beach to ourselves. Shall we paddle?'

'Paddle?'

'Yes. It's such a hot day, it will cool us down.' She sat down on a rock and pulled her boots off, tossing both them and her stockings aside.

'Sadly, my valet won't be very pleased if I get sand in my Hessians.' He extended a hand to help her up, clearing his throat at the sight of her bare ankles.

'Ah. Luckily for me, Jane is in such a good mood now that Mrs Fitch has left, I think she'll forgive me no matter what state I go home in.' She ran past him down to the water. 'Pity for you, though!'

'Mmm.' He made a sound of assent, though he was somewhat preoccupied with the view again. Both her calves, as well as her ankles, were clearly visible now as she tugged the hem of her skirt up to keep it out of the water.

'How is it?' He wrenched his gaze up with an effort.

'Quite bracing!' She turned around, hunching her shoulders, though her eyes were sparkling. 'A little colder than I expected, but very refreshing.'

'I'll take your word for it.'

'This is officially my new favourite place in the

world.' She spread one arm out, twirling around in the shallows.

He smiled, heat radiating through his chest at the words. It felt strangely good to hear her say them. The idea of her being homesick had bothered him more than he would have expected. 'I should have thought to bring a picnic.'

'That would have been lovely, although I think Mrs Hotham has enough to do today preparing for the fair.' She looked over her shoulder at him. 'By the way, I told her we'd be happy with a light dinner tonight. I hope that's all right?'

'Of course. I should have thought of it myself. Look out!' He sprang forward, catching her around the waist and lifting her backwards as a particularly large wave hurtled towards her.

'Oh!' She clamped a hand to her mouth, laughing. 'Thank you. That would have soaked my dress.'

'Here.' He lowered her back down to the sand, his fingers tangled in the folds of her close-fitting riding-habit, though he found himself extremely reluctant to take them away. Instead he tightened his hold, sliding his hands down to her hips.

'Leo?' she whispered, her eyes widening as she looked up at him.

'Florence.' He murmured her name back, dropping his gaze as a pink flush swept up over her throat and across her cheeks. She looked—she *was*—so unutterably perfect, it occurred to him again that she was exactly the kind of wife he might have chosen had he felt himself free to choose. Whatever anger and resentment he'd once felt towards her had ebbed away completely. Now, with their breaths mingling, all he felt was an irresistible desire to kiss her.

Slowly he tilted his head, giving her time to pull away if she wanted, bringing his lips towards hers and nudging them gently apart.

She didn't respond at first, as though she needed a few moments to think, before making a soft sound in the back of her throat and lifting her hands, slipping them over his shoulders, and kissing him back.

He didn't know how long they stood that way. He was dimly aware of the sound of the waves lapping on the beach, of the sharp cries of seagulls circling overhead. He could smell salt on the air and on her skin, could taste it too, along with a sweetness like honey on her tongue. He could feel his skin tingling and his blood throbbing heavily in his veins, filling him with a new sense of exhilaration as time seemed to slow and stretch. Their kiss might have lasted for a few seconds or an hour, but by the time they broke apart, both of them panting, he felt as though the whole world had shifted on its axis.

'Leo,' she whispered again, pressing a hand to his chest as she opened her eyes to look at him with a half-confused, half-dazed expression. 'You kissed me.'

'Yes.' His voice sounded husky.

'But you resent me.'

'I did. Before. Not any longer.' He swayed forward, pressing his forehead to hers. 'I'd rather kiss you again, if you have no objection?'

'No.' She slid her tongue between her lips in a way that sent a hot pulse straight to his groin. 'That is, no, I don't have any objection.'

He hesitated, trying to make sense of the negatives.

'I mean, I want you to kiss me again,' she clarified.

'Ah.' He breathed a sigh of relief. 'Thank goodness.'

He bent his head once more, claiming her lips just as a large wave swept over their feet, soaking them up to their ankles.

'Oh!' Florence gave a startled yelp.

'Damn.' Leo pulled back to look at her wet skirt. 'It seems I should have carried you a little further up the beach.'

'And your poor boots!' She pointed at them in dismay. 'If your valet doesn't like sand, he's really going to hate salt water.'

'Come on, we'd better get you back to the house before you catch a chill.' He bent down, reaching for her sodden hem and wringing it out, before sweeping one arm around her shoulders and the other beneath her knees.

'Wait! You don't have to carry me.' Florence laughed. 'It's a wet dress, not a twisted ankle.'

'Humour me. It was my fault.'

'How so?'

'I distracted you.'

She coiled her arms around his neck as he carried her back up the beach, shingle crunching beneath his ruined boots. 'Actually, I think we may have distracted each other.'

'And how do you feel about that?' He tightened his hold on her. 'As distractions go, I mean?'

'Well…' she tipped her head against his shoulder '…as distractions go…it was quite enjoyable.'

'*Quite* enjoyable?' He lifted an eyebrow. 'So you wouldn't mind being distracted again? Once the fair is out of the way, of course?'

There was a momentary pause before she cupped a hand around the back of his neck and gently touched a thumb to his nape. 'I think I should like it *very* much.'

Chapter Seventeen

Today was the day, Florence told herself, seized with a burst of nervous excitement the moment she opened her eyes the next morning, the first Saturday of August, the date of the annual summer fair.

She rolled onto her back and stretched, revelling in the cocoon of warmth she'd made under her blankets. She'd slept well, better than she'd expected considering how anxious she felt, which was surely a good sign, but what *was* that sound? Faint but persistent, a soft tapping, like fingertips beating gently against a drum. Slowly she lifted her head, looking around her bedchamber for the source. A small fire was roaring in the grate and her curtains were open, though her room was still a shadowy grey thanks to the rain.

The rain?

She jolted upright and stared at her window in horror. Rain was lashing against the glass, and not just a little, but a practical deluge. So much so that she wouldn't have been surprised to find somebody standing outside throwing buckets of water up at the house.

Oh, no. No, no, no… Her spirits plummeted to the soles of her feet. There was *never* rain on fair day. Wasn't that what Leo had told her? And yet here it was, in her very first year as the marchioness…

'Leo!' She leapt out of bed and ran to the door between their bedrooms, bursting through without bothering to knock because this was an emergency and she needed to speak with him right away or…

She skidded to a halt. Her husband was climbing out of bed, presumably thanks to her panicked shout, looking as if he'd just woken up, with a smattering of dark stubble across his jaw and his hair sticking out at comical angles. More to the point, he was also completely stark naked.

Her eyes dropped before she could stop them. With five brothers, she wasn't exactly ignorant about the male body, only she'd never seen one so…fully grown before. Goose-pimples erupted over her skin. And this was the man she'd kissed on the beach, whose lips had moulded to hers as though they'd been made for each other, who'd scooped her into his arms and carried her back to their horses…

'Oh!' She spun around, mortified to realise she'd been staring. 'I'm so sorry. I should have waited. I just needed to tell you…' She flailed her arms towards the windows. 'Rain!'

'Ah.' She heard a rustle of clothing, followed by footsteps. 'So there is.'

She darted a quick look sideways. Leo was already standing beside the window, his body now concealed beneath a long, dark green dressing gown, while she… She glanced down, suddenly acutely conscious of the fact that she wasn't wearing any kind of dressing gown herself, just the revealing nightdress that Cassie had given her. And if he looked rumpled then so must she. She hadn't even glanced in a mirror before rushing in here. Her hair could be standing on end for all she knew.

'I just can't believe it.' She attempted to focus on the problem at hand, folding her arms around herself in a belated attempt to preserve her modesty. 'After eighty-five years of sunshine! What are the chances?'

'Quite low.' He sounded contemplative. 'It's certainly a surprise.'

'It's more than that. It's a calamity! The whole day is ruined!' A shiver rippled through her. 'And it's *cold*! I don't know how, but this is all Mrs Fitch's fault. She's probably laughing to herself right now, thinking it's a sign that everything's going to collapse without her.'

'Sewell too probably.'

'Do you think it might pass?' she asked hopefully. 'Bad weather usually clears in four hours.'

'Unless there's no wind, which unfortunately appears to be the case.'

'Argh!' She flung her head back. 'It doesn't even matter. Even if the rain was to stop right now, there's so much of it, the grass would still be too wet for a picnic this afternoon.'

'I'm afraid you're right.' His footsteps approached. 'Fortunately, it's only a summer fair. In the grand scheme of things, it's not hugely important. Nobody's sick or injured.'

'Maybe not, but—'

'*And*,' he went on, slowly unpeeling her arms from around her chest, 'we have a ballroom.'

'We…what?' Her pulse jumped as he laced their fingers together.

'We have a ballroom,' he repeated, his eyes warm. 'As well as several reception rooms we barely use. If we clear away some furniture, we should be able to bring the fair inside.'

'That could work.' Her breath caught. 'We could fill the ballroom with flowers from the orangery so it looks like a garden. Then we could lay blankets on the floor and put a hamper on each. And we could use the long gallery for the children's races and set out tables in one of the drawing rooms for all the competition entries…'

'Exactly.'

'And then, when the picnic is finished, we can clear the blankets away and have dancing!'

He smiled. 'It's beginning to sound better than the original plan.'

'So we don't have to cancel?'

'And let Fitch and Sewell win? Absolutely not.'

'This is going to work. Leo, you're a genius!'

'I'm glad you think so.' His gaze dipped to the top of her nightdress. 'I like this.'

'Do you?' Her voice sounded curiously high-pitched all of a sudden. 'It was a present from Cassie.'

'I like that less.' He gave her a wry look. 'But you look very pretty. Mornings suit you.'

'Oh.' She ran her tongue between her lips as the air around them felt very dry suddenly, despite the rain outside. Half of her was distracted by the long list of jobs already stacking up in her head. There was just *so* much to think about. Aside from moving furniture, messages needed to be sent out all over the estate. People needed to be told about the change of plan before they assumed everything was cancelled. Only the other half of her didn't care about any of that, not when Leo was standing right in front of her, his eyes smouldering so intensely that she felt as if a match had just been struck between them.

It was almost funny, she thought, considering how fast she'd run into his bedchamber, how impossible she found it to move now. Only it wasn't *actually* funny and she wasn't completely still either. Her insides were swirling wildly, making her tremble with nervous energy. It occurred to her suddenly that she no longer thought of him as the scowling and severe Marquess of Rainton, the man with storm clouds for eyes, who'd arrived in London and begun paying court to Amabel. Whoever that man had been, the one standing before her now was somebody else entirely, somebody who'd kissed her on the beach yesterday and who she wanted to kiss again, even though now really wasn't the time.

'You're shivering.' His hands skimmed the sides of her waist. 'I'd offer you my robe, only...'

She didn't let him finish, lifting up on her toes to press her lips against his.

He gave a low moan and then swept his arms around her, pulling her flush up against him, until she was completely enveloped in his body heat and the swirling sensation was a practical hurricane.

'We could just cancel the fair,' he murmured.

'We can't.' She kissed him one last time before pulling away reluctantly. 'It would let too many people down.'

'Then we take this up again later. Tonight.'

'Tonight,' she agreed.

Three hours later, Florence stood in the middle of the ballroom and marvelled at the transformation that had occurred since that morning. The huge empty space had metamorphosed into a countryside idyll. There were tubs of flowers all around the walls—

considering the number of children attending, vases had seemed like an invitation to trouble—garlands and ribbons around the windows, and an assortment of brightly coloured blankets on the freshly polished floor, as well as a few tables and chairs for the older guests.

'That's it!' She wiped the back of her wrist across her forehead. 'I think we've done pretty well.'

'We've done more than that. We've worked wonders.' Jane, standing beside her, exhaled loudly. 'I never imagined that being a lady's maid would involve quite so much flower arranging.'

'It's just for today, I promise.' Florence smiled apologetically. 'At this rate I'll have to promote you to Housekeeper.'

'No, thank you. Clothes and hair I can manage. The rest of the house, absolutely not.'

'Fair enough.' She braced her hands on her hips. 'You know, His Lordship said he was going to write to his man of business in London to fill the position, but is there anybody downstairs you might recommend instead?'

'I don't think so.' Jane scrunched her mouth up thoughtfully. 'Mrs Fitch was so strict that most maids left after a couple of years. And those of us who stayed were hardly ever given any additional responsibilities. That's how she kept control of everything.'

'So there's no natural successor?'

'Not really, except…' Jane snapped her fingers '… Catherine Chenoweth. She stuck it out as a maid a good fifteen years before taking another position last November. I suppose she gave up hope of Fitch ever retiring.'

'Was she good at her job?'

'Very, and we all liked her. She was the one everyone went to with problems when we knew Fitch would only have scolded us. I don't think I ever heard her raise her voice or say a bad word about anyone. She's Housekeeper to Squire Norris now, but I'm sure she'd jump at the chance to come back.'

'That sounds promising.' Florence pursed her lips. 'But the squire might not be pleased if I poach his housekeeper.'

'Don't worry about that. He'll be thrilled if he can tell people his former housekeeper now works for the Marquess of Rainton. His wife might be more of a challenge, but I'm sure if you pay her a call, she'll forgive you. Throw in a dinner invitation and they'll probably pay you to take her.'

'In that case, do you think you could get a message to her?'

'I'm sure Mr Rimmer could.'

'Wonderful.' Florence looked around the ballroom one more time, starting to feel anxious again. 'Will this really work? Or will everyone think there would have been sunshine if Mrs Fitch were still here?'

Jane snorted. 'Trust me, everyone's just going to be grateful the fair's still going ahead. And no one's going to miss that old tyrant. She would *never* have allowed tenants inside the house.' She gave Florence a nudge. 'I don't suppose the new marquess would have thought of it either if it wasn't for you.'

'Actually, it was his idea.'

'Really?' Jane looked taken aback. 'Well, then, you must be a good influence.'

'Who's a good influence?'

Florence gave a start of surprise at the sound of Leo's voice behind them, at the same moment as Jane gave a squeak of alarm and plummeted into a curtsey.

'Nobody.' She recovered herself first. 'We were just discussing a possible new housekeeper. She was a former maid here and I'd like to ask her back, if you have no objection?'

'None at all.' He smiled. 'That's your department now, remember?'

'So it is.' She glanced at his rolled-up sleeves. 'What have you been doing?'

'Moving furniture. With the help of a couple of footmen, I should add. The carpets are all rolled up in the long gallery and we've moved everything we don't need out of the second drawing room and the Green Room, as instructed. Rimmer tells me one of them is going to be an impromptu nursery.'

'Um…yes.' She blinked rapidly, still distracted by

the sight of his uncovered biceps. 'You've really been moving furniture?'

'Yes. It didn't seem right to just stand by and watch.' He clapped his hands together. 'So what next?'

'Next I think we should all have a rest.' She turned to Jane, who was still looking red-faced. 'Tell everyone downstairs to take a break too. And please tell them tomorrow will be a holiday as a thank-you for today.'

'Yes, my lady. I'll go and tell them now.'

'A holiday?' Leo cocked an eyebrow as Jane bobbed another curtsey and hurried away. 'It really is a new regime.'

'It only seems fair considering how hard everyone's working today. They might all walk out otherwise.'

'Actually, I don't think so.' He moved closer, slipping his arms around her and lacing his fingers across the small of her back. 'The footmen are more motivated than I've ever seen them, and I believe I heard a few of the maids singing this morning.' He glanced over her head at the ballroom. 'This looks very impressive.'

'Thank you.' She lifted her own hands to his chest with a proud smile. 'I'm quite pleased with it. I thought the older children could start off with games in the long gallery while the adults have some tea and look at the competition entries in the Green Room. If I go with the children and you stay with the adults, it should work. Then, when the children are all tired out, we can send them to the "nursery" to be supervised by a few of the maids while we hand out prizes and you give a speech.' She paused for breath. 'After that, we can have the picnic in the ballroom, and then clear all the hampers and blankets away for music and dancing. What do you think?'

'I think there's no way Mrs Fitch could have devised anything like this, especially so quickly.'

'Well, I don't know about that, but I'm starting to feel excited.'

'Good.' He dipped a kiss onto her nose. 'But now we really should sit down for a while or we'll have no energy left to greet everyone.'

'True.' She laughed as he caught hold of one of her hands, pulling her along behind him. 'Where are we going?'

'To my study. It's officially out of bounds to everyone else, but I suggested we store a few surplus pieces of furniture in there.' He opened the door and gestured towards a crimson velvet chaise longue. 'I thought it would make a perfect place if you feel like you need a few minutes alone.'

'That's for me?' Her heart thumped with pleasure at the sight before her. The chaise longue had been placed a few feet from the fireplace, where a roaring fire was crackling in the grate. It looked so cosy and comfortable, part of her wished she could spend the rest of the day here.

'Officially reserved for the marchioness.' He smiled. 'Now, why don't you lie down while I fetch us some tea?'

She opened her eyes wide as he headed back towards the door. 'Wait! You're not going downstairs, surely? Mrs Hotham will have conniptions at the sight of you.'

'Yes, she almost did earlier when I went down to ask for some help with the long gallery.' He looked faintly sheepish. 'I had no idea it was so shocking for a man to enter his own kitchens. I just thought, with everyone being so busy, it made more sense for me to go downstairs than ring for someone, but it caused quite a commotion.' He shook his head. 'Even Rimmer looked scandalised.'

'Oh, dear.' She pressed a hand to her mouth. 'Well, at least your intentions were good, but maybe this time you should use the bell?'

'I would, except that you just asked your maid to tell everyone to take a break.'

'Oh, yes.' She bit her lip. 'So I did.'

'How about I call out from the top of the staircase so that everybody knows I'm coming? Now that I've been downstairs once, a second time shouldn't cause quite so much panic, should it? I can make my own damn pot of tea if necessary.'

'I'm sure it won't come to that.' She chuckled. 'Just be sure to call loudly.'

'Understood.' He made a bow. 'I won't be long.'

Florence laid herself down on the chaise longue as he shut the door behind him, flinging her arms over her head and stretching her legs out. It was so soft and comfortable, and the fire was so delightfully warm, she thought it would be easy to drift off to sleep here in his study. She could have a quick nap, surrounded by books and…

She opened her eyes again with a snap. She was in his study. Alone. And Mrs Fitch had told her that he kept his letter of 'instructions' from his father on his desk. This would be the perfect opportunity to take a look.

If she wanted to take a look, that was.

She sat up, her heart pounding. Did she? Should she? Impulsively, she leapt up and hurried across the room, telling herself she could decide on the way because, whatever she did, she needed to make up her mind quickly. It wouldn't take Leo long to fetch a tray of tea. The kitchen staff would want to be rid of him as soon as possible…

She went round to the far side of the desk and quickly surveyed the objects laid out on the surface. Two candles, a pen, a quill pot and, peeking out from beneath a large ledger…a letter, folded but with the seal broken.

Before she could think better of it, she slid it out and opened it up.

'To my son, Leopold Claridge, on his elevation to the marquessate...'

She diverted her gaze mid-sentence, struck with a sudden pang of guilt. The letter was addressed to him, not her. It was his private correspondence, which meant that it really wasn't any of her business...except that it *was*, wasn't it? If her husband was living his life according to some 'instructions' laid out by his father, didn't she at least deserve to know what those instructions were? And if Mrs Fitch and Mr Sewell both had copies, why shouldn't she read it too? Besides, if Leo really wanted to keep the contents of the letter secret, he wouldn't leave it on his desk where anyone could read it...would he?

She threw a swift look at the door and then carried on reading.

'Your first and most urgent task is to secure the future of Rainton through marriage and the siring of an heir...'

Chapter Eighteen

It wasn't going to be a summer fair in the traditional sense, Leo reflected, standing at the front door with Florence. It certainly wasn't going to be anything like the ones he remembered from his childhood. Back then, the sun had always shone, the birds had always sung, the butterflies had always danced, and the whole event had looked like a painting of some bucolic wonderland. Today, by contrast, the skies were a heavy slate-grey, the birds and butterflies were sheltering in trees and hedges—if they had any sense anyway—and even the most talented of artists would have struggled to make the scene look inviting. And yet…for the first time in a very long time, he was actually looking forward to it. This fair, he suspected, was going to be fun.

'Here we go.' He smiled at Florence as the first cart-load of guests arrived in the courtyard. In a few minutes, the house would be filled with his tenants and their families. It was strange…and slightly nerve-racking. His father, though adamant about the fair's always going ahead, had only ever made token appearances, walking through the crowd like a king in front of his subjects, judging the competitions and then making a brief speech, before retreating back to his palace. He and Florence, on the other hand, would be acting as hosts, opening their home and welcoming everyone inside…mingling.

His father had never mingled with anyone outside the *ton* in his life.

'Here we go,' Florence echoed, her eyes fixed on the approaching cart.

Leo kept his gaze on her, trying to read her expression. She'd been acting differently ever since he'd proudly carried a tea tray back to his study, a feat he'd achieved despite the half-horrified, half-amused reactions of his kitchen staff. It wasn't an obvious change. Nobody else would likely have noticed, but the sparkle in her eyes had faded again, replaced by a muted, withdrawn look. For the life of him, he couldn't understand why. One minute they'd been laughing and teasing each other and then…this.

'Is everything all right?' he murmured.

'Of course.' She gave him a swift sidelong look. 'I'm just nervous.'

'Ah.' He nodded with understanding. That made sense. He was feeling moderately anxious about the situation himself. Only something told him there was more to it than that…

There was no time to enquire further, however, as people were already heading up the stone steps, *also* looking nervous. Or, in several cases, downright terrified. He couldn't blame them. Tenants had never been allowed anywhere near the front door in the past. His father would have had apoplexy at the very idea. Some of the new arrivals probably thought the message they'd received that morning had been a mistake and they were about to find themselves thrown out on their ear, which meant that it was *his* job to set them at ease.

If only he knew how. How did one go about setting people at ease?

'Welcome to Rainton.' He inclined his head to the new arrivals, hating how stiff and formal he sounded.

There was a flurry of bows and curtseys while he racked his brains for something else to say. Should he mention the weather? Several people looked quite soggy, but it seemed rude to mention the fact.

Fortunately, Florence saved him by stepping forward and gesturing to the small army of footmen standing to one side. 'Please come in. If you'd all like to leave your coats and hats, Mr Rimmer will take you inside for some tea. I'm sure everybody would like to warm up. Then we have some activities set up for the children in the long gallery.'

'Thank you,' Leo said as people scurried away.

'Don't worry, I know how to do this, even if I'm

not…' She stopped abruptly, as if she was biting her tongue. 'Never mind.' She gave her head a small shake. 'Our next guests are arriving.'

The games had been a little more raucous than she'd planned, Florence had to admit as she descended the grand staircase an hour later. So loud, in fact, that her ears were still ringing. Thankfully, however, nothing was broken, only a few small children had cried— mainly about not winning, though thankfully a few mothers had been on hand to comfort them—and it was time for the grown-up competitions.

'Now, if the children would like to go with Jane…' she announced once they reached the hall, throwing a grateful smile at her maid, who was standing by with a stalwart expression, ready to take her new charges away. 'It's time for the prize-giving.'

There was a scurry of feet as they all hurried away, leaving her free to draw in a deep breath, smooth her skirts, lift her chin, and then go to join Leo in the Green Room. It had taken a couple of hours, but she'd finally recovered from the initial shock of the old marquess's letter. As she recalled, Mrs Fitch had called it a list of 'kindly meant' instructions, but in her opinion there had been nothing kindly about it. Leo's father had wanted to control every facet of his son's life—first and foremost, his choice of wife.

'Select a bride whose fortune will enhance the es-

tate, whose temper will benefit your domestic harmony, and whose bloodline is worthy of our illustrious family.'

The words were seared into her brain. She'd suspected something of the sort, but seeing them written down in black and white had shaken her more than she'd anticipated. Now she knew that Leo's father wouldn't just have disapproved of her. He would have detested her, just like Mrs Fitch and Sewell had no doubt detested her. As Leo himself had at first detested her! And even though she wasn't ashamed of who she was and where she came from—only what she'd done to Leo—now she truly realised the size of the gulf between them, and she couldn't help but feel humiliated and insulted, and hurt too. Because she was the very antithesis of the woman he'd been supposed to marry! A bride without any fortune, with too many opinions, who didn't possess a single drop of 'illustrious' blood! And there could be no making the best of anything because, in his father's eyes, their union was the worst thing that could possibly have happened, not just to Leo, but to the estate. How was it possible to 'make the best' of that?

The blunt truth was that she didn't belong at Rainton and she never would. And what if the old marquess was right about her? What if she'd already ruined Leo's life by trapping him? And then kept on ruining it by encouraging him to go against his father's 'instructions', by getting rid of Mrs Fitch and Sewell? What if everything she'd done, and was doing, was just the first step towards…what were the words again…'*the ruination and the collapse of everything I have spent so many years striving to achieve*…'? What if, in a few days or weeks or a year even, Leo came to think that way again too? What if she really was the worst thing that could ever have happened to a man she was falling in love with?

She pulled her shoulders back as she made her way to one of the competition tables. It was laden with at least a dozen plates of biscuits, the kind she would normally have been salivating over, if the knot of misery in her stomach hadn't completely destroyed her appetite. It was a stark contrast to the way she'd felt that morning. She'd been so excited about the fair, but now just keeping her head up felt like an effort, as though she was holding herself together by the thinnest of threads.

'Are we allowed to taste them, do you think?'

She half turned her head as Leo's breath skimmed her cheek. 'Yes…' She felt the knot twist even tighter. 'It's a baking competition. We probably ought to.'

'It's hard to know where to start. They all look delicious.' He picked up a biscuit with raisins and held it to her lips. 'Judging contests is more fun than I expected.'

'Mmm.' She managed to twist her mouth into some approximation of a smile as she chewed.

Leo held on to her gaze, his eyes darkening as he lowered his head. 'By the way, I have a surprise for you later.'

Her stomach lurched so violently, she almost brought the biscuit up again. All she wanted to do later was curl up in a corner and scream her emotions into a pillow. 'Oh?'

'Yes.' He winked, as if he was genuinely enjoying himself, as if he didn't know that she was everything his father had loathed... 'But you have to wait and see.'

She gritted her teeth, then kept them gritted as the afternoon dragged on. After the baking competition came flower arranging, then embroidery, then wood carving and finally landscape painting, after which she presented the prizes to loud applause, and Leo gave a speech, thanking everyone for coming despite the weather and suggesting they all adjourn for the picnic.

'Ready for your surprise?' Leo murmured as the crowd headed towards the ballroom. 'It's upstairs.'

'Now?' She stiffened, every nerve suddenly on high alert. 'What about our guests?'

'You said we ought to make ourselves scarce.' He offered an arm. 'We can show ourselves again later at the dance. In the meantime, Rimmer will keep an eye on things.'

She nodded reluctantly, unable to think of an excuse. 'Very well.'

They climbed the staircase and made their way along the upstairs gallery in silence. Florence kept her feet moving, though her pulse was racing so fast, she felt as if the world was spinning around her. Their kiss that morning played itself over and over in her mind. '*Later*...' he'd said. Did he mean *now*? Because there was no way she could even think about anything like that, not when her emotions were still so raw. She sucked in a breath, wondering how to tell him as he opened his bedroom door, then released it again as he led her straight through his chamber, past the bed, and on into a dressing room.

'It's a private picnic,' Leo announced. 'When I went down to the kitchens for tea, I asked Mrs Hotham to make us a special hamper.'

'Oh…' She placed a hand to her chest, touched despite the tension now pounding in her head. A large white blanket had been spread out over the carpet, surrounded by cushions, while a red bow had been tied to the top of the hamper. 'It looks lovely.'

'I'm glad you like it.' He waited for her to sit before crouching down beside the basket. 'Although I have to admit, I'm still quite full from all the biscuits. Sandwiches might have to wait.'

'Yes.' She tried to laugh, but it was impossible. She felt too overwhelmed, as if she might break into tears at any moment.

'Florence, what is it?' His expression softened. 'Has something happened?'

'No. Yes. I can't…' She closed her eyes.

'Try.' Their shoulders touched as he sat down beside her. 'Whatever it is, it can't be so bad. Or, if it is, we'll deal with it together.'

'I read your letter!' The words erupted out of her, the sympathetic look in his eyes making her feel even more wretched. 'I know I had no right and I should have asked your permission first, but it was just sitting on your desk and I wanted to know what Mrs Fitch meant about a warning.'

'I see.' His voice sounded blank.

'I'm sorry. I know I did a terrible thing when I tricked you into marrying me, but I had no idea how terrible, making you choose between doing the honourable thing and fulfilling your father's expectations.' She hung her head miserably. 'I'm not the kind of woman he wanted for you and I never can be. And I don't know what to do about that. I don't know how to fix it. I just know that I don't belong here.'

There was a long pause, disturbed only by the continued patter of rain against the window.

'You're right,' he answered finally, his tone thoughtful. 'You're nothing like the woman my father wanted me to marry. You're a hundred times better.'

'What?' She raised her eyes back to his.

'What lady of the *ton* could have offered me so much advice and practical support today?' He gave a soft laugh. 'I admit I was furious about our marriage at first, but now I'm glad we were compromised. From the moment I inherited my title, my whole life became about order and restraint and tradition. When I went to London the first time this year, I was the man my father raised me to be, another version of him, cold and unfeeling and hard. And I would have carried on that way, doing everything the way it had always been done, marrying Miss Wadlow, following Sewell's advice, living in a cage, no matter what I really wanted.'

'A cage?'

'That's how it felt. I could see out, but I didn't know how to escape, how to live the life I really wanted. With you.' He lifted a hand, gently caressing the side of her face. 'I didn't realise it at the time, but I think I fell in love with you the first time we met.'

'But…' she felt stunned '…you were courting Amabel.'

'Yes.' He made a face. 'I admit, the fact that you were friends gave me pause, but I also knew she was exactly the kind of woman my father would have chosen for me, so I convinced myself that my attraction to you didn't matter. I thought I could ignore it.'

'That's…'

'Deluded? Crazy? I know. Then we were compromised and I was so angry and resentful, I didn't even notice that the door of my cage had just sprung open. Instead, I was rude and hurtful and ungentlemanly, for which I'm deeply sorry.' He made a rueful expression. 'You know, marrying you was the first time I ever disobeyed my father's instructions, and once I'd done that and the sky didn't fall on my head, I started doing other things. I came home and ordered a herd of cows.' His lips curved. 'I've been disregarding his letter ever since our wedding day because, despite everything, you gave me the confidence to try new things, to make changes and be myself. And since we came back here the second time, you've made this whole house better. Even now, you're chasing away the shadows and turning it into a home. So don't say you don't belong, Florence, because you do. We belong here together.'

'How can you be sure?' Her voice cracked. As much as she wanted to believe him, it seemed too good to be true. 'What if this is a mistake and it all goes wrong, like your father said it would?'

'Then at least I'll have chosen my own path.' He smoothed his thumb across her cheek. 'And this—us—isn't a mistake, I already know that. I'm not just making the best of things any more. I want this. I want you.'

'I want you too, but there's still a whole month that I can't remember. What if I did something even worse than tricking you into marriage?'

'Such as?'

She dipped her head evasively. 'I don't know, but now I know what I'm capable of, I'm frightened that maybe there's more, and until I remember the whole truth about myself—'

'The truth is that we've both made mistakes,' he interrupted her. 'All I need to know is who you are now. Today. That's enough.'

She caught her breath as he cupped her face in his hands, the expression in his eyes making her heart melt. Now was the time to tell him about the love letters, but there was still no proof they were hers. And if he meant what he said, about this moment's being enough, then maybe she could finally let them go, throw them into the fire and forget about them once and for all…

'Do you truly mean that?' Her insides were swirling again, the way they had been that morning when he'd said *Later*… And suddenly, with every fibre of her being, she really wanted that to be *now*.

'Yes.' He slipped a hand around the nape of her neck, drawing her face towards him and touching his lips to hers. 'I do.'

Chapter Nineteen

'Leo...' Florence murmured, letting the past melt away as she slid her hands over his shoulders and opened her mouth to his. And then the rest of the world seemed to fade away too and there was only the two of them as her senses unravelled and something clicked into place in both her head and her heart. He was right, this was where she belonged, no matter what anyone else said—or wrote. This was what she wanted too, this sense of shared understanding and closeness with him.

He wrapped his hands around her waist, lifting her up and over his lap, deepening the kiss as she settled her legs on either side of his thighs. It felt so intimate, so shockingly new and exciting, she couldn't hold back a moan from escaping her throat.

'Can I take this off?' He bunched his hands in the fabric of her dress, his voice a rough scrape of sound that sent tingles of vibration along all her limbs.

'Yes.' She pulled back, lifting her arms for him to draw it over her head.

'I've been thinking about this all day, ever since I saw you in that nightdress.' He moved his lips to her ear, touching the lobe softly with his tongue. 'I wanted to carry you to bed right there and then.'

She sucked in a breath, glancing towards the door at the mention of bed. 'Should we go…?'

'If you want.' A wicked smile spread across his face. 'Although these cushions look quite comfortable. It's up to you.'

'Oh…' She caught her bottom lip between her teeth, feeling as if a fire had just ignited inside her, shooting hot sparks along every nerve… 'In that case… I think I like it here.'

'I was hoping you'd say that.' He reached behind her, pulling at the lacings on her stays, but she arched away from him, curving her hands over his shoulders and squeezing tight.

'Wait.'

He froze. 'What's wrong?'

'Nothing.' She splayed her fingers, relishing the feel of the muscles beneath. Her breasts felt heavy with want and her whole body was coiled tight with desire, but she only had a vague idea of what she was doing and she wanted to prolong every sensation for as long as possible.

'Forgive me.' He pressed his forehead to hers. 'It's

your first time. I didn't mean to rush you.' He started to lift her off his lap. 'We can wait.'

'I don't want to wait.' She clenched her thighs around him, refusing to go anywhere. 'But it's my turn.'

'Turn?' He sounded confused.

'Yes.' She licked her lips, looking pointedly at his cravat. 'That looks so tight. It must be uncomfortable.'

His eyes widened before flaring with heat. 'It is.'

'I'd better remove it, then. May I?'

He made a sound of assent like a growl.

She leaned forward, pressing her breasts against his chest as she slowly unravelled the knot, then slid the fabric from around his neck and tossed it aside. 'Now you.'

'Thank you.' He grinned, holding eye contact as his hands moved back to her stays, hurling them in the same direction as her dress.

'Mmm. What next?' She tapped a finger lightly against her chin for a few seconds before slipping her fingers beneath the shoulders of his jacket and pushing it down his arms. 'How about this? *And* this…' she moved her hands quickly to his waistcoat '…since you're wearing more clothes than me.'

'I'm aware.' He made a low rumbling sound, waiting until she'd finished before smoothing his hands along her thighs and down her legs, slowly unrolling her stockings.

'Then I'd better hurry with this…' She moved on to his shirt, her fingers fumbling a little with the buttons.

'Let me.' He wrenched it over his head, while she did the same with her chemise, then lowered his head to one of her breasts, tracing his tongue around the nipple in a way that sent a thrill of sensation shuddering straight to her core, causing a rush of molten heat between her legs.

She tipped her head back, her heart pounding so heavily, she thought he must be able to feel it through her skin, but she didn't care. The touch of his lips felt so good, she didn't want him to stop. Ever. It made her feel shameless too, so much so that she couldn't even bring herself to blush as she writhed and strained against him.

He stiffened at the movement, muttering something she couldn't understand before lifting his head again. 'Florence…' his breathing sounded as ragged as hers '…did your mother or Lady Wadlow tell you what to expect?'

'No.' She gave a shuddering laugh at the idea. Her mother probably hadn't thought it was necessary before she went to London and she didn't suppose Lady Wadlow would have said anything even if she *had* been talking to her.

'Oh.' He swallowed, his expression taut.

'But…' she put a finger to his lips as he opened

them again '… I grew up on a farm. I have a rough idea.'

'You have no idea how glad I am to hear that.' He gave a ragged laugh, his muscles loosening again with relief. 'Only our game isn't over quite yet. I'm still wearing too much.' He tilted his head. 'Maybe you should make yourself comfortable?'

She smiled slowly as she slid off his lap, laying herself down on the cushions to watch as he removed his boots and breeches. It wasn't the first time she'd seen him naked, but the sight was just as stirring as it had been that morning, the broad lines of his body so toned and chiselled, she felt her fingers twitch with the urge to reach out and stroke them.

'That's better.' He threw the rest of his clothes aside and then lowered himself on top of her, one hand on either side of her body, his gaze roaming over her face as if he was searching for the answer to some question there. In response, she threaded her fingers into his hair and drew him towards her. And then there was no space, no air, no anything between them. Their tongues met, tentatively at first, then hungrily, tangling and sucking and tasting each other, while his hands smoothed a path over her skin, exploring and caressing her in such places that it made her feel light-headed, coaxing out sensations and sounds she'd never even imagined making before.

'Leo?' She gasped as his fingers slid between her legs, stroking her gently.

'Is this all right?' His voice was so deep, it seemed to vibrate all along her spine.

'Yes.' She nodded frantically. 'Don't stop.'

'I won't.' He kissed her again, even more deeply than before, while his fingers moved in slow, tantalising circles that made her mind reel.

'You feel so good...' He released her lips finally in order to slide downwards, touching his tongue to the hollow at the base of her throat.

'So do you.' She was panting now, her skin so hot, she thought her blood must be boiling in her veins.

'It might hurt a little at first.'

'I know.' She dug her nails into his back, squirming against him. 'I don't care.'

Although maybe she *did* care a little, she thought, crying out as he settled between her legs, nudging gently at her entrance before pushing deep inside, causing a sharp, stinging sensation. He was too much and she was too tight, even though she had a feeling he was holding himself back.

'Florence?' He sounded as if he was the one in pain.

'Wait a moment.' She took a deep breath, letting her body slowly adjust to the feeling of him inside her, then cautiously rolled her hips, pulling away before pushing herself up again.

'Florence.' His voice was more urgent now.

'Yes,' she breathed as she wrapped her legs around his waist, drawing him deeper inside her. There was another moment of pain, but then it eased and the friction between them transformed into something else, a wet heat that soothed the ache and enveloped her in pleasure from the very top of her head to the tips of her toes. Their pace increased and the pleasure became even more intense. And then she couldn't—wouldn't—stop, so caught up in the feeling, she thought she wouldn't even have noticed if all their guests had burst into the room at that moment. There was only the two of them and the friction still building between them.

'Leo!' She screamed his name as her inner muscles spasmed and contracted around him suddenly, making her whole body shake. Wave after wave of sensation flooded through her, tipping him over the edge too. He gave an incoherent shout, shuddering violently before collapsing on top of her.

It was some time before he twisted his head, pressing his lips into her hair.

'Yes.' She answered his unspoken question, still panting. 'Yes, it was.'

'Do you think anyone will notice if we don't show our faces again?' Leo drew Florence back against him, holding her close as he pressed a trail of kisses slowly along her shoulder blade, amazed by how relaxed and content he felt. No matter what his father would have thought, being with her felt right. Better than right. Perfect. And he wasn't going to spoil the moment by thinking about his father any more...

'I'm afraid they might,' she murmured sleepily, turning around in his arms and slipping a leg over his thigh. 'We should have at least one dance.'

'I was afraid you'd say that.' He pressed his lips to hers, plundering her mouth in a deep, searching kiss that made his body twitch with need.

'Again?' She broke the kiss as one of his hands trailed lower, curving over her buttock. 'You wouldn't be trying to get an heir in me, would you?'

'I'm afraid my motives are more base than that.' He caught her bottom lip lightly between his teeth.

'Mmm, mine too.' She sighed. 'But we should dance first.'

'You're probably right.' He moaned and pulled his hand away. 'No regrets?'

She looked startled by the question. 'None. Why? Have you?'

'Only that we've wasted so much time. We could have been doing this two or three times a day for the past two months.'

'Only two or three?' She laughed, rolling away to reach for her clothing.

'I meant at night. We could have been doing it during the day as well.'

'Oh, really? Then maybe you should keep the chaise longue in your study?'

He gave a surprised laugh, though, as ideas went, it wasn't a bad one. The thought of making love in what had once been his father's study gave him a wicked surge of pleasure.

'Do you think people will guess what we've been doing?' she asked anxiously, pulling her chemise back over her head.

'With any luck, everyone will have been too busy enjoying themselves to even notice we were gone.'

'I hope so.' She caught her reflection in a mirror and winced. 'Although my hair might give me away. It's a total mess, but if I call for Jane she'll definitely know what we've been up to.'

'You look beautiful.' He propped himself up on one elbow to watch her. 'But if you're worried, maybe we should change your appearance completely. Why don't you wear your ballgown from London?'

'Do you think so?' She opened her eyes wide. 'Isn't that a bit too much?'

'We're the marquess and marchioness. We're acting our parts, that's all. And I'll wear evening clothes too. Then people will think we simply came upstairs to change.'

'For two hours?'

'Perhaps we've also been discussing philosophy?' He chuckled and pushed himself to his feet, catching her eye in the mirror as he walked up behind her. 'Besides, does it matter what anyone thinks?'

'I suppose not.' She tilted her head back, resting it against his chest as he coiled his arms around her waist and held her close. 'You're right, it's our business.'

'Then let's get dressed and go dancing.'

In the absence of either a valet or lady's maid, they helped each other to dress. It was a surprisingly erotic experience, Leo thought as he tightened Florence's laces, fully intending to loosen them again within a couple of hours. Resisting the temptation to kiss every inch of her skin before covering it up with layers of silk and organza was driving him to distraction, but she was right, they needed to show themselves at least once more downstairs before he took her back to bed. A real bed this time. One with soft pillows, a firm mattress and a warm eiderdown to pull over their heads and shut out the rest of the world while he made slow and steady love to her all night. Just the thought of it made his trousers feel too tight.

He had to make a concerted effort to think *unerotic* thoughts as they descended the staircase, heading towards the sound of fiddles and dancing feet coming from the direction of the ballroom. Judging by the clapping, even those who weren't dancing had found a way to join in with the music.

'It sounds like everyone's having a good time.' Leo smiled as they approached the doors, where Rimmer was standing in the same place they'd left him. 'How are things going?'

'Very well, sir.' If Rimmer thought anything about their change of attire, he didn't show it. 'As you can hear, the dancing has begun. I hope that isn't a problem, only we didn't wish to…ah…disturb you.'

Which meant he definitely knew what they'd been up to, Leo thought, quickly offering a hand to Florence as a faint blush stole across her cheeks. 'Excellent.' He made a deep bow. 'Shall we dance, my lady?'

'My lord.' She cleared her throat, avoiding looking at Rimmer as she dipped into a matching curtsey. 'I'd be honoured.'

Chapter Twenty

The buzzing sound was back.

Florence opened her eyes with a jolt, dismayed to realise she didn't recognise the view before her. It wasn't her bedroom in Grosvenor Square *or* the blue and silver one she'd grown accustomed to at Rainton, or even her red room at Cassie's. It was a different room again entirely, decorated in shades of teal-blue and green. Her mind started to spin with panic. Had she lost her memory again? Was this her life now? To lose her memory over and over until she had no idea who or where she was…?

'Florence?' a familiar voice murmured in her ear, at the same time as warm fingers slid their way tenderly around her waist. 'Bad dream?'

The buzzing receded as the world suddenly made sense again. She *did* know this view, after all. She was still at Rainton Court, only she was lying in the massive oak bed in Leo's chamber, and the voice and hand were both his. Because she'd slept here last night.

Slept and…done other things, in several new and surprisingly inventive ways. It was no wonder she hadn't recognised the room at first. She'd been far too distracted to notice the furnishings.

'No.' She wriggled back under the covers as her heartbeat slowed down again. 'I just forgot where I was for a moment.'

'Ah.' His hand tightened around her waist, a reassuring pressure against her skin. 'So this must be a surprise.'

'It is.' She smiled at his cautious tone. 'But it's a pleasant one.'

'Thank goodness. How did you sleep?'

'Very well.'

'Me too. Better than I have for months.'

'Perhaps we should hold fairs more often?'

He chuckled. 'As successful as that was, I'm pretty sure the fair had nothing to do with it.'

'I've no idea what you mean.' She laughed, snuggling closer.

'What are you thinking?' His lips nuzzled her ear after a few moments.

'Honestly? I'm thinking that even if my memory never comes back, at least we've found a way to move on and be happy.'

'I couldn't agree more.'

'And maybe…' She stopped with a sudden jolt, her eyes catching a flutter of movement at the window.

'No!' She pulled herself up to a sitting position. 'That is *so* typical!'

'What is?'

'Sunshine again!' She waved her hands. 'Glorious sunshine after all the rain we had yesterday. Look! There's a sparrow on the window ledge taunting us.'

'He looks quite friendly to me.' Leo leaned back against the pillows, folding one arm behind his head. 'It seems that we forgot to close the curtains last night.'

'Doesn't your valet usually do that?'

'Yes.' He waggled his eyebrows. 'Obviously he thought we shouldn't be disturbed.'

'You mean...' She groaned. 'I knew Rimmer could tell when we went downstairs yesterday. All the staff probably know, don't they?'

'Not *all*, I'm sure.' He laughed at her mortified expression. 'But they're also discreet. You were absolutely right about them deserving an increase in their wages.'

'And additional days off.' She lay down again, nestling her head against his shoulder. 'Speaking of which, we'll need to fend for ourselves today.'

'What about food?'

'Oh, I told Mrs Hotham we still had plenty left in our hamper, so there was no need to worry about it.'

'What did she say to that?'

'She said she couldn't possibly *not* worry, so I insisted.' She lifted her head slightly, propping her chin on his chest. 'I doubt we'll need any fires in this weather either, although if we do, I'm perfectly capable of building one myself. A marchioness might not be supposed to get her hands dirty, but I'm still a work in progress.'

'You're more than that…' He lifted a hand, stroking it gently over her hair. 'However, if the staff are all allowed a day's holiday, I think we're allowed one too. Starting with spending the rest of the morning in bed.'

'That sounds good to me. Although bowls in the long gallery also looked quite fun. We could have a game of our own later?'

'I'd like that.' His gaze wavered, drifting towards the bedside cabinet. 'In the meantime, I have a question.'

'Mmm?'

'It's about your locket.' He tilted his head to where she'd placed it last night. 'Whose picture is inside?'

'Why?' She looked at him suspiciously. 'You're not jealous, are you?'

'That might depend.'

She laughed. 'Well, then, you'll be relieved to hear that it's nobody.'

'It's empty?'

'Not exactly.' She reached across, scooping the necklace up by its chain. 'It's hard to choose one picture when you have such a large family, so I decided it should contain something else instead. Look.'

He peered inside as she opened the oval-shaped locket. 'Is that your house?'

'Yes. This way, I'm including everyone who lives inside.' She arched an eyebrow. 'Happy now?'

'Yes.' He rested back against the pillows again. 'You know, maybe we should pay them a visit?'

She caught her breath. 'Do you mean it?'

'Of course. You left your family, expecting to see them again in two and a half months, and it's been almost four. I know you said you didn't want to see the inside of another carriage for a long time, but if we wait until the autumn, the roads might be in too poor a condition for travel. If you'd like to go, we should go soon.'

'I'd like it very much.' She beamed at him. 'I'd like for my parents to meet you too. The letter I received from them when we got back from London was...odd.'

'How so?'

'It's hard to explain. Just...distant somehow, and formal, as though they thought they shouldn't be writing to me now I'm a marchioness. I know our marriage must have come as a shock, but I'd like to go and reassure them that I'm still their daughter.'

'Then that's what we'll do.' He lifted the necklace and clasped it around her neck. 'It's about time I explained myself to your father as well.'

'What do you mean?'

'I married his daughter without seeking permission.

I wrote him a brief letter soon after our marriage, but it was remiss of me not to visit him in person.'

'I'm sure he'll appreciate that.' She leaned over to kiss him. 'So will I. And don't worry, I'll make sure my brothers don't hurt you.'

'Is that likely?'

'Well…' She scrunched her mouth up to stop herself from smiling. 'Like you said, you *did* marry me without my father's permission. And they *are* all quite large, not to mention protective.'

He looked mildly alarmed. 'Just how large and how protective exactly?'

'Nothing you can't handle, I'm sure. And I'm certain everything will be all right once you tell them what a wonderful marchioness I am.'

'Why am I suddenly having second thoughts about this trip?'

'Too late.' She grinned. 'You've suggested it now. We're going to Cumberland, even though it means spending a whole week in a carriage together.'

'A whole week?' He found her lips again before rolling her over onto the bed. 'Whatever will we do to pass the time?'

'Was that a knock?'

'Mmm?' Leo prised his eyelids open, vaguely aware of Florence shaking him awake. They'd made love twice that morning, before eating a hamper picnic in bed and then dozing off in each other's arms.

'I think somebody just knocked on the door.'

'Ignore it. Hopefully they'll go away.'

'There it is again.' She lifted her head. 'It must be important.'

'It had better be.' He groaned and swung his legs over the side of the bed, pointing a stern finger at her as he pulled on his dressing gown. 'Don't go anywhere.'

'I didn't intend to.' She gave him a coy look before snuggling back under the eiderdown.

'Rimmer?' Leo found his butler standing outside the door. 'What can I do for you? And why aren't you taking the day off?'

'I thought it best for one person to stay on duty, my lord.' Rimmer cleared his throat, looking more than a little awkward. 'Some guests have arrived.'

'Guests? Please don't tell me they got the wrong date for the fair.'

'No, my lord, it's nothing like that. However, they say their business is quite urgent.'

'Of course it is.' He ran a hand over his face, stifling a yawn. 'I suppose that means I should get dressed. Did they give their names?'

'Yes, my lord. Major and Mrs Vaughan.'

'Vaughan…' He drew his brows together. The name sounded familiar, but he was still too sleepy to place it.

'Apparently they've just arrived from Ireland.'

'Ireland?' That also sounded as though it should mean something to him, but… He shook his head. 'I've no idea who they are.'

'I do.' He looked over his shoulder to find Florence standing behind him, wrapped in a sheet, her face as white as…well, that same sheet. 'It's Amabel.'

'Amabel?' He stared at her for a long moment before turning back to Rimmer. 'Put them in the drawing room and tell them we'll be down shortly.'

'Very good, my lord.'

'And offer them some refreshments, if you can find anyone in the kitchens.'

'I'll make tea myself if necessary, my lord.'

'Thank you.'

'Amabel…' Florence repeated as he shut the door, her cheeks completely bloodless now. 'What do you think she's doing here?'

'I don't know.' He wrapped his arms around her. 'But if you don't want to see her—'

'I do. Of course I do. It's just a shock, that's all. I thought she didn't want anything to do with me.'

'Maybe she's changed her mind. Come on.' He gave her a quick squeeze before stepping back. 'The sooner we get dressed and down there, the sooner we'll find out.'

'Major Vaughan, Mrs Vaughan, this is a surprise.' Leo stood by Florence's side as they entered the drawing room only ten minutes later. She was putting on a brave face, but her skin was still much too pale, her hands were trembling and her eyes had a stunned look. Suddenly he wished he'd taken the opportunity to stop outside the door and give her one last supportive embrace.

'My lord, my lady.' Miss Wadlow, or Mrs Vaughan as he supposed he ought to think of her now, stepped forward from where she was standing by the window and curtseyed, looking as beautiful and elegant as ever, her sable hair artfully styled into a braided bun and her glowing complexion perfectly complemented by an apricot-coloured day gown. 'Please forgive the intrusion. We would have sent word ahead, but we came in such a rush and…well…' She twisted her hands together as her gaze moved between them. 'We thought, given the circumstances, you might not mind too greatly.'

'You're here…' Florence sounded as if she couldn't quite believe the evidence of her own eyes.

'Yes.' Amabel half turned towards the auburn-haired man standing soberly beside her. 'This is my husband, Major Vaughan. James. You met him a few times in London, if you recall?'

'I remember.'

'An honour to meet you, Major.' Leo gestured towards a collection of leather armchairs. 'Shall we all sit down?'

'Thank you, my lord.' Major Vaughan made a formal bow before taking the chair beside Amabel's. 'I'm afraid the matter we've come to discuss is somewhat delicate.'

'Yes, *delicate*!' Amabel seized on the word. 'And… difficult.'

'I don't care. I'm just so glad you're here.' Florence sank down onto the chair opposite. 'I wanted to write, but I didn't know what to say, where to begin—'

'Then let me. Please. If I don't do this quickly then I might lose my nerve.' Amabel reached for her husband's hand. 'The fact is, I recently received a letter from Mama. She told me about your visit to her in London and that you'd lost your memory in an accident. Is that true?'

'Yes.' Florence nodded slowly. 'I lost a whole month, from the night before your parents' ball.'

'That's what she wrote.' Amabel swallowed. 'It's why I had to come back. I had to see you.'

'Truly?' Florence's chest heaved with emotion. 'So you don't hate me?'

'I could never hate you.' Amabel's eyes began to glisten. 'You're my dearest friend. You always have been.'

'But I betrayed you. I stole your future.'

'No.' Tears were already sliding down Amabel's cheeks. 'That's what I came back to tell you. When I learned about your accident, and that you'd gone to

London looking for answers, I realised how it all must have seemed, what everyone would say and what you would think... I've felt perfectly wretched ever since.'

'I don't understand.' Florence shook her head, un-comprehending. 'Why would *you* feel wretched?'

'Because none of it was your fault. It was all mine.'

'Mrs Vaughan.' Leo sat forward, feeling a prickling sensation on the back of his neck. 'On the night of the ball, you were as shocked as anyone to find Florence and myself together. You said—'

'I lied,' Amabel interrupted.

There was a heavy moment of silence.

'You...lied?' He repeated the words heavily.

'Yes. She wasn't the one who trapped you into marriage. I was.'

'But...' Florence put a hand on his arm '... *I'm* the one he married.'

'I know.' Amabel lowered her head, pressing her lips together tightly before answering. 'Because I trapped him into marriage with *you*.'

Chapter Twenty-One

'It wasn't supposed to happen the way it did.' Amabel sat forward on the edge of the armchair, her gaze fixed on Florence as she spoke. 'But I had to find a way to stop the marquess from proposing to me.' Her eyes flicked guiltily towards Leo. 'Apologies, my lord.'

'You didn't want to marry him?' Florence's hand was so tight on his arm, he thought she might be trying to constrict his blood flow.

'No. I was in love with James. Desperately so, but my parents would never have agreed to the match while a marquess wanted to marry me.'

'Didn't it occur to you to simply tell me that?' Leo interjected. 'If I'd known your affections were engaged elsewhere, I would never have proposed.'

'Honestly? No.' Amabel looked awkward. 'Forgive me for saying so, my lord, but you aren't the easiest of men to talk to.'

'Then why not simply refuse my proposal? Or compromise yourself with Major Vaughan?'

'Because it wasn't so easy. My parents must have suspected there was some affection between James and me because he wasn't invited to the ball. As for saying no, if they'd thought for even a moment that I was giving you up for him, they would have cast me off without a penny and we'd never have been able to marry.'

'So you arranged to meet me in the library and then sent Florence in your stead so we could be caught together?'

'No!' She jerked her head back. 'You weren't supposed to be caught, but it all went wrong.'

'What did?' Florence spoke softly, letting go of his arm finally. 'Amabel, what really happened?'

'The truth is, I told you everything that day. When we went for a walk in Hyde Park, I told you all about James and how I was afraid that my parents had other plans for that night. I said that I didn't know what to do and then…well, we agreed that you would talk to the marquess for me. You know, explain the situation and ask him…politely…*not* to propose to me.'

Florence's shoulders went rigid. 'You mean, I volunteered?'

'Not exactly.' Amabel squirmed in her seat. 'I asked you if you would mind saying something, and you agreed…eventually.'

'Eventually?'

'I was too frightened to do it myself!' she burst

out. 'I knew I'd babble and say the wrong thing and just make everything worse, whereas you're so practical and resourceful, you were bound to do it right. It seemed like such a good plan. So I arranged the meeting in the library and then gave you a signal.'

'That's why you seemed nervous.' Leo twisted towards Florence, remembering the strange way she'd behaved that evening. 'You weren't stalling for time. There *was* a message. You were just trying to decide how best to tell me.'

'There was hardly time for her to tell you anything.' Amabel sounded exasperated. 'My father decided to show the Malverns his first edition of Fielding, and then more people joined in, and I didn't know how to stop them. I followed them all to the library, thinking that perhaps I could cause a distraction, but it was too late. They walked straight in and found you.' She heaved a deep breath. 'Even then, I thought it would only be a minor scandal. I thought that my parents would just give Florence a scolding and send her home.' She gestured around the room. 'I never imagined it would lead to all this.'

'Let me get this straight.' Leo sat forward. 'You thought that half a dozen members of the *ton* could find us alone together and it could all be brushed aside and forgotten?'

'Yes.' Amabel lowered her head again. 'I know it sounds foolish now, but I wasn't thinking clearly.'

'I even asked you about the message. I asked you and you denied any knowledge of it.'

'I panicked.' She peeked back up at Florence. 'I know it was awful of me not to defend you, but if I'd told the truth my parents would have been furious with me. And what good would it have done when you were already compromised? Whereas keeping quiet...' She swallowed visibly. 'It was the only way I could be with James. And it worked. My parents agreed to our marriage just a week after your wedding.'

'In other words, you traded Florence's future for your own?' Leo narrowed his eyes.

'Not intentionally.' Amabel looked pained. 'And I thought that maybe you could find a way out of it, but everything just happened so fast.' She stretched a hand out to Florence. 'And you forgave me. When you were locked in your room, I bribed one of the maids to let me in, and you said you understood and forgave me.'

'So you knew the truth on our wedding day?' Leo turned towards Florence, his heart twisting. She hadn't spoken for a few minutes now, staring straight ahead with an oddly detached expression, a stillness about her he'd never seen before. She hadn't even seemed to notice Amabel's outstretched hand. 'You told me it was a misunderstanding, that the circumstances weren't what they seemed, but you wouldn't explain. Why didn't you just tell me? Why take the blame?'

'Because she was protecting me,' Amabel answered.

'I knew that if she'd said anything at that point, you might have been angry enough to tell my parents, so I begged her to stay quiet. But it wasn't going to be forever. Once James and I were married and the announcement was published, we agreed she could tell you everything.'

'Only she hit her head and forgot it all first.' He glowered.

'The love letters...' Florence murmured suddenly. 'They're yours, aren't they?'

'Love letters?' He gave a start. 'What love letters?'

'Mine.' Amabel turned to gaze lovingly at her husband. 'The most beautiful words you've ever read. I gave them to Florence for safekeeping on the day of the ball in case Mama searched my room. I thought I'd be able to reclaim them later.'

'But I found them.' Florence's voice sounded distant, as if she were speaking from a long way away. 'I came across them a couple of days after I woke from my accident. I had no idea who they were from, but I thought I must have been corresponding with another man.' She pressed a hand to her forehead. 'I felt so guilty about it. I thought that I was a wicked person.'

'You thought you were corresponding with another man?' Leo felt an ache in his chest at the idea. 'Why didn't you mention it?'

'Because it seemed like you already hated me enough.' She grimaced, though she didn't look at him.

'Besides, I didn't know the truth. I didn't see how it was possible, but… I couldn't be sure of anything.'

'You're not wicked.' Amabel came to crouch on the floor in front of her. 'You're the best, most loyal friend a person could ever ask for.'

'Or the stupidest.' Florence rose slowly to her feet. 'You used me.'

'No! That is…yes, but I never meant to. I was desperate.'

'You used me,' Florence repeated. 'You let me take the blame for something *you* arranged and then you swore me to secrecy about it. You let me be condemned and insulted, not just by other people, but by myself too. This whole time I've been so worried about how much you must hate me and now it turns out I was innocent all along.'

'But that's why I came back!' Amabel jumped up too. 'Once I received Mama's letter, I knew I had no choice. I wanted to put things right.'

'How good of you.'

'My lady,' Major Vaughan spoke this time, standing up as Florence walked away, 'I know it sounds bad, but I assure you, Amabel has been distraught over the whole situation. And this is as much my fault as it is hers. When she told me what had happened at the ball, I knew we should step forward and tell the truth, but I was too much in love and this was the only way for us to be together.' His gaze softened. 'Anything we did, we did for love.'

'So the ends justify the means?' Florence stopped by the door, her voice distant again.

There was a brief pause before he shook his head. 'No, but I'm grateful none the less.'

'I'm so sorry, Florence.' Tears were rolling steadily down Amabel's cheeks now, turning her beautiful face blotchy. 'I'm truly sorry.'

'I know, but I need to be alone for a while.' Florence turned away. 'I'm going to my room. Please don't follow me.'

Leo clenched his jaw as she closed the door behind her. He had a strong suspicion those last words had been aimed at him. It also occurred to him that for the past ten minutes his wife hadn't so much as glanced in his direction. Worst of all, his gut was telling him that he deserved it.

Florence kicked her heels against her horse's flanks, pelting headlong across the lawns on the eastern side of the house towards the woodland that divided the estate and the village. She'd walked out of the drawing room with every intention of going upstairs to her room, only once she'd stepped into the hallway, her feet had taken her in a different direction entirely, through a door at the back of the house and on to the stables. Aside from a few boys playing football in the courtyard, the whole place had been deserted, allowing her to saddle a horse on her own and then ride out with no idea where she was going until she was halfway there and then…then it seemed so obvious… Of course she knew where she was going. She was going back.

Because she'd remembered.

Her whole body had gone completely numb while Amabel had been talking, as if she'd been armouring herself against the words. She hadn't wanted them to be true, even though they'd made sense. A horrible, shocking, hurtful kind of sense, in which her best, closest and oldest friend had persuaded her to do her dirty work for her, and then, when things had gone wrong, walked away. No wonder she'd lost her memory. She'd probably wanted to forget. She'd been used, abandoned and then married off to a man who'd blamed her for all of it!

Images had crowded into her head, images so real she'd known they couldn't be anything but memories, unspooling so fast she could barely keep up, as if Amabel's arrival had been all that she'd needed to push through the fog in her mind: the way her friend had clutched her hand in Hyde Park, begging her to speak to Leo on her behalf, the way she'd thrown her arms around her when she'd reluctantly agreed, swayed by sympathy and a sense of indebtedness, then the gasps of the people entering the library that night, the sea of shocked faces, followed by Leo's expression, a combination of horror and anger, swiftly hidden behind an aristocratic mask of disdain. He hadn't paused for a second before assuming the worst of her. He'd simply walked away, leaving her at the mercy of the Wadlows, then sent a curt message the next day, stating that he was arranging a special licence and would collect her at the end of the week. There had been no proposal, no conversation, no attempt to get to know her, just a short ceremony followed by a long carriage ride to Dorset and then almost three weeks of angry silence and pretending she didn't exist.

So she'd run away.

She pulled on her reins, slowing her mare to a trot as she entered the woodland, following the path for a little way before stopping in the middle of a grove. There were so many trees here, slender hazels as well as massive oaks and horse chestnuts, their canopies all tangled together as they pushed their way up towards the sunlight. Without a breath of wind to stir them, they were still and silent today, but there were signs of recent storm damage, fallen leaves and scattered branches scattered over the ground. She remembered this place. She'd been riding through it when she'd heard a noise like a groan, as though one of the trees had been calling out a warning to her, followed by a loud crack, before a dark shadow had swung into the corner of her vision, knocking her off her horse and onto the ground, taking her memory with it. Until now.

She slid down from her saddle and crouched beside a fallen branch, smoothing her hand over the rough surface of the bark. Running away... *Of course* she'd been running away. Both from her husband and her marriage, planning to catch the stagecoach from the village to London, where she'd intended to find another to Cumberland. That was why she'd risked riding out in a storm, why she'd had her clothes and keepsakes with her too, *and* the letters, because despite everything she'd still been keeping them safe for Amabel.

That was it, the whole story, the truth about her marriage and her husband. She'd thought he was cold and aloof the first time they'd met, but she hadn't appreciated just *how* cold he could be until after their wedding. And even though she could understand why he'd behaved that way, even though he'd apologised for it since, it turned out that knowing what he'd done and feeling it were two very different things. Because now she remembered the way she'd felt during those first three weeks of her marriage, the pervasive, almost overwhelming sense of misery and emptiness and entrapment. He might not have physically mistreated her, or insulted her outright, but his chilly silences, combined with an excessive civility whenever he *had* been forced into speaking, had made it abundantly clear that he'd wanted nothing to do with her. He'd been as cold as a snake—a lizard—a shark! And she'd loathed him! She'd thought if she ran away he would have some grounds for an annulment or a divorce, anything he'd wanted, because that way she'd never have had to see him again. She'd never wanted to see him again. If her plans hadn't been thwarted by a knock on the head, she could have happily lived out the rest of her life without *ever* seeing him again!

Only he wasn't cruel now. Another memory rushed in on her, from that morning when she'd woken up in his arms, when she'd felt cosy and happy and content. Over the past few weeks his coldness had melted away, turning him into a completely different person, the kind of husband she might once have wanted…

A warm nose prodded her shoulder. The mare was nuzzling her, just as she'd probably done the last time they were here. Florence tilted her head sideways, grateful for the comfort, wishing she could go back to that morning. If she could only forget everything again and *not* know the truth about Leo, maybe she could still be happy…

But there was no way back. Her heart felt heavy at the realisation, as if there were some kind of weight attached, dragging it down to the very pit of her stomach. But at least she knew who she was again. She was the person she'd thought she was when she'd woken up in confusion almost a month ago, the person she'd hoped she was all along. And now that she had her answers, she had some accusations to make of her own.

Chapter Twenty-Two

'Can I come in?' Leo knocked gently on the door to Florence's bedchamber. He'd respected her wishes by not following her out of the drawing room, staying to say an awkward goodbye to the Vaughans instead, but after a couple of hours spent pacing his study, he hadn't been able to restrain himself any longer. After everything they'd learned that afternoon, he knew she must be in shock and he needed to comfort her. And, when he'd done that, he needed to apologise.

The longer Amabel had spoken, the more he'd become aware of a heavy, guilty feeling building in his chest. Because Florence had been innocent. Every time she'd told him that the circumstances of their marriage weren't what he thought, that she hadn't set out to trap him, that she wasn't a fortune hunter, she'd been telling the truth. And he'd dismissed her.

'Florence?' He tapped again when there was no answer, then twisted the handle, but the room was empty.

Muttering an oath, he turned around and went back

down the corridor, trying to remember what exactly she'd said when she'd left the drawing room. Definitely something about going to her bedroom. So where was she?

He ran down the staircase, charging through each reception room in turn. Damn it, why did he have so many rooms? And why hadn't he gone to check on her sooner? If she'd sneaked out of the house again, in a distressed frame of mind... It wasn't stormy today, but what if she'd had another accident? His heart stalled at the thought. He had to go after her...

Except apparently he didn't have to. He came to an abrupt halt as he strode back into the hall. There she was, coming through the front door at this very moment, looking utterly calm and composed, as though she'd simply stepped out for a breath of fresh air.

'Florence.' He hurried to greet her. 'Are you all right?'

'Yes.' She didn't look at him.

'I thought you were in your bedroom?'

'I changed my mind. Where's Amabel?'

'She and Major Vaughan left, but they're staying at the inn in the village for a couple of nights. I offered them a room, but they thought it best to give you some time.' He put his hands on her shoulders. 'How are you feeling?'

She blinked, as if the question puzzled her, before taking a step backwards, so that his hands fell away again. 'About as good as you might expect. We need to talk.'

He frowned, taken aback by the coolness of her tone, following as she led the way into his study. 'Where did you go? I was worried.'

'Were you?' She walked straight past the chaise longue, going to stand beside his desk.

'Of course.'

'It's not such a strange question. A month ago when I was really in trouble it took two hours for anyone to even notice I was gone. You weren't so worried then.'

'I wasn't here. I told you that.'

'But were you worried when you heard what had happened? Or did some part of you feel disappointed that I was found at all?'

'No!' He staggered as though she'd just struck him. 'I've never wanted anything bad to happen to you, Florence.'

She narrowed her eyes, studying him intently for a few seconds. 'Maybe not, but I doubt you were too bothered either way.'

'You're upset. It's understandable, given what Amabel just told us, but, Florence, we're in the same boat. We were both tricked into this marriage.'

'The same *boat*?' She gave a disparaging laugh. 'Oh, no. We may be on the same ocean, but our boats are completely different! *You* were tricked. *I* was tricked and then blamed for it.' She pointed a finger at him. 'And you never even gave me the benefit of the doubt!'

'You're right.' He bowed his head as he walked towards her. 'I completely misjudged you, but only because all of the evidence pointed in your direction. There was no other explanation.'

'What about *my* evidence? I told you at the time I was innocent, but you wouldn't listen. It never even occurred to you that I was telling the truth. You believed Amabel because she was one of you, one of the *ton*!' She seemed to hurl as much contempt as she could muster into the word. 'Whereas I was just a nobody.'

'I never said that.' He clenched his jaw. 'You were never a nobody.'

'But you assumed I was a fortune hunter! Because what woman *wouldn't* have seized a chance to marry the great and dignified Marquess of Rainton?'

'Florence—'

'That's what you thought, wasn't it? That any woman would be honoured to marry you.' She pushed her face closer to his. 'How does it feel to know that Amabel went to such extreme lengths just to escape your proposal?'

'She was in love with somebody else.'

'Because obviously there *had* to be a reason. It couldn't simply have been that she didn't like you.'

He stiffened. 'You're upset.'

'Yes, I'm upset.' Her eyes flashed. 'Because I remember.'

'Your memory…?' He felt very cold suddenly.

She nodded jerkily. 'It all came back to me while Amabel was talking. The ball, our wedding, our life here.' Her voice wavered. 'Most of all, I remember how you treated me.'

'That's…' He pushed a hand through his hair. 'Florence, I'm so sorry.'

'I believe you.' She looked at him and then away again, her profile hardening. 'You're sorry now, but you weren't then. You were cold and disdainful and so completely sure you were right. You walked away from me every time I tried to speak with you. You punished me for a crime I would *never* have even dreamed of committing and then, to compound it, you made me believe I was guilty too. You convinced me that I was a terrible person.' She sniffed. 'I could forgive you for everything else, but not that.'

He flinched. It was true, every word. His behaviour had been horrible. He'd been just like his father, heartless and dictatorial and remote. 'If I could go back—'

'But you can't! And wishing for it won't fix anything.' She swung back towards him, her expression fierce again. 'Do you know what the worst part is? That I was grateful to you for forgiving me. *Grateful!*' She clenched her fists. 'But I'm not just angry at you. I'm angry at myself as well, for not trusting myself when I knew, deep down, I would never have done something so awful.' She lifted her chin. 'But I know who I am again now and I'm not the one who should be feeling ashamed. You are. Because I know that if our roles had been reversed, I would have listened to you. I would have given you a chance.' She rocked back on her heels, swaying away from him. 'I detested you! That's why I was out in the woods that day. Because I never wanted any of this and I thought I might freeze to death here!'

He felt a heavy thud in his chest. 'What do you mean?'

'I mean that on the day of my accident I was running away. Leaving you. I couldn't even wait for the news of Amabel's wedding so I could tell you the truth about what happened at the ball. I couldn't see how it would make any difference, so I was going back to Cumberland. Then I thought you'd be able to get an annulment for desertion and it would be the best thing for both of us.'

'I see.' He swallowed hard. All this time, he'd simply assumed she'd been out riding. It had never for one moment occurred to him that she might have been leaving him. Because he was just as arrogant as she'd said... 'And now?' Somehow he kept his voice even. 'Is that what you still want?'

'I want the Leo I've known for the past two weeks.' Some of the fire in her eyes faded. 'But when I look at you now, all I can see is the man who turned his back on me. And I can't bear to be anywhere near him. I almost died because of him.' Her eyes glittered, pinning him to the spot. 'Do you understand that? How horrible the atmosphere was here? How much it hurt?'

'Yes.' He nodded. 'I do. I grew up in it and it's not what I want either, but I can fix this. Just tell me what to do to prove how sorry I am. Ask me anything and I'll do it.'

'It's too late.'

'It can't be.' He felt a surge of panic. 'The Florence I know doesn't give up. Please.' He moved closer, lowering his lips until they were within a hair's breadth of hers. 'I love you. Give me one more chance.'

He heard her sharp intake of breath. 'You love me?'

'Yes.'

He clutched desperately at her waist. It was true. The moment Amabel had told them the truth, the last defences around his heart had fallen away. He was in love with his wife, more deeply than he'd ever imagined possible.

'We can get past this.' He pulled her closer. 'I've changed. I'm not who I was before. You've made me a better person.'

'Maybe I have, but you made me believe I was a worse one.'

'I'll make it up to you.'

She looked up into his face, her own stricken. 'Even

if you can, even if you *have* changed, how could I ever be certain you won't change back?'

'Because I won't turn into my father, I promise.'

'Won't you?' She twisted her face towards the letter still sitting on his desk. 'I know your behaviour wasn't entirely your fault. It was because of the way he raised you. But, Leo, I've known you for two months. He had twenty-four years. How do I know that one day you won't look at those "instructions" and think he was right, after all?'

'Florence…'

'You know, I think I loved you too.' She lifted a hand to his face, smoothing the backs of her fingers across his cheekbone before pulling them away again. 'When I thought I knew who you were, but now… I can't tell any more. Maybe I love and hate you at the same time. All I know is that now I've remembered, I can't make myself forget, and I'm not certain if I can forgive.' She pulled away from him. 'That's why I have to leave. I need some time to think.'

'How long?'

'I don't know.'

'Will you come back?'

'I don't know that either.' She lifted a shoulder. 'I think I need to wait until I'm not so angry any more and then decide.'

'Wait.' He caught at her wrist as she turned to go. 'I'm your husband. I could order you to stay.'

'You could,' she agreed, gently extricating herself before continuing towards the door, 'but that would only prove that you're like your father. I'll leave first thing in the morning.'

And then she walked out, leaving emptiness behind.

It was surprising how much fondness she still felt for the place, Florence thought, looking over her shoulder at the massive structure of Rainton Court. Now that her memory had returned, she remembered how it had felt during those first few weeks of her marriage, like a great stone prison, but now it saddened her to think she might never come back. Then again, maybe it was possible to hold two opposing ideas in the mind at the same time and find a way to reconcile them into something positive. With places anyway. People were more complicated.

'I'm going to miss you, my lady.' Jane came to join her as two footmen staggered past, hauling a large trunk between them.

'I'll miss you too.' Florence reached for her hand, squeezing it tightly for a couple of seconds. 'I don't know how I would have managed here without you. I'm just sorry that you won't get to be a lady's maid any more.'

'Don't worry about that. They'll find me something to do, I'm sure.' Jane looked down at the carriage. 'Are you certain you don't need me to travel with you?'

'I have four grooms. I'll be quite safe, don't worry.'

'Safe, yes, but bored out of your mind too, most likely.'

'Perhaps.' She smiled sadly. Truth be told, she was looking forward to having some time alone to think about nothing. Her mind had been whirling ever since the moment Rimmer had woken her with news of Amabel's arrival. Now all she wanted to do was lean back, close her eyes and *not* think. Hopefully she'd manage to doze too, after getting next to no sleep the previous night. She and Leo had gone to bed in their own separate bedrooms, but knowing he was so close had done nothing to ease her inner turmoil.

'Safe travels, my lady.' Jane stepped away, scurrying off as Leo emerged from the house and walked towards them.

'Florence.' He looked as perfectly groomed as ever, though his face was drawn, as though he hadn't slept either.

'Leo.' She pulled her shoulders back, wondering if he'd come to forbid her from leaving after all. If he did, it would truly mean the end for them.

'Rimmer told me the carriage was being brought round.' A muscle ticked in his jaw as he spoke. 'Is there anything else you require for the journey?'

She shook her head, feeling relieved and a little disappointed at the same time. 'No, thank you. Mrs Hotham prepared me a basket.'

'Good.' He turned his face to one side, his expression so pained that, for a moment, her heart stuttered and she almost relented.

'Might I write?' he asked, twisting back again suddenly.

She hesitated only briefly before nodding. 'Of course.'

'Thank you. I can let you know how the herd is getting on.'

'I'd like that.'

'And perhaps you could…' his voice faltered '…if you want to, that is.'

'Yes.'

She clamped her lips together, not knowing what else to say. They were being so polite, she thought, as if she was only leaving for a couple of days, while the memory of everything they'd said yesterday hung heavy in the air between them.

'Florence,' he cleared his throat finally, 'I know it's too late, but for what it's worth, I truly am sorry for the way I behaved. Of all people, I should have known how hurtful it was. At the very least, I should have listened to you.' He stepped forward to open the carriage door. 'That's all I wanted to say. I hope your journey is uneventful.'

'Thank you.' She paused as she climbed in, her throat stinging as she leaned back to lay a hand softly on his shoulder. 'Goodbye, Leo.'

'Goodbye, Florence.'

Slowly, she pulled her fingers away, keeping her gaze averted as he closed the door behind her.

'I won't be long,' Florence called up to the driver as she stepped down from the carriage outside the village inn. Ironically, it was the one where she'd intended to catch the stagecoach to London when she'd run away. Now she was leaving openly, but she still had some unfinished business to attend to.

'Florence!' Amabel came racing across her private sitting room when she walked in. 'I'm so glad you came! James has gone for a walk, so it's only the two of us.'

'Good.' She put her hands out before Amabel could embrace her. 'I've come to say goodbye. I'm on my way north, back to Cumberland.'

'You're going home?' Amabel looked startled. 'Because of what I told you?'

'In part.' She moved across to the window, looking back in the direction she'd come from. She couldn't see the house from here, but she still felt a tug towards it. 'And because my memory returned yesterday. It made me see my marriage in a different light.'

'Oh.' Amabel's voice had a quaver in it. 'Florence—'

'You don't need to apologise again. What you did was…hurtful, and I can't pretend that I'm not upset, but I also appreciate the fact that you came straight back from Ireland when you heard about my accident.'

'I still wish—'

'So do I.' She turned around, cutting the words off. 'And I hope that some day we can put it behind us and be the way we used to be, but not yet.'

'I understand.' Amabel bowed her head.

'I wanted to give you these too.' Florence reached into her cloak and pulled out the bundle of letters she'd found in her saddlebag.

'Oh!' Amabel seized hold of them gratefully. 'Thank you. I know it probably seems ridiculous, but they mean so much to me.'

'How did you ever receive them?'

'One of the maids at Grosvenor Square was susceptible to bribery.' Amabel lifted a shoulder. 'She's the one who let me in to see you after the ball.'

'I see.' Florence managed a small smile. 'And they're not ridiculous. I read a few of them when I didn't know who they were from and they show how much you and Major Vaughan love each other. I suppose that's why I can understand what you did... You wanted to be with the man you loved.'

'Yes.' Amabel blinked a few times, as if she was trying not to cry again. 'What about you and the marquess? Is your marriage so terrible? Is he as bad as he seemed?'

'No.' She shook her head quickly. 'He's not bad at

all. We actually came to care for each other, but I need to think and I can't do it here.'

'And he's just letting you go?' Amabel sounded surprised.

'Yes.'

'Then he really isn't the man I thought he was. He told my father he wanted an heir as soon as possible. I think if he could, he would have added it to the marriage contract: an heir nine months after the wedding night.'

'That sounds about right.' Florence's lips twisted. 'It's on his list of instructions.'

'His what?'

'Nothing.' She took a deep breath and then held a hand out. 'In any case, I didn't want to leave without saying goodbye and good luck.'

'Thank you.' Amabel clutched at her fingers. 'Florence…please say you don't hate me.'

'I don't hate you.' She pursed her brow, as it occurred to her that maybe Amabel was just as much a victim of her parents as Leo was of his father. They'd both been raised with such high expectations, maybe it wasn't their fault they'd both behaved badly because of it. 'Now I'd better go.' She turned for the door. 'Just be happy with your major, Amabel. Then, whatever else happens, all of this will have been worthwhile.'

Chapter Twenty-Three

Three weeks, five days, six hours and… Leo glanced at the clock on the mantel…twelve minutes.

He dropped his pen onto his desk and rubbed a hand over his face. Apparently there was no point even trying to do his accounts today, since he'd been staring at the same page for approximately forty minutes now. He wasn't entirely sure why he'd bothered. He'd done the same thing yesterday, and the day before. Thank goodness his enthusiastic new steward, Macauley, had settled in so well or the estate would be in a complete mess by now.

Slowly he pushed himself to his feet and walked across to the window. The day was grey and overcast, just as it had been for the past three weeks. Or had it? He frowned. Maybe it had only seemed that way.

Things actually hadn't been so bad to begin with. In an attempt to distract himself from missing Florence, he'd launched into several new projects, but gradually his spirits had sunk so low it was an effort to get out of bed every morning. His carriage had returned, with confirmation that she'd reached her parents' house safely, but there had been no word, no letter, no sign that she was ever coming back.

He'd written her letters, thirteen in total, all of which he'd deposited in the fireplace, since they were either dry reports about cattle behaviour or passionate pleas for forgiveness, neither of which were quite what he wished to convey. Surely there had to be some romantic middle ground between cows and begging? If he could only find the words, the *right* words…maybe he could truly convince her he'd changed?

He looked around at the sound of a commotion in the hall. He could hear the sound of voices, along with doors opening and closing, and running footsteps. His heart lifted, right up until his study door opened and two boys came charging into the room, closely followed by his sister, carrying a toddler in her arms.

'Patrick! Anthony!' Cassie's face was flushed. 'Oh, for pity's sake, I know you've been cooped up in a carriage for three days, but stop running around like you're in the park. Put. That. Figurine. Down!'

'Cassie.' Leo lifted his brows. 'This is a surprise.'

'I should imagine that's an understatement.' George was the last to appear. 'We've come to visit, by the way. I apologise in advance.'

'Nonsense.' Cassie approached his desk. 'Leo's invited us plenty of times.'

'Under the mistaken belief that we'd never come, no doubt.' George grasped a juvenile collar in each hand and hauled his sons back to the door. 'I'll take these two outside for a while. Hopefully they'll wear themselves out.'

'Thank you, darling.' Cassie blew him a kiss. 'And for goodness' sake, don't let anyone give them cake. The last thing they need is sugar.'

'I'm well aware.'

'But if there *is* cake, I'm feeling rather peckish myself!'

'I can ring for cake.' Leo smiled, coming to kiss first her cheek, then the top of the toddler's head. 'To what do I owe the honour? I thought you hated travelling anywhere, especially here.'

'I do, which just shows you how devoted a sister I am. Oh, Rimmer?' Cassie called over her shoulder.

'Yes, my lady?' The butler's head appeared around the door.

'Please tell Mrs Fitch that I need a room preparing as soon as possible. My head is ringing from being cooped up with those boys.'

'I think you mean Mrs Chenoweth, my lady?'

'Do I? What happened to Fitch?'

'She's enjoying a well-deserved retirement.' Leo grinned. 'Sewell too.'

'Well, good gracious.' Cassie looked thunderstruck.

'If I weren't here on such important business, I might swoon.'

'Business?' Leo propped himself on the edge of his desk.

'Yes. And don't pretend that you don't know what it is.' Cassie deposited the toddler on the floor. 'What really irks me is that I had to hear it from somebody else. Why didn't you write?'

'About what exactly?'

'Oh, I don't know. Maybe about your wife leaving you?'

He winced. 'That's not exactly true. She needed some time away to think, that's all.' He narrowed his eyes. 'Although I'm curious about how you know any of this.'

'I make it my business to know things.' Cassie pursed her lips as she drew off her gloves. 'I heard it from Lady Fox, who visited the Parkers on their estate last month.'

'Ah.' The Parkers' estate was twelve miles away. Gossip clearly travelled between the two houses.

'Of course, they didn't say that Florence had left you. They simply said that she was away for a while, but I guessed the rest. So...' she braced her hands on her hips '...*what* is going on?'

He sighed. 'Very well, if you must know, it turns out you were right and that she didn't trap me into marriage, after all. Her friend Miss Wadlow was behind the whole thing.'

Cassie's eyebrows rose. 'The one you intended to propose to?'

'Yes. Florence was as much a victim of her deception as I was.' He spread his hands out. 'So go ahead and say you told me so.'

'Oh, Leo.' Cassie came to sit on the desk beside him. 'I may be tactless, but I'm not entirely heartless.'

'I know.' He nudged her shoulder. 'Then Florence's memory came back and she remembered how unpleasant I'd been to her and...well, apparently it made it somewhat difficult to stay with me. She said she couldn't forget how bad I'd made her feel.'

'Oh, dear.'

He rubbed a hand over his face. 'I acted just like him.'

'Ah.' She didn't ask who he meant.

'So maybe I deserved to be left.' He winced at the thought that had been crushing his spirit for the past few weeks. 'Maybe I'm already too much like him and she's better off with her family, where I can't hurt her again. Maybe we're better off apart. Maybe if I really love her, I should just let her go.'

'Nonsense.' Cassie tipped her head against his. 'This is all my fault. I should never have gone to London and left you alone with him all those years ago.'

'It wasn't your job to take care of me.'

'But you had no one else to love! No one to show you that you were worthy of love too. But you are. Do you think I would have come here if you weren't? You know how much I loathe this house.' She lifted her head again. 'Do you truly love Florence?'

'Yes.'

'Do you think there's a chance that she loves you?'

'She said she thought she did before, so…' he grimaced '…maybe.'

'Well, if you do and so does she then *neither* of you is better off apart! How long has she been gone?'

'Almost a month.'

'Then maybe it's time to go after her?'

'I can't.' He clenched his jaw. 'She said that she needed some time to think and I have to respect that.'

'Mmm… As pleased as I am to know you're not a domestic tyrant, there are times when a woman needs a gesture.'

'What do you mean?'

'I mean, you've given her time. Maybe now you should show her how you feel.'

'How? I told her I'd changed, but she said she couldn't trust me not to change back.'

'So find some way to prove that you won't.'

'It's not quite so easy, not when she's in Cumberland and I'm…' He stopped talking abruptly.

'Leo?'

'Maybe I *can* prove it.' He turned around slowly, reaching for the letter on his desk.

'Urgh, is that what I think it is?' Cassie gave a shudder as he opened it up. 'You know he sent me one of those too.'

'What did you do with it?'

'Well, I wanted to throw it into the fire, but…it was too hard. So I gave it to George. I've no idea what he did with it.'

'He gave it to me on his deathbed. It felt like a set of orders.'

'He had no right to dictate to you.'

'I know.' He stared at his father's signature for a long moment and then tore the letter through the middle.

'Oh, well done.' Cassie put a hand on his shoulder. 'That was worth coming two hundred miles for. Now do it again. Tear it to shreds!'

'No.' He shook his head. 'I need it like this.'

'Why?'

'Because you're right, I need to make a gesture. Florence needs to know that I've changed and this is my proof.'

'You mean, you're going to Cumberland?'

'Yes.' He felt his muscles coil in readiness for the journey ahead. Maybe he was already a bad son, but he could still be a good husband. A good marquess too, only he'd do it his way from now on. 'Will you be very offended if I leave you to fend for yourselves?'

'Don't be ridiculous.' Cassie clapped her hands delightedly. 'I was rather hoping you would.'

Florence sucked in a deep breath, filling her lungs with air as she stood on top of the hill that marked the northern limit of her parents' land, on a boulder that might once have been part of the ancient Roman wall, gazing out over mile upon mile of verdant farmland and forest, towards the lowlands of Scotland. This was exactly what she'd needed. This hill, this view, this sense of isolation and peace, even this boulder; these were the things she'd missed so terribly during those first miserable weeks of her marriage. Coming back had been good for her, a balm for her soul as well as her bruised heart, although, ironically, now she was here she found herself missing the rolling pastures and jagged coastline of Dorset instead, as if she was torn between two places at once.

She also wished that she'd worn more than a woollen spencer over her dress because the wind was a great deal stronger than she'd anticipated, with a biting edge that meant she probably ought to leave soon or she'd catch a chill. Autumn was definitely in the air. In a few short weeks, the green landscape would have faded entirely to muted brown, but for just a little while longer she wanted to stand here and breathe it all in.

She twisted around, looking south this time. From this vantage point she could see a scattering of villages, as well as the Wadlows' large manor house and her parents' farm. There was a rider coming from that direction, she noticed. Thomas probably, her second oldest brother, going to visit Miss Ogden, the vivacious daughter of the local doctor, just as he'd done twice already that week. Something told her there was going to be another wedding in the family before the year was out.

She heaved a bittersweet sigh at the thought. As happy as she was for them, she couldn't help but feel a little bit jealous too. It must be nice to be courted, to enjoy the first flush of uncomplicated, innocent romance. Nothing about her relationship with Leo had been uncomplicated, and as for innocent…but there was no point looking back any more. That was the conclusion she'd come to after a month of soul-searching. She'd spent enough time being angry and dwelling on the past. Now she simply had to decide on her future, whether to forgive or simply give up.

Now, at last, she thought she knew the answer.

As if in reply to her decision, a particularly strong gust of wind buffeted her so hard, she almost tumbled backwards off the boulder. Meanwhile, her bonnet made a bid for freedom, tearing loose of its ribbons and blowing off down the hill.

She took the hint and ran back towards the farmhouse after it. Her parents' cook had been baking when she'd left, meaning there would probably be something hot and delicious waiting in the kitchen. Maybe she would take a tea tray up to the parlour, where her mother and Hannah, her sister-in-law, were no doubt still busily sewing baby clothes, just as they had been when she'd left. Maybe she'd stay and make a pair of booties herself.

Life with her family was back to the way it always had been, although there had been some uncomfortable moments when she'd first arrived, stepping down from her carriage to find them all standing in an awkward-looking receiving line. They'd greeted her with trepidation, avoiding eye contact and making stiff half-bows and curtseys, as if they hadn't known how to behave, but after a couple of days her brothers had started to tease her again, and by the end of the first week any shows of deference had been abandoned. Now everyone accepted that she was still their sister and daughter as well as a marchioness, and she felt completely at home again. She'd also shared the story of her marriage with her parents and, to her immense relief, they hadn't told her it was her duty to go back to her husband, or asked her how long she intended to stay. They'd simply given her her old room back and let her work out the answers herself.

She hooked her skirts over one arm, picking up speed as she charged down the hill, sending a flock of sheep scattering around her. Bother! Her bonnet was caught in the rushes of a small stream, now far too soggy to wear, though thankfully it was only a ten-minute walk back to the farmhouse. She scooped it up, dangling the ribbons from her fingers as she started along the track that ran through the middle of the valley, surprised to see the horse and rider coming towards her. That was odd, since the village was in the opposite direction. Did Thomas want her to accompany him? Although, looking closer, she didn't recognise the horse. And it didn't look like Thomas or any of her other brothers either. It looked like…

'Leo?' She stopped in the centre of the track, opening and closing her eyes a few times to make sure she wasn't hallucinating. When she'd left Rainton, she'd wondered how she would feel when she saw him again and now she knew. Her heart was leaping so high, it was halfway up her throat. Unfortunately, she was also conscious of being dressed in one of her oldest gowns, with mud around the hem and her hair loose and knotted from the wind. As usual, she looked nothing like a marchioness, although, at this precise moment, he didn't particularly look like a marquess either. Quite the opposite: he looked positively dishevelled, his greatcoat creased and travel-stained, his boots caked in dirt and his face dusty. If she hadn't spent so much time thinking about him over the past month, she might not even have recognised him.

'Florence...' He dismounted before his horse had even come to a halt and strode towards her, dark eyes blazing.

'What are you doing here?' She felt a pang of alarm. 'Have you come to take me back?'

'No.' He stopped abruptly, a hurt expression crossing over his face. 'Not unless you want to come.'

'Oh... Sorry.' She gave him an apologetic look. 'You just looked so purposeful.' She peered closer. 'And exhausted. Are you all right?'

'I've been riding for five days.'

'You came all this way on horseback?' She gasped. 'Alone?'

'I brought one of the grooms with me, but I left him at the local inn.' He cleared his throat. 'I'm sorry I came without sending a message ahead, but once I made up my mind, I wanted to get here as soon as possible. Your parents said you were out walking.'

She tensed. 'You've met my parents?'

'I have. They were very courteous.' He removed his hat, so that his dark hair tumbled forward over his forehead. It was longer than before, she noticed, and in desperate need of a comb. 'I also met four of your brothers, at least three of whom I think wanted to attack me.' He threw a quick glance over his shoulder, as if he thought they might be in pursuit. 'You were right, they are very large.'

She put a hand to her mouth to stop a laugh from escaping. 'Don't worry, I'll protect you.'

'Thank you.' He dipped his head and then reached into his greatcoat, pulling out two pieces of torn paper and holding them out to her. 'This is the reason I came. You said you needed proof that I've changed.'

She held on to his gaze for a moment before looking down and inhaling sharply. 'Your father's letter?'

'Yes.'

'You tore it up?'

'Yes.'

'I don't…' She swallowed. 'You didn't have to do this.'

'Yes, I did. And this.' He took the paper back and tore it again, into fragments this time, then turned and strode away up the hill.

'Where are you going?' Florence shouted after him, too stunned to move.

'To let it go!' he shouted back, reaching the top and throwing the pieces high into the air. As she watched, the wind caught them, tossing and whipping them around in a spiralling motion for a few seconds as if it were playing with them before blowing them up and away over the fields.

'I can't believe you just did that.' She gaped incredulously as he came back down.

'That's not all I've done. My new steward has arrived, along with your housekeeper, and the house is completely different. As for the estate, I've made lots of plans. The new cottages are finished and we're building some more. We're also planting different crops and expanding the herd.'

'Oh.' She closed her mouth, aware that she was still gaping.

'I know that not everything will work. Some of my ideas will fail, but I can live with that.' He moved closer, until they were standing only a foot apart. 'What I can't live with is failing you.'

'Leo...' She felt a lump swell in her throat.

'I know I hurt you,' he went on. 'I was an arrogant, close-minded fool. I don't expect you to forgive me for the way I acted, but if you come back I promise I'll never make you feel bad about yourself ever again. I'll be the man you deserve, if you'll just give me one more chance...' He crouched down on one knee.

'Stop! Leo, you'll get covered in dirt!' She grabbed at his shoulders, trying to hoist him back up again.

'I already am.' He reached for her hands, folding his own around them. 'Florence, I've never done anything like this before. I've never had any kind of emotional outburst. Honestly, I didn't think I was capable of one, but I need to ask, will you marry me?'

'Marry you?' She shook her head in bewilderment, her heart pounding with a combination of nerves and excitement. 'We're already married.'

'No, we're not.' He paused and made a face. 'Well, all right, officially we are. But that was the old me. This is the new one. And if you say yes we'll do it again, properly this time, so your family can be there too. I'll put an announcement in the newspapers telling everyone I'm marrying the woman I love.'

She bit her lip, laughing and crying at the same time. 'Just inviting my family will be enough.'

His face lit up. 'Is that a yes?'

She nodded, a wide smile spreading over her face. 'Yes. I've thought about what happened a lot over the past few weeks, and I can understand why you assumed I was the villain, but from now on I want to be the heroine of my story.'

'You will be. I promise.'

'Good. Because when I left Rainton, I didn't know which would be stronger, anger or love, but as it turns out, love won.'

'Florence...' He stood up and took her in his arms. 'I know we had a bad start, but I promise you, we're going to have a wonderful future.'

She closed her eyes as their lips met and all her fears and worries fell away. Because now she knew who she was and where she wanted to be. She was the scandalous Marchioness of Rainton and in a few days, once she'd properly introduced her husband to her family, she would go home.

Epilogue

The first Saturday in August, eleven months later...

'Anthony! Patrick!' Cassie bellowed over the lawn, making her now three-year-old, Edgar, give a startled yelp and drop a piece of cheese pie onto the picnic blanket.

'I'd leave them to it, if I were you.' George chuckled, picking it up again.

'But they're running Florence's poor brothers completely ragged!'

'I think they're enjoying themselves,' Florence replied, turning towards her mother for confirmation. 'Don't you think, Mama?'

'I know they are.' Her mother rolled her eyes fondly. 'They'll still be playing football when it gets dark, if we let them. Besides, it's not just them. There are some local children playing too.'

'Well, if you're certain...' Cassie sounded appeased.

'I don't know how I ever came to have such energetic children.'

Florence smiled, angling her head towards Leo, sitting nestled beside her. 'Wouldn't you like to join in?'

'No, I'm saving myself for the cricket match tomorrow.' He grinned. 'Anyway, I'm much too comfortable here.'

'Me too.' She leaned back into his arms, tipping her face up to the sky with a sigh of contentment. The lawn in front of the house was a sea of picnic blankets and people. Unlike last year, the weather for today's summer fair was perfect. Everything was perfect. The prize-giving, which had taken place in a tent beside the lake, was over, she and Leo had both made speeches, and now everyone was basking in the August sunshine. Everyone including her parents, the three brothers who were now playing football, Samuel, sitting on an adjacent blanket with Hannah, and their ten-month-old baby, Laura, and Thomas, who'd just gone for a stroll with his new bride, the former Miss Ogden. Now that she thought of it, a walk sounded like an exceptionally good idea. It would give her an opportunity to discuss a recent and somewhat important piece of news with her husband.

'Come on.' She pushed herself to her feet and reached for Leo's hand. 'Let's go for a walk.'

'Didn't we just agree we were comfortable?'

'Yes, but if I don't move now, I'll fall asleep.'

'Go along, Leo.' Cassie twirled her parasol in a queenly fashion. 'I'll deal with any problems while you're gone.'

'Is that so?' He quirked an eyebrow at her. 'You know, if I didn't know better, I'd think you were beginning to feel at home here again.'

'Oh, I'm enjoying myself immensely. I've already decided, we'll be coming to your summer fair every year from now on.'

'See what you've done?' George lifted his eyes skyward.

'You'll be very welcome.' Florence laughed, linking her arm through Leo's and pulling him along beside her. 'We won't be long.'

'You know, we *could* take our time,' he murmured, wrapping an arm around her waist and pulling her close against his side. 'There's all sorts we could get up to in the woods.'

'Not with my family and all of our tenants here, there isn't.' She nudged her hip against his. 'What if somebody saw us?'

'Good point. That could be awkward.' He pressed his lips into her hair. 'In that case, I suppose we'll just have to wait until tonight.'

'We will, but then I'll be all yours.' Heat rippled through her veins as she cast him a sidelong look. 'Just like last year.'

'I'll find us some cushions.' He waggled his eyebrows and then stopped abruptly, spying a couple strolling arm-in-arm along a nearby path. 'Good grief. Is that—are *they*—who I think they are?'

'Mmm? Oh, yes.' Florence nodded complacently. 'I invited them.'

'You invited Fitch and Sewell?'

'Yes. It only seemed polite.'

'It might be, but I'm still amazed they came, given how much they disapprove of everything we do.'

'Actually I think those days might finally be over. I visited Mrs Fitch's cottage to ask in person and she was much too embarrassed to be disapproving.'

'Why embarrassed?'

'Because when I arrived, Mr Sewell was already there, looking *very* comfortable.' She smiled smugly. 'I do believe they're courting.'

'Fitch and Sewell?' Leo sounded disbelieving.

'Yes. Isn't it delightful?'

'No.' He put a hand over his face. 'I don't want to picture it.'

'All right, but I'm still glad they're here. Everything's just as I hoped it would be.' She took a deep breath. 'Especially since I have an ulterior motive for inviting you to walk with me.'

He gave her a confused look. 'I thought you just said that we couldn't?'

'Not *that*.' She rolled her eyes and placed a hand

on her stomach. 'There's just something I need to tell you.'

He looked down and then up again, his jaw dropping with the motion. 'You mean…?'

'Yes.'

He caught her up in his arms and then quickly put her down again. 'Sorry. I shouldn't lift you.'

'Of course you should. I don't even have a bump yet.' She beamed. 'It seems you've fulfilled your "*first and most urgent task*", after all.'

'I don't care if it's a boy or a girl, so long as it's healthy.'

'Me too, but if it is a boy, we are *not* naming him after all the former marquesses.'

'Agreed. And if it's a girl…' he crouched down, plucking a small white flower from the grass '…what do you think of the name Daisy?'

She gave him a suspicious look. 'I thought I told you about that poem?'

'You did. It's why I tried writing you a new one.'

'You wrote me a poem?' She pressed a hand to her chest, touched.

'No.' His expression turned sheepish. 'I *tried* to, but it turns out it's a lot harder than it sounds. I came up with a few rhymes. Petal and metal. Rose and nose. Leaf and thief. Only I couldn't seem to put them together.'

'Oh. Well, it's the thought that counts.'

'True, but it also occurred to me that Mr Archer was right the first time. You *are* a daisy.'

'Sturdy and reliable?'

'Innocent.' He tucked the flower behind her ear. 'That's what daisies symbolise. That's what I should have seen about you all along. Only try finding a rhyme for innocence...'

Florence stifled a laugh, batting away a bee as it buzzed too close to her ear. 'Well, then, we'll put Daisy on the list, since we have several months to decide on a name while it's still just the two of us, the Marquess and Marchioness of Rainton, laughing stocks of the *ton*.'

Leo grinned, lowering his forehead to hers. 'I wouldn't have it any other way.'

* * * * *

*If you loved this story, you're sure to love
Jenni Fletcher's other historical romances:*

"The Christmas Runaway"
in Snow-Kissed Proposals
The Highlander's Tactical Marriage
Cinderella's Deal with the Colonel
A Wedding to Protect Her Fortune

*Why not pick up her
Regency Belles of Bath miniseries?*

An Unconventional Countess
Unexpectedly Wed to the Officer
The Duke's Runaway Bride
The Shopgirl's Forbidden Love

MILLS & BOON®

Coming next month

THE DUKE'S MEDDLESOME MATCHMAKER
Emily E K Murdoch

Book 1 in The Unconventional Oliver Sisters trilogy

'You are not my client,' said the proposal planner slowly.

Henry turned back to Miss Oliver. 'Absolutely not,' he said firmly.

She examined him for a moment, and heat grew in his chest at the attention. Not because it was her, naturally. He would have felt discomforted if it had been anyone.

'Well,' said Miss Oliver finally. 'Well. That changes things.'

'So you'll stay?' Henry said eagerly. He wouldn't be the one to ruin things for Charles. After all, it had been the one thing their father had asked of him, on his deathbed, Henry's years of medical training still not enough to keep the man he loved alive.

Look after your brother, whatever you do.

The proposal planner stepped down from the dog cart—which he had to assume was a good sign.

'My brother is a good man,' Henry snapped, trying to ignore the heat roaring through his body as she stepped closer. 'I want him to be happy.'

'Even if you think I am some sort of charlatan,' Miss Oliver said, halting before him and gazing up at him through long eyelashes.

Henry swallowed. Charlatan? Yes, that was one word for her. It wouldn't be particularly accurate. *Beauty*. That was more accurate. *Temptress*, for it was tempting to lean down and taste—

He stiffly stepped back, half wondering how he'd managed to get himself into such a situation. *Honestly, man. Pull yourself together!*

Miss Oliver was examining him closely. 'It appears most difficult to please you, Mr. Paisley.'

God in His heaven... 'All I am asking is that you fulfil your agreement with my brother,' was all he could manage. 'He is the only family I have left.'

Something flickered in Miss Oliver's gaze. 'I'll stay,' she said shortly, walking around for her trunk.

Henry almost tripped over his own feet to get out and retrieve it for her. It was the least he could do.

'Good,' he said, handing her the heavy thing. *What did she have in there?* 'I'm glad you're staying.'

'I'm not staying for you!' Miss Oliver bristled. 'I—I am already fatigued by avoiding your displeasure.'

They stood there for a heartbeat, glaring at each other, until Miss Oliver snorted, turned around and stamped over to the inn.

Henry watched her go. *Well!* That would be the last time he'd ever be tempted by Miss Oliver!

Continue reading

THE DUKE'S MEDDLESOME MATCHMAKER
Emily E K Murdoch

Available next month
millsandboon.co.uk

COMING SOON!

We really hope you enjoyed reading this book.
If you're looking for more romance
be sure to head to the shops when
new books are available on

Thursday 15th January

To see which titles are coming soon, please visit
millsandboon.co.uk/nextmonth

MILLS & BOON

LET'S TALK

Romance

For exclusive extracts, competitions and special offers, find us online:

f MillsandBoon

X @MillsandBoon

⊙ @MillsandBoonUK

♪ @MillsandBoonUK

Get in touch on 01413 063 232

For all the latest titles coming soon, visit
millsandboon.co.uk/nextmonth